DISCLAIMER

This book is a work of fiction. Names, characters, businesses, places, schools, events and incidents are either the products of the author's imagination or have been used in a fictitious manner. Any resemblance to actual persons, living or dead, or actual events is purely coincidental.

Trigger Warnings: This book contains scenes briefly describing or depicting rape, sexual deviant behavior, sex trafficking, gun violence, and physical assault.

EDDIE MORRISON

AN AGENT WHELAN MYSTERY THRILLER

KIRK BURRIS

Look for titles by Kirk Burris:

The Agent Whelan Mysteries
12 PILLS
MURDER AT PARKMOOR
EDDIE MORRISON
THE KITTIMER JOURNEY (coming in 2024)

You can find purchase links on his website:
www.KirkBurris.com

Follow Kirk on Twitter: @BurrisKirk
Follow on Facebook: @KirkBurrisAuthor
Follow on Instagram: @KirkBurrisAuthor

ISBN 978-1-7355864-7-2   Hard Cover
ISBN 978-1-7355864-4-1   Paperback
ISBN 978-1-7355864-5-8   eBook

Dedicated to Robert.
Thank you for your unending support.

For my dad, whose love of mysteries and
reading inspires me daily to be better at my craft.

Chapter 1

FBI Special Agent Whelan ducked behind the dumpster outside the backdoor of Kung-Pao-Now. The stench of rotting chicken bones and three-day-old grease stung his senses as much as the bullet grazing him stung his ear. He wiped at it with his left hand. Cartilage could pour blood if pierced in the right spot. He wondered how many shirts he'd explained to the dry cleaners over the past nine years. *No, it's blood, not ketchup. Do your best.*

"Cannon?" he yelled over the gunfire.

"I'm okay!" a voice returned, somewhere thirty yards to the left.

Each time Whelan stuck his head up or out to the side, another bullet zinged by, plunking into cars or shrubs behind him.

"You're trapped, Eddie!" he yelled again toward the back of the strip center. "You and your men drop your weapons, or we'll have no choice but to take you down!"

Whelan wanted to do precisely that—vengeance for a previous undercover partner in the field, Special Agent Jay Pierson. Eddie Morrison killed him right in front of Whelan's eyes. After hunting him for another two years, Whelan had Morrison trapped like this once before. He could have killed him, but what kind of federal agent would he be if he didn't bring the criminals to trial? What kind of world would his son grow up in if he contributed like that?

So Whelan brought Eddie to justice: three life sentences plus forty years for murder, drug smuggling and trafficking, and illegal firearms trafficking. Eddie was also involved in sex trafficking, but his victims wouldn't testify. The rest was enough. Three months after sentencing, Eddie escaped prison with help from the inside and outside.

And now, after a six-month manhunt, Special Agent Thomas Whelan and his rookie field partner, Special Agent Phil Cannon, once again had Eddie Morrison cornered and ready for capture in Temple City, California, a suburb of Los Angeles.

Whelan took a long breath. *Am I going to take him back to prison after this? Maybe I should end it here.*

He contemplated the L.A. SWAT officers taking up guarded positions on either side of him. It would be challenging to kill Eddie without witnesses.

Whelan watched two officers on his right move in tighter to the building. He turned and saw four more on his left do the same. *There's Cannon! He's moving in.* He realized the hail of bullets from the back door to the Chinese takeout had ceased. Peeking around the dumpster's edge, no more shots rang out, and he joined the group in moving closer.

It was dark inside the kitchen. Egg rolls burned in a fryer. Whelan had smelled worse. Much worse.

A SWAT officer looked at him inquisitively, and Whelan gave a nod. The officer launched two smoke grenades, and seconds later, four men came out with their hands in the air. It was over.

Whelan rushed to them, his old and trusted Glock pointed at their heads. "On the ground! On the ground!"

SWAT rushed them and tackled anyone who failed to comply, zipping their hands together behind their backs, their faces shoved into asphalt full of old chewing gum and rat feces.

Two more men gave themselves up after trying to hold their breath inside. Six were now in custody.

Whelan went by each and grabbed their chins, pointing them toward him. None of these men were Eddie Morrison.

"Where's Eddie?" he shouted.

They stayed silent.

"Eddie!" Whelan screamed into the doorway, still billowing a thick cloud of tear gas.

He yelled to one of the officers, "Mask!"

They tossed him one. He had it in position after a brief wrestling match. He fired up his flashlight, holding it alongside his firearm, and stepped into the doorway. Two SWAT team members backed him up. He'd made it clear earlier this was his show.

"Eddie!" he continued to yell. "Come out, Eddie! There's nowhere to run."

The smoke started to clear. SWAT officers were coming through the kitchen from the front of the building.

"He didn't get past you?" Whelan asked them.

"No. No one has come this way."

"He was here!" shouted Whelan. "I saw his face not ten minutes ago!"

A tap on Whelan's arm jolted him, and he spun around. His flashlight lit up Agent Cannon's face.

"Whoa, Tom, watch where you point that thing," said Cannon. He knew Whelan was wound up more than usual.

"Sorry." Whelan lowered his weapon. They located the light switches for the tiny kitchen. It had only two stoves with woks on them, a deep fryer, storage shelves, and not much else. A small walk-in refrigerator about four-by-six feet revealed nothing.

"Where the hell did he go?" Whelan was dumbfounded.

"Here?" asked Cannon. He moved a storage rack loaded with jugs of soy sauce and bottles of hoisin out from a side wall to reveal a door.

It connected to the store next door, a bagel shop. They rammed the door open, nearly knocking down a young girl in the stock room. The agents aimed their weapons at her. "On the ground!"

She dropped in tears. "Don't shoot! I'm Carmina! I work here! When the firing started, I wasn't sure where it came from, so I hid here! Please don't kill me!"

They handed her off to the police and saw another door connected to the adjacent bay in the strip center. Again, it was rammed in by a SWAT officer. This store was a consignment shop for women's clothing, with no one left inside. Another door revealed the stockroom for a soft serve yogurt joint, and through there, the break room of a Marshall's.

Whelan asked Cannon, "All of these stores are connected? Do you find that unusual? They're locked. Did Eddie have a key?"

"Must have. We did trace this to one of his shell corporations. He owned this building. Maybe he left all these doors for a day just like this one?"

"Maybe. But if he owned this building, I'm sure it was part of his master plan for more unscrupulous activities. He would have loved to set up a huge operation in L.A. He always tried to grow it, but the competition continually pushed him down. Still, he had a minor hold here."

Whelan turned red. "I thought we had the bastard! He must have slipped out with the crowds down at this end while his boys kept us busy."

Whelan tapped the button on his radio. "Morrison's out of the building! We need to set up a search parameter. He has to be within six square blocks of here."

The SWAT member still with him called in the search to his superior. "We're on it."

They all moved outside. The remainder of the stores in the strip mall were thoroughly searched, and a four-hour manhunt in the surrounding streets discovered nothing. Eddie Morrison evaded capture yet again.

By the time the SWAT team rammed in the first door from the Chinese kitchen, Eddie was grabbing a ball cap off a rack inside Marshall's.

He moved quickly, yanking a brown barn coat off another, and drifted out with a handful of people as his men kept the SWAT team busy with bullet fire.

He followed a woman to her car and shoved his gun in her gut. On the right end of the parking lot, a second SWAT armored rescue vehicle was stationed near the end of the building. No officers were this far down yet, monitoring the fleeing shoppers.

He hopped in back and sank low, pushing the nose of his SIG P226 into her side. "Drive!"

"Where?" she asked. She was shaking visibly.

"Las Vegas."

"Vegas! I have to pick my kids up at school."

"If you ever want to see them again, get me to Las Vegas."

"I need gas," she stalled.

Eddie raised his head high enough to read the meter. It registered half full. "We'll fill up on the way. Give me your purse."

"Take what you want. I don't have much. We can stop at an ATM, and I can withdraw up to $600 for you. Maybe you'll get lucky on the tables. I bet you're a blackjack man."

She handed him her bag. He searched through it. "Where's your cell phone?"

"Please, let me call my husband to have him pick up the kids. Then you can have it."

"Cell phone!" he snapped. "Now!"

She looked between her legs where the 9 and 1 were already dialed on the keypad. She closed all windows and handed it to him as he shoved his gun deeper between her rolls, landing against a rib bone.

Eddie was in her rearview, and their eyes met. Hers were full of tears.

Silently, she navigated her way to the 605 and the 210. As she approached Interstate 15, she made a final plea. "We need gas."

The meter had dropped an eighth of a tank. "Keep driving," said Eddie. He sat up to get his bearings and ensure she was going the right way.

"Once we enter the mountains, we can't get gas for an hour," she persisted.

Eddie smiled. She was trying her best. "I'll take my chances."

He started watching the landscape after they passed Cajon Junction. In a few minutes, he pointed at a turn-off to the left. "There! Turn there!"

"We can't. It says 'Wrong Way.'"

"Do it." He fired a round into the side of her seat cushion before jabbing it into her rib bone again.

She veered onto the small road for emergency and government personnel connecting north and southbound lanes. The two highways were a quarter mile apart here. The road swerved right, then left.

"Stop!" yelled Eddie. "I'll drive now."

The woman complied. A well of tears continued to wash down her face, but she managed to keep her silence as she handed the keys over the headrest as demanded.

Eddie jumped out of the car before her, and grabbed her arm when she opened the door. He marched her west, up and down small hills, until they were out of sight of either traffic lane.

"On your knees," he ordered.

"Please, let me phone my husband. I need to tell him I love him. We fought this morning, and I can't have the last thing he hears from me be my screaming what a little shit he is. I didn't mean it. I was just—"

The sound of gunfire echoed all around the couple as the woman dropped to the ground. Eddie had learned from past mistakes to put a second bullet into someone when you needed to make sure they were dead. Shockingly, people survived all kinds of crazy things you'd never expect them to.

He plugged her head again, this time closer.

Eddie switched up cars at a taco joint right off Ranchero on the other side of the pass. He traded again in Barstow, this time driving himself to Vegas. He hated leaving a trail of three bodies, but it wouldn't matter. By the time any of them were discovered, he'd be long gone.

He was aware that Vegas maintained traffic cameras on practically every corner. He kept his cap and sunglasses on, even as night set in. Daylight could not have been brighter than the millions of lightbulbs and neon glow the Las Vegas Strip generated.

He navigated side streets to the North Las Vegas Airport.

A flash of cash and the first private charter pilot he approached flashed his pearly whites. "Where to?"

"D.C."

"Oh, Washington's lovely this time of year," cooed the pilot. "Cherry blossoms will be coming into bloom soon."

Eddie's foreign connections were no longer returning his calls since his incarceration. If he wanted to get his business running again, he needed to stay in the States. A handful of people were willing to work with him now, and they were all here.

"Are you visiting family in D.C.?" asked the pilot as they began taxiing.

"Someone's, yes."

By 6:45 p.m., Eddie Morrison was in the air and headed east. He was tired of running from Special Agent Thomas Whelan. It was time to end the nonsense. And he'd finally obtained the address of Connor, Whelan's son.

Chapter 2

Connor Whelan was playing the first little league game of the Spring season about a mile from his home in the greater Washington D.C. area. His team was ahead, four to three. He batted in two runners and cast his eyes into the stands from third base, searching for his mom's face. He found it wrapped in a scarf to shield a late March blast of wintry air, and he could tell she was smiling. She gave a 'thumbs up' when she saw him looking at her.

It was her turn to host the after-game lunch. Little Jimmy's Pizza Parlor soon buzzed with twelve and thirteen-year-olds celebrating a victory. She handed Connor her credit card for the arcade in the back and nestled herself into a booth when her phone rang.

"Georgia!" yelled her ex-husband and Connor's dad, Thomas Whelan. "We had him, Georgi, and he got away! Eddie was right in front of me and then gone. Just gone!"

"Oh, Tom, I'm sorry. I know that must have been hard. When was this?"

"Yesterday. Where are you? It's noisy."

"You think?" she asked, while fourteen boys devoured pepperoni slices and tried to talk with full mouths. "They played their first game today. We're all at Little Jimmy's. Not the best time to talk, but he'd appreciate a call from you this evening."

Tom withdrew on the other end. He hated missing out on his son's life. "Did he score?" he whispered.

"Three of the eight points the team made. We may have a future pro on our hands."

"Fantastic. I'm glad he's active and participates in sports and other activities. Takes after your side of the family."

"And you too, Tom. He's razor-sharp—still straight A's at school. You *are* still coming in three weeks during his spring break, I hope? Bring Phil. He and Connor have grown pretty close playing their online video games these last few months."

"I don't know, Georgi. I have to play it by ear. If we get a lead on Eddie…."

Georgia Whelan took a slow inhale, holding it as long as possible before letting it whistle through her lips. "Well, if you don't, I'll expect to see you on the fifteenth as planned."

She hung up the phone, unsure if her ex had anything more to say, but didn't much care. His repeated failures as a father were the primary reason she insisted on a divorce two years ago.

Sure, he's out there, heroically risking his life to save others.

But she needed a man who could be home for his son on a nightly basis—and for her.

Finishing the final bite of her pizza, Georgia hopped up and checked on the boys in the back, making sure they weren't disrupting the other patrons. On the way, she caught a man staring at her. He was too old for her, so she moved quickly by him, inadvertently brushing an elbow against his brown barn coat.

Whelan clicked the "end call" button on his phone. He shook his head at Cannon.

"She'll come around," offered Phil. "One day, it'll get easier. For both of you."

"You're invited to join us in three weeks if I still go. Probably more so if I don't. I know Connor's been dying to get you in front of the latest game. Online is okay, but sitting side by side makes it more fun for him.”

Phil became like a younger brother to Tom Whelan over the last eighteen months, and especially the last six, chasing Eddie around the country. He was now the “fun uncle” to his son Connor. His real brother certainly never fit that bill.

Patting Tom on the shoulder, Phil said, “I think you should go by yourself. You need some one-on-one.”

The pair were sitting in the L.A. field office for the FBI, filing their report. The flight home to Kansas City was uneventful, and by 9:20 p.m., Whelan pulled into the driveway of his small house in Westport.

He channel-surfed for twenty minutes before hitting the power button on the remote and picking up his phone. He pressed the third speed dial. “You busy? I need a drink.”

Fifteen minutes later, he plopped into a booth at his new watering hole across from his Assistant Special Agent in Charge for the Kansas City FBI office, Miranda Jones. They worked a couple of cases together before her promotion the previous summer and formed a tight bond. He trusted her implicitly and needed some honest advice. More than his ranking superior, Miranda had become his closest friend and confidant. Thankfully, she lived a mile away and was available on short notice.

“So, should I turn this manhunt over to someone else or stay on him?” asked Whelan, referring to Eddie Morrison.

Miranda smiled at him. It always warmed him from the inside with its legitimacy. Her ebony curls hung loose around her shoulders tonight.

Whelan fought an attraction to her since the day they met nearly two years ago. Of course, now, with her promotion, any relationship was definitely off the table—as if it were ever on it.

"What does your gut tell you?" she asked.

"To stay after him. He's running right now, not holed up, which makes him scared and prone to mistakes. He'll make another one soon enough."

"And what does your head tell you?"

Whelan stared at her. "I'm not sure."

"Then continue to trust your gut. It's usually right. How's Cannon holding up out there? You two haven't been home in over a month."

"He's amazing. He has an energy I haven't felt since Pierson was killed. I find it annoying sometimes," Whelan grinned. "But it keeps me up and reinvigorates me on days when I need it. By the way, he's tired of us referring to him as a rookie. Wants to know when we'll start thinking of him as a regular Special Agent."

Miranda laughed. "I already do."

"So call him and let him know."

"First thing tomorrow."

"And now I'm sure I can't turn the case over to someone else."

"Like you were going to," said Miranda.

They ordered another round.

"How's Derrick?" asked Whelan, inquiring about her ex-fiancé. They had officially called it off a few months prior when his fitness and modeling career took off, and he was forced to be in New York if he wanted to grow his brand. "When's the last time you spoke to him?"

Miranda Jones sipped her bourbon. "At least six weeks? Seven? I've stopped counting. He's doing well. Saw him in a deodorant commercial the other day. Didn't even know he was pursuing acting now."

"How was he?" asked Tom.

"Good. Funny. Of course, they wanted to show his body off, so they have him all shirtless in a bathroom, stroking up his pits under those massive arms with some clear goo. If he gets any bigger, he won't be able to model anything but fitness gear."

Whelan glanced at his scrawny arm, flexing in the mirror behind Miranda's head.

"You can stick to modeling suit coats," she jested. "They like tall skinny white boys for those."

At thirty-four, Thomas was developing significant crow's feet and appeared older than most men his age. This career could deteriorate you, fast and harshly. He sighed and took a drink of his beer.

"Next time I'm in New York, I'll see if Derrick can hook me up with his agent," he said.

They sat quietly for a minute, each reflecting on their choices in recent months. And years.

A few minutes after 10:00 p.m., Whelan's phone rang. "Whelan."

He spoke in quick snippets of acknowledgement, his face brightening with each utterance. When he hung up, his whole perspective changed to the positive.

"That was the L.A. office. A woman went missing this afternoon, and the police ran her car's GPS. It was abandoned off I-15, north of the San Bernardino Mountains. Miranda, the woman is on video inside the strip center where we lost Eddie yesterday! Parking lot footage showed a man getting into the backseat of her car when she left. They can't identify Eddie in it, but it has to be him. He's headed to Vegas!"

"Did they find the woman?" asked ASAC Jones.

"Not yet. But it's doubtful Eddie let her live. I'll bet he dumped her body on the way. California Highway Patrol is searching for her, and so is Nevada's on their side of the line. The Vegas office is running facial recognition on all the cameras in the city. I'm going to grab Cannon and head out there. I wonder if there's a red-eye."

He started Googling on his phone.

"If he's still there, he'll be there in the morning. Go, sleep a few hours. Catch a morning flight."

Whelan opened his mouth to protest.

"That's an order," insisted Jones.

Whelan jumped up from the table and tried to get the waitress' attention.

"I've got this," said Jones. "Go." She waved him off.

When the server made it to the table, Jones raised her head. "Bring me the check, please. And put one more bourbon on there first."

Chapter 3

Whelan arrived at the airport by 7:35 a.m. the following morning. Cannon was ten minutes behind.

"It's not like you to be late," chided Whelan.

"My bed wouldn't let go of me this morning. I had to beat it into submission. You should see my poor pillows. Innocent bystanders, casualties of war. Sad, really."

"I've been there."

They landed in Las Vegas four hours later and headed to the local field office.

The Las Vegas special agent in charge greeted them in their bullpen. "You boys let him escape Friday in L.A.? I heard you had eyes on him."

"Yes, sir. We did. He's a slippery bugger."

"Uh-huh. I've got men in the field already today, flashing his photo to car rentals, hotels known to take cash without asking too many questions, et cetera. He'll be staying off-grid as best he can. No reason to even check the strip."

"Swell."

Whelan ignored the jab at their incompetence for letting Eddie Morrison get away. Safety comes first in these situations. None of the good guys were injured. That was important, especially during an onslaught of heavy fire. He put enough blame on himself the past three years. Nothing this man might say could make it worse.

"How sure are we he's still in Vegas?" asked Cannon. "Eddie's smart. I'd wager he planned on us figuring out he was headed this direction. He owned the strip mall where we had him holed up. He knows it's loaded with cameras. I doubt he's sticking around."

An agent in the Vegas office raised her head up from her monitor. She tapped a button on her headset. "We received a call from San Bernardino Sheriff's Office. A man was reported missing this morning outside Barstow. We ran his tags and picked up the plate in North Vegas last night."

"What's in North Vegas?" asked Whelan.

"An airport."

Whelan chewed his inside lip. "Shit. He could have gone anywhere."

"Doesn't look that way. I've cross-referenced all the flight logs, and only one was scheduled at the last minute. I think your man headed to D.C."

Connor Whelan opened the back door to take the trash out.

"I'm starting it!" yelled his mother from the front room.

It was 7:30 p.m., and he was trying to race back to the television to watch the baseball game with her. The Washington Nationals were playing the Houston Astros in Spring Training, and it was being broadcast by one of the cable sports networks.

A gloved hand caught his arm and yanked him to the back porch. It threw his balance off, and he dropped the trash bag. Before he could scream, another hand wrapped itself over his mouth and tightly held him in place. He wriggled against the man holding him, and tried not to breathe as a sweet chemical scent overtook his senses.

He gave one last attempt to shout, but when he managed to open his mouth, his head grew dizzy and his mind spun. He felt the pressure release against him as his body collapsed into waiting arms.

The man carried Connor to a car in the alley and lay him in the trunk before racing away.

"Connor?" his mother shouted again.

After two minutes with no response, Georgia Whelan made her way to the back door in the kitchen. She stuck her head out. "Connor?"

The bag of trash was at her feet. She picked it up and took it to the cans near the alley. The light of dusk was enough to see up and down both directions, and there was no sign of her son.

She searched both sides of the house. It was unlike him to disappear without telling her where he was going. An uneasy feeling began to crawl up her spine, and by the time it reached her neck, the hairs on its nape stood up at attention like little soldiers.

Glancing at the television as she returned to the living room, she noted the game paused on the screen. Connor's favorite player was up at bat.

She picked up her phone and pressed the speed dial button for Connor. Her neck's little soldier hairs nearly snapped it in two as she whipped around when her son's phone rang loudly right beside her on the end table.

He'd never leave the house without his phone!

She hung up and dialed her ex-husband.

"Tom! Connor's missing!"

"What do you mean, missing? How long?"

"A few minutes. He went to take the trash out and disappeared. The trash was sitting on the back porch. His phone's here!"

"Georgi, a few minutes isn't exactly long enough to be considered missing. Is he playing a trick on you? Would he run over to a friend's house and forget to tell you?"

"No. I don't think so. Tom, a horrible feeling came over me. I can't explain it, but something's wrong. I know it."

17

"Call 911."

"And they're going to say the same thing you did. A few minutes doesn't constitute a missing person. But…he's *missing*!"

It was Whelan's turn to have the hairs on his neck rise. He gazed at the monitor in front of him, showing a list of the private airlines flying in and out of the North Las Vegas Airport the night before. His eyes were focused on the last-minute flight to D.C. at 6:42 p.m. He turned slowly in horror to Cannon on his left.

He still held his phone to his ear. "Georgi, hang up now and dial 911. Tell them he's the son of an FBI agent, and you have reason to suspect he was abducted. I'll be on the next flight to D.C."

He hit the "end call" button.

Phil Cannon raised his brows along with widening, questioning eyes.

Whelan was already dialing another number on his phone as he spoke to his younger partner. "I know where Eddie Morrison is."

Chapter 4

"Please, no," said Cannon.

Whelan hung up the phone. "I'm booking us a flight in twenty minutes."

He pointed to the second name on the list of private airlines.

The special agent in charge was filled in and vowed to contact the D.C. office on their behalf. Agents would be dispatched to the residence of Georgia and Connor Whelan immediately.

"Go!" he barked at them. "Catch your plane, and get this bastard!"

Whelan stopped cold, with a retort on his tongue, but he swallowed it and ran out the door. Cannon was fast on his heels. They raced their rental car to the airport in under eight minutes and threw their travel luggage on the floor of the plane. The hatch barely shut when they started taxiing down the runway. They'd chartered an older Falcon 50 EX and were soon cruising at over 500 miles per hour.

"Get settled, even at max speed, it's going to be four-and-a-half hours," said the pilot.

Agent Cannon stripped off his Kevlar vest so he could relax and get comfortable. He wore it almost non-stop the past few months, whenever a lead on Eddie surfaced, and he thought they were close to capturing him.

Whelan usually kept his in his luggage. He didn't wear it often since it hindered his freedom of movement, and opted to leave it in the trunk more than he should.

He lowered the visor over his window and hunkered down for a power nap. He normally fell asleep on airplanes, the motion and the humming knocking him out. He wrestled his body for an hour, trying to find a comfortable position, but his nerves wouldn't let him drift off this time. Erratic thoughts jolted his core as his mind played a game of "what-ifs."

Instead of dwelling on his next steps, he focused on the past, recalling the first time he ever heard the name Eddie Morrison and the proceeding manhunt. The haunted memory loaded in his head like film in a projector. He'd played this one over a thousand times, but guilt subjected him to his self-induced punishment.

Three and a half years' prior, a man approached thirty-year-old Agent Thomas Whelan in the bullpen of the Washington D.C. Field Office of the FBI.

"Agent Whelan," he began. "I'm Special Agent Jay Pierson, New York office."

Whelan took a break from his computer screen, where he was entering a few notes on his report from a multi-state case involving a gang of drug mules. "How can I help you, New York?"

"I'm putting together a task force to go after a trafficker. Nasty fellow named Morrison. He's set up a new operation here in D.C. It's the fourth major city we know of, the others being L.A., Miami, and New York. We know he has connections in New Orleans and Houston as well. He's trying to expand and step up to the big leagues."

Whelan was interested, but this sounded like significant traveling, and his son Connor recently turned nine. He'd be entering the fourth grade, and his personality was growing and changing as fast as his physical body. Thomas didn't want to miss any of it.

"How long before you expect this task force will be able to capture this guy? Realistically?" he asked.

"We've been building evidence and our case for nearly two years. But with his recent growth, he's getting sloppy. Three, maybe six months? We're holding off until we're certain we can bust the whole nut at once, not just him."

"And why me?" Whelan was curious about what Pierson specifically saw in his record that made him a candidate.

"Your last three busts show you work cleanly, and I need someone who can keep the rest of us from getting too gritty."

The comment surprised Whelan. "I have a son—well, of course you know that. I need to be in D.C. full-time again by Christmas."

"That's probable, but I guarantee nothing. And if you join us, you're in for the long haul. I won't have time to bring others up to speed once this starts rolling. We'll be undercover, and things could get ugly. It's why I want you. You're fresh. Fresher, anyway, than the others."

"Others?" asked Whelan.

"Agents Lee Saunders, Joyce Cliburgh, and Steve Beatty. They like rolling in the muck. I need arrests that stick. Everything by the book."

"Ahh. A goody-two-shoes? That's what my record says about me?"

Agent Pierson leaned in low and dropped his voice. "It says you get convictions. I've been on this for two years already. I need this asshole put away. For life. And if you're worried about being known as a prig, this is the kind of case that'll put hairs on your chest. Some of them gray."

Whelan rocked back in his chair, considering the offer. He'd been attracted to more dangerous cases lately, and was the first to jump up when anything drug-related came through their office. His interest and near-PhD in pharmacology were part of it, but the other half of him longed for more action. He was growing bored at the bureau.

He gazed at his wedding ring. *Georgi's going to kill me.* "I'm in."

Three months later, Saunders and Beatty were killed during a drug bust in New Orleans.

The feds were lucky to have recovered their bodies. Agents were known to disappear and never be seen again in this line of undercover work.

When the paper trail dead-ended with no ties to the other cities' operations or Eddie Morrison himself, Supervisory Special Agent Jay Pierson re-assigned Joyce Cliburgh to infiltrate the Miami outfit, while he and Whelan headed back to get in tighter with the development in D.C.

Another two months passed. Whelan and Pierson were blending in, laundering money. It was menial. Cliburgh was getting cozy with the Miami crowd, working to find out who was in charge of trafficking young women for prostitution. Miami was the largest sex ring operation of all the cities where Eddie was established.

After four months, Cliburgh asked Pierson if she could be reassigned out of Miami. Things were getting rough, and she wasn't making any progress digging up dirt to put Eddie away.

Pierson instructed her to embed herself even deeper. Clearly, she wasn't gaining any trust with Eddie, or she'd have something they could use by now.

A turf war killed thirteen of Eddie's outfit. They were notified that Joyce Cliburgh was among them. Jay Pierson's original special task unit was down to two. And they were spending all their time counting twenty-dollar bills.

When word came that Eddie's cabin on Cacapon Mountain in eastern West Virginia, near Cumberland, Maryland, was a storage and layover hideout for arms dealing, it was time for the agents to make their move.

Cumberland is a hundred miles northwest of D.C., spread among the foothills of the Appalachian Mountains on the edge of West Virginia. Based on the north branch of the Potomac River, Interstate 68 runs through it, and there are major AMTRAK and CSX railway stations. If smuggling is your game, you can efficiently move your merchandise by car or train through Cumberland.

Eddie Morrison's goons ran multiple operations around the country—drugs, hookers, guns, and children—all for sale to the highest bidder.

With intel from FBI teams working in other states, Whelan and Pierson let it slip they'd heard of a drug bust going down in Cumberland and were on the first flight out to share their knowledge firsthand.

When they arrived, expecting to meet Eddie Morrison, they were routed to his right-hand man, Angel Baylor.

Baylor was known throughout the area by his nickname, Lil' Baby. He was a dwarf, barely topping three-foot-eight. What he lacked in athletic prowess, he made up in loyalty, intelligence, and organization. Cumberland was one of Eddie's most profitable operations thanks to Lil' Baby keeping expenses at a minimum and leveraging favors for discounts on shipping charges.

"I don't know you," Lil' Baby spit at them. "You tell me there's a drug bust going to go down here next week, and you happened to hear about it from a truck driver in Baltimore?"

"As I said," Pierson explained for the third time, "we were doing a drop-off to Baltimore at Eddie's slip in the Northwest Harbor. We took one shipment, and this truck driver took another. While waiting on the boat, he mentioned a bust coming here in Cumberland. Didn't say how he knew, but he sounded scared, like he was ready to get out of the business. He didn't want any part of it. We thanked him for the intel and went our separate ways."

Lil' Baby gawked at the new arrivals. "And *you two* want a part of it?"

"Eddie's growing fast and needs more men he can trust," said Whelan. "Yeah, we want a part of it. And we're here to show him we're ready to level up and be bigger players."

"And you expect what out of this, exactly?"

"A larger cut of the pie."

"More demanding work demands more apples," chimed in Pierson.

He felt a nudge against his crotch.

Lil' Baby was pressing a tiny Ruger SR40c pistol against Pierson's left testicle. "If you want to *keep* your apples, you'll lose the bravado."

Chapter 5

Whelan snapped himself from his memory of Lil' Baby when the plane's wheels hit the runway at Reagan National Airport in Washington, D.C.

His watch read 12:52 a.m. Eddie had his son for nearly six hours now.

"You've been staring into the darkness for two hours. Care to share?" asked Cannon beside him.

"I was thinking about one of Eddie's old goon-squad leaders, before the big bust last year, Lil' Baby. He's one of six we didn't catch from the eighty-seven we knew about. And the *only* one who wielded any real power in Eddie's original outfit."

"You think he's hooked up with Eddie again since his escape?"

"I have no idea," said Whelan. "Possibly." He returned his gaze out the window while they taxied to a small hangar for private airline use. A blast of wintry night air hit them in the face when they ran down the steps.

"I forgot how much chill North Atlantic air can have in it," said Whelan.

Their rental SUV awaited them, and they raced northwest along the Potomac toward Palisades.

Tom Whelan burst through the front door of his ex-wife's home—a home he once shared. Georgia was sitting on the sofa, surrounded by agents and police.

She allowed him to hold her, and the pair stood embracing for two minutes, oblivious to all the eyes on them.

"I haven't told your mother yet," Georgia said.

"Thank you. This will kill her. Let's not until we have concrete news to share."

Georgia nodded. She saw Phil Cannon waiting by the front door. "Phil?" she asked. They'd spoken many times over the past year but never met in person.

Phil opened his arms wide, and she gave him a generous hug.

"So this is the face keeping my son up until two a.m. on school nights playing online games?" she teased when they separated.

"Not guilty. Not on school nights. If he's online that late, it's with someone else."

He gave her a "scouts honor" salute.

She let a few tears fall without warning. "No. He's pretty good about going to bed on time. He's so *good*."

She wheeled on her ex. "Why Tom? Why Connor? How'd he find us? What does he want?"

"Me. He wants me. Dead. So I can't catch him and put him away again."

"Why doesn't he leave the country?"

"He's never developed a strong foothold outside the U.S. I doubt he'd even know where to start in his current status as a hunted fugitive. I'm sure he's luring me with my son, so he can get me close and kill me. I know how he thinks, how he moves. Phil and I have worn him down over the past six months. He's tired and cash poor. He's desperate."

"Won't that make him dangerous?"

"He's already dangerous. It *will* make him slip up, however. His first call would normally be to me. He'll want to encourage me to meet him alone. He wouldn't have Connor with him, nor tell me where he is, until we meet."

"And if you meet, he knows you'll wear a wire. He wouldn't tell you even then," said Georgia.

"No. He knows I would never truly be alone. The bureau wouldn't allow it. The director would never accept those terms."

Cannon stepped into the ring. "So, his first call will be to…? Georgia?"

"Maybe."

Whelan stood silent, working out multiple scenarios in his head. Georgia took Cannon's arm and led him to the kitchen.

"Can I fix you a coffee? Tea?"

"No, thank you." He felt as though he'd known her for many years. He'd grown to love her child over the past year like his own nephew. And when you share a love for a child, there's already a bond.

"Georgia," he said softly, "Connor's strong. More than you know. He'll be fine emotionally. This won't break him or mess him up."

She let a tear streak her cheek as she turned into him. "Thank you, Phil. I pray you're right. But you see the 'rough and tough' side to him while you shoot bad guys or play space cowboys with him online. I see the side that still cries when he skins his knee or gets depressed when his dad doesn't call him for over three weeks. I see the side still wanting peanut butter and jelly instead of tuna salad and hugging me when I cut the crusts off."

Phil squeezed her arm. "How about I make *you* a cup of tea?"

She smiled. "Yes, lovely. Thank you. Third cabinet from the right."

Georgia took a seat at the kitchen table as Tom entered. He pulled out a chair beside her and took her hand, holding it like the past four years hadn't ripped their lives apart. She allowed it, but retrieved it back into the safety of her lap after a few seconds.

"Tom? Tea?" asked Phil.

"Please. Orange Spice, decaf."

The trio was silent for a few minutes while the kettle came to a boil. Its whistle scared the life out of all of them. Three sets of nerves precariously on edge, lost in the same nightmarish thoughts.

Whelan helped himself to the sugar bowl on the table. There were many late winter nights sipping tea around this table during the "worthwhile years." Now it was a reminder of his failures as a husband *and* a father.

Phil saved him from torturing himself further. "So, what did you decide will be Eddie's next move?"

"There will be someone we don't know who makes contact. It's the only way."

"Why not have someone kill you outright? Why go through kidnapping Connor?"

"He needed to make sure of my location. And he wants me to suffer first, like we've made him suffer lately. This has grown personal to him. It's been personal for me since…Jay Pierson. I can't believe Kendrick didn't give the Oklahoma lead last summer to Miranda and me. Two more weeks, and we'd have captured him then. *This* wouldn't have happened!"

His grip tightened around his teacup, nearly cracking it. Georgia leaned over and put her hand on his until it relaxed, and he was calmed somewhat.

"What's *our* next move?" she asked.

"We wait. It's in his hands now. Unless we get a break, we just wait."

"Then I'm going to wait in bed." She stood. "There are blankets in the closet. Tom, you can have the sofa, and Phil, you'll have to make the most of the loveseat."

"I'll be fine, thank you."

They adjourned to the living room. Agents were stationed out front, and they shut the lights off.

Cannon was beginning to drift into sleep two hours later when the house phone rang.

Whelan was on it by the third ring. "Eddie?" he answered.

There was silence on the other end and then a click.

Georgia ran into the room. "Was that him?"

"Presumably. And now he knows I'm here."

Chapter 6

No one slept the rest of the night. Coffee was put on around 6:00 a.m. Silent, confined thoughts wore on them all.

"How long will he drag this out?" asked Georgia, unable to sit still. "All day? Two? A week? This will drive me mad. I'm already losing it."

"You're holding up incredibly well," offered Phil. "Most parents in your situation would have already needed tranquilizers."

"So glad to know I'm normal," she said, popping a small pill into her mouth she'd hidden in her hand.

"I'd offer you boys one, but I need you both to stay sharp. Do your damned jobs," she continued.

She topped off their coffee cups. "Drink up."

Georgia retreated to her bedroom for a shower.

"Whelan," said Cannon, "we should get to the local office. Get in front of this. Get updated. See what the SAC has to offer from here."

"Agreed. You shower first. I'll go after you. Towels are in the linen closet beside the hall bathroom."

When Phil left, Tom opened the door to the rear porch. He stepped out, scrutinizing the yard and the alley. It was twenty-eight degrees out, but he inhaled it deeply, letting it revive him. Eddie Morrison had a six-hour head start. *Come on, Eddie. Take a shot. I'm right fucking here! Come and get me. Give me back my son, you bastard. Take your shot!*

He closed his eyes and spread his arms wide to the sky. He rose on his tiptoes, a sense of elated acceptance having washed over him.

When he landed hard on his heels, he jolted to reality with renewed determination. *I'm coming for you.*

The Washington D.C. field office was a few blocks northeast of the bureau's main headquarters, six blocks from the Capitol Building. Each time Whelan visited Washington, he felt like he was home again. He loved Kansas City, but being closer to the heart of the bureau stirred emotions and renewed his passion for service to his country.

Perhaps it was due to being closer to his son. He always wanted to make his son proud. He'd attained that, but it cost him his wife along the way.

If I put Eddie away again, maybe Georgi and I can try once more. Harder. It shouldn't have to be hard, but it simply was in his line of work.

He and Cannon were asked into the SAC's office.

"Here's what we know," he started. "Based on Morrison's pattern of stealing cars, we're theorizing he stole the one he kidnapped your son with. The closest traffic cameras picked up eight cars coming from your neighborhood around 7:30 last night. Footage wasn't clear enough to see inside any vehicles. If your son was in the back seat, or…"

"The trunk," Whelan finished his sentence for him.

"Or the trunk, we wouldn't have seen him anyway. And the drivers' images were too blurry to get any hits on facial recognition. We've been able to rule out five of the eight cars so far. The owners of the other three have yet to be contacted. I've got agents door knocking this morning."

"What areas are the three remaining vehicles from?" asked Whelan.

"Chevy Chase, Falls Church, and Gaithersburg."

"Gaithersburg?" asked Cannon. "That's pretty far out. Twenty, twenty-five miles?"

"That will be it," said Whelan quietly. "It's off local radar, and he's familiar with all the areas between here and Cumberland. It's Baltimore's jurisdiction."

"Yes," said the SAC. "They're cooperating. They've got four agents on their way."

Whelan stood. "We need to be there."

"Why don't you sit tight until we get their report? Should have it by early afternoon."

"No, that's it," said Whelan.

He looked directly at Cannon and lowered his voice. "Let's go."

Cannon popped up without question. He opened the door and headed down the hallway.

The special agent in charge made another plea. "Agent Whelan, you're too close to this now. Sit here and wait for the report. You might be wasting time heading north if Morrison is discovered in one of the other neighborhoods."

Whelan's voice grew stern. "Sir, are you ordering us to stay?"

"No. This is still your investigation. But I need to make sure your head is on straight. Morrison's got your kid, making you no longer an objective lead on this case."

"I've *never* been objective when it comes to Eddie Morrison," retorted Whelan.

He left the office and shouted over his shoulder as he rushed to catch up to Cannon. "And I'm not about to start now!"

Whelan and Cannon stopped in the bullpen to obtain the specifics: addresses, agent names, and other intel they'd obtained on the case.

When they arrived at the address in Gaithersburg forty minutes later, the home was surrounded by police tape, and four squad cars were out front.

Badges were flashed as they lifted the yellow tape marked with bold CRIME SCENE lettering. The garage door was open, and a gold Mercedes was parked inside. Its doors were open, and someone was scraping and bottling blood samples out of the back seat.

Whelan's stomach turned when he walked by and peered inside. The amount of blood was significant. His mind conjured an image of his son, riddled with bullet holes and lying in an inch of blood.

Cannon read Whelan's thoughts and put his hand on his partner's shoulder. "It wasn't Connor. Morrison needs him alive until he guarantees he can get to you."

"Thanks. That helps."

They stepped into the home and raised their identification a second time.

A police officer greeted them in the room. "The sergeant should be here in ten if you'd prefer to speak to him."

"Will he know more than you?" asked Whelan.

"No. I guess not. We've only been on the scene a few minutes. Given the situation's urgency, we didn't feel we could afford the time to wait for a SWAT unit. This is all moving quickly, and we're collecting and preserving evidence until CSI can get here. But there's no sign of anyone in the house. I don't believe any of the beds were slept in last night."

"Do we have the name of the owner?"

"Angela Roffler."

Another officer came in through the front door. "Neighbor confirms Ms. Roffler lived here alone. She's divorced, kids are all grown and live out of town."

"You think it's her blood in the car?" asked the officer to Whelan and Cannon.

The two feds exchanged glances, wondering how much they should share.

Whelan was less concerned about protocol since his son was missing, and relied somewhat on Cannon to help guide his response.

Cannon could care less about protocol under the circumstances as well, however. "Yes, given what we know of the probable assailant, she was likely killed in the back seat and her body dumped. It wasn't personal. He just needed a vehicle."

"I understood from the call that a child was kidnapped? Why would he bring him back here after stealing the car? And whose car are they in now?"

"We need the whole place fingerprinted," said Whelan. "Kitchen, fridge, bathrooms, shower handles—everything. Make it a priority."

The other officer raced out to the car to get a kit.

"The CSI guys should start with the bedrooms," continued the officer. "Maybe I watch too many movies, but it's likely the reason he brought the boy back here was to molest him. Probably raped and killed the kid, then took off with the body. A lot of sick fucks are out there."

Whelan's face grew red, and his voice was tight. "That's not what happened," he snapped.

"How can you be sure?" asked the police officer.

"Because *the kid* is my son!"

Chapter 7

Three hours passed, and they were still investigating leads and awaiting lab results at the home in Gaithersburg.

The local police detective and the department sergeant were all in attendance, more to put on a show for the feds than to be of any genuine assistance. The FBI's evidence response team was critical now. They were working in tandem with the four agents from the Baltimore office.

A neighbor three doors down reported her stolen car to the officers out front. They were now working on the assumption Eddie hotwired it, a white 2019 Ford Escape. A BOLO, "Be On the Look Out," was issued.

Fingerprints throughout the home matched Connor's. Thankfully, Whelan was smart enough to have his son printed three years' prior in the event of a situation like this. It was utter irony that he was still trying to protect his family from Eddie Morrison after all this time.

Fate is cruel and unoriginal.

Connor's prints were all over the house. It appeared he and Eddie ate at the kitchen table, showered, and possibly changed clothes.

The closets were ransacked, and some boys' shirts were scattered about the closet floor. They were likely left there for visits from one of Ms. Roffler's grandchildren.

The TV remote had Connor's prints, in addition to one end table and the coffee table in the living room.

Cannon was checking out the powder residue running up the door frame to the kitchen. He turned back to the living room and shouted to the local CSI agent.

"Does that look like a 'U' and an 'M' to you?"

The man turned and glared at the table, slowly approaching. Connor's prints were tightly gathered on the tabletop and seemed to form letters. He grabbed one of the forensics team members and instructed him to dust more heavily around it, further out, side to side.

"Whelan!" shouted Cannon out the back door.

Whelan was consulting with the police sergeant near the double doors to the basement.

He came inside and followed Cannon's arm and pointing finger. Written on the coffee table in his young son's fingerprints, clear as could be, were the letters CUMBERL.

Emotions of pride and fear welled within Agent Tom Whelan quickly, and he choked as he mumbled, "That's my boy."

He ordered the other federal agents, "Focus the BOLO on all the roads between here and Cumberland. That's where they're headed!"

"Yes, sir."

Cannon was confused. He'd studied Whelan's case reports on Morrison over and over. He knew it as well as anyone who worked it.

"Why go back to Cumberland? It doesn't make sense. He has to know it's on our radar. The local authorities were alerted to his escape last year and are keeping extra eyes out for him. Why chance it?"

"Because he has connections there?" suggested Whelan. "Someone still in his loop, who we never associated perhaps, working from the area?"

"I can't imagine you missed anyone. Your bust took down eighty-one men and women in his outfit, in six cities around the country. You were hailed as a hero. I still hear people talking about it at the office. Well, *did*, until we hit the road these past few months."

"I'm no hero. Too many honorable men and women lost their lives along the way—agents, consultants, civilians. There are six we never caught who we know of, and it's possible there were others we never discovered."

"Cut yourself some slack," ordered Cannon.

Whelan acquiesced with a nod.

"Do you think he's dumb enough to return to his old cabin on Cacapon Mountain?" asked Cannon.

"Dumb enough? No. *Desperate* enough? If there was something still there he needed? Something we missed? Maybe."

"What might that be?"

"Guns. Ammo. Cash. He'd have to have them buried somewhere nearby. They ran imaging in a two-hundred-yard radius around the home, but they wouldn't go digging or metal detecting more than fifty yards out in all directions. They were there for four days as it was. They did put motion-detecting video cameras around the area. They're solar-powered and still operational. All I get clips of are deer."

"*You* get those?"

"Of course."

"I figured someone from tech was monitoring it."

"They are. I'm on a 'cc' list. There was a huge, ten-point buck last month."

"Are you a hunter?" asked Cannon.

"Only of people," responded Whelan. His mind drifted to the memories of his first hunt for Eddie Morrison. *What are you up to now, Eddie? What's your endgame this time? Where's my son?*

Frustration grew quickly in Whelan, and he threw his empty water bottle across the room. It struck a small figurine on the fireplace mantle, sending it smashing into the edge of the wall nearby. It just missed the head of Agent Luke Garrity from the Baltimore office as he was coming from the bedroom hallway.

"Are you fucking insane?" he snapped at Whelan before turning his head to Cannon.

"Is he fucking insane?"

"Of course not," Cannon defended.

He stepped directly in front of Whelan. "You're *not*, are you?"

"Not yet. I hope that wasn't valuable. Make sure it's written up so I can compensate someone for the accident."

"You got it."

Whelan cleared his throat. "Agent Garrity, I apologize. My mind is elsewhere. We're headed to Cumberland. Please let Baltimore know."

The man confirmed there were no eavesdroppers nearby and addressed Whelan in a low tone. "Why don't you wait? This is going to wrap up shortly. All lab work can be emailed to us."

"Morrison's still ahead of us."

"Agent Whelan," Garrity began, "I don't know you. But I have orders to keep my eyes on you, given your closeness to the situation. I need you to wait here."

"Orders from who?"

"My SAC, who took them straight from Director Commerson. And from that little display of anger you just put on, I have to say, I agree with their concern."

Whelan's head shook. "No. I'm sorry, but circumstances haven't changed. It's a manhunt, and the man's on the move. Did Commerson put you in charge of this investigation? Because no one told me I was no longer lead on this."

"No."

"All right. Leave the other agents here. You ride along with us and keep your eyes on me. You won't be disobeying your SAC or the Director. It's a win-win. But remember, I *am* in charge of this case, and you'll follow my orders."

"I understand."

Whelan opened a closet door in the kitchen and retrieved a broom and dustpan he'd noticed earlier. "Least I can do," he said as he cleaned up the porcelain remnants. "Inform your team and let your SAC know our plans. We leave in five."

"Yes, sir."

Whelan sighed as he knelt to collect the debris.

Cannon squatted beside him. "You okay? Maybe you *are* too close on this one. You sure you want to take this on? Maybe you should stay with Georgia. Let me head over to Cumberland."

Whelan glowered at his partner, who had become like a brother to him over the last year, and like an uncle to his son. "Has to be me. I was there. Before. Has to be me."

He took a deep breath and counted to ten in his head before releasing it.

"Whelan, I…" started Cannon.

"Yes?"

"Nothing."

"Good. Then let's go find my son."

Chapter 8

Cumberland, Maryland, was battling an early spring blast of cold when the three agents drove into town in Whelan's fleet SUV. Late March could still drop the temperature, and the streets were carrying a dusting of white from the previous night's snowfall. The town was on the western edge of a major storm cell which blew down from Canada.

They weren't sure where to begin, and hungry stomachs were growling. They stopped at a diner downtown and took a back booth, eating clam chowder and sipping coffee.

"This is delicious," said Cannon to their waitress.

"Yeah, the cook makes a mean chowder. And he puts more clams than potatoes. Other restaurants add a bunch of filler."

She studied Whelan's face longer than was considered socially acceptable.

He twisted his neck directly at her. "Can I help you?"

"I've seen you here before. A few times. Cheeseburger, extra pickles. That's you, right? Been a while."

Whelan was impressed. "About three years ago, yes. I spent a couple of months here. The cook makes a mean burger, too."

"Yes, he's a keeper, that's for sure. All those burgers, and still skinny as a rail. I wish I had your metabolism."

She turned to Garrity. "I can't remember what you used to order. Pulled pork with extra slaw?"

"I've never been in here," he smirked. "I was cursed with one of those faces everyone thinks they know."

"Oh. Well, you…" she gawked at Cannon. "You've definitely never been in here. I'd remember a cutie like you for sure."

She moved on to another customer.

Cannon's face reddened. "You were here two months?" he asked Whelan.

"Pierson and I were fitting in, proving ourselves. It was right before Eddie killed him."

Whelan's memories drifted back three years. "Jay and I worked to show Lil' Baby we were worth our weight. But for those two months, we never met Eddie Morrison face to face. I made sure our names—well, our aliases—hit the reports Lil' Baby sent him. It was crucial to get inside Eddie's inner ring."

Cannon had heard some of these stories before, but Garrity leaned in close, hanging on to every word out of Whelan's mouth as he began recounting the past to the other agents.

Three years' prior, Jay Pierson reached down and moved Lil' Baby's Ruger from his left testicle to his right. "If you want to do some damage, shoot this one. It's the only one of the two still in production."

Lil' Baby broke out in a boisterous laugh. "Welcome to the Queen City, gentlemen."

He tucked his gun away and motioned them to follow.

Cumberland's "Queen City" nickname dated back to the 1800s and was derived from its service to the "King City," Baltimore, via an early highway and the railroad.

Two nights later, the drug transfer was scheduled to go down on that same railroad at the CSX classification yard. This hub is where new trains are assembled as cars are sorted and classified according to destination.

CSXT-389074, a refrigerator rail car, was supposed to arrive and offload a massive shipment of methamphetamines, fentanyl, and hydrocodone. It was being shipped to Lil' Baby's unit so they could divide, repackage, then redistribute the merchandise via other railway cars to nine cities around the country.

Whelan, Pierson, Lil' Baby, and two of his trusted henchmen stood on the roof of a building eight blocks away with high-powered binoculars.

Whelan held his breath as the listed refrigerator car slowly arrived from the east. There was no sign of FBI or police action, and all seemed quiet. The car was silently detached from its current train by the few men working the graveyard shift and pushed over the "hump" so gravity could slowly carry it down the track to join other cars waiting to be connected.

As it rolled slowly along one of twenty-two adjacent sets of track in the hump yard, Whelan turned to his undercover partner and felt a lump in his throat.

Were we wrong? Do we have the right car? Is this the right night?

Lil' Baby must have been thinking the same thing. His face became more soured by the minute. "I hope you two haven't cost us thousands of dollars and delayed our shipment for nothing. If you're wrong about this, you'll be feeding fish in the bottom of the Potomac."

Three long minutes ticked off the clock. A brutal north wind whistled around the compressors on the building's roof.

He and Pierson had been stripped of their firearms. If Lil' Baby's men wanted to shoot them then and there, they could put up no resistance. Their lives hinged on the intelligence provided to them by the bureau. Whelan began counting the number of past cases where that intel proved incorrect.

Without warning, the entire train station lit up and came to life. Federal, state, and county cars were suddenly ablaze in red and blue swirling lights. Six spotlights from multiple directions and heights ignited the middle of the rail yard, focused on the white refrigerator car. It was blinding, like staring into the sun.

Twenty-six men and women from two SWAT teams and four jurisdictions swarmed in and took all the poor working souls to the ground.

Once frisked and any weapons confiscated, they were marched to the refrigerator car and commanded to open it.

Lil' Baby managed to whisper his normally gravelly voice. "The one in the green down coat, he's my man."

Three sets of binoculars shifted to him as he retrieved a set of keys from his pocket. He sneered at the officers and agents but tromped to the refrigerator car, unlocked a padlock on the side, and slid open the side door.

Three agents jumped inside with flashlights and guns held high. No one was inside.

The rail car was set up as a freezer and set to minus forty. It was much colder than the outside air and brutal to stand in for more than a minute without your nose hairs freezing over and your lungs working overtime to breathe.

For over an hour, agents took turns opening boxes. They were marked on the outside with words like "Hamburger," "Turkey Breasts," and "Chicken Pot Pies." When cut open and inspected, the feds uncovered hamburger, turkey breasts, and chicken pot pies.

Cars around the rail yard started turning off their flashing lights one by one. Spotlights on the action dwindled to one.

The man in the green down coat folded the warrant and tucked it into a pocket. When the all-clear was given along with an apology to him, he pretended to be angry and yelled at them, questioning who would pay for any damaged or undeliverable products.

But when he found a free moment, he turned toward the building undercover agents Whelan and Pierson were standing on. He took off his ski cap for the first time all night and scratched his ears before replacing it and disappearing back inside the refrigerator car, presumably to work on closing up boxes and putting things back in order.

"That's the signal," muttered Lil' Baby. "It's over."

He held out his hand to the two agents. "Thank you. You've saved our organization a four-million-dollar loss and kept me and my men out of jail."

Jay Pierson shook his hand. "As we said, we're ready for a bigger piece of the pie. When can we meet Eddie and finalize all this?"

"No one meets Eddie until they've proven themselves at least a year under my watch. He trusts me completely. Once you're ready to move up from here and take on a territory of your own, *then* you'll meet the big guy. But relax, you both got a huge bump in salary today."

While he was blowing up on the inside, Whelan forced a smile to his lips. "Thanks, Lil' Baby. We look forward to building our relationship and proving our worthiness. What's next?"

"Tomorrow, you two go find apartments and take the day exploring the town. I'll have assignments for you on Wednesday. Good job, boys."

They all filed down the stairwell and went their separate ways.

Once safely in their double-bed motel room, and after their nightly sweep for listening devices and hidden cameras, Whelan unloaded on Pierson. "You said this would be over by Christmas! It's now March! I haven't seen my boy in four months! What happened to fast-tracking this? We have a ton of evidence and witnesses. We can bring this operation down!"

"This one, yes, but without a link to Morrison or the five other outfits around the country. I need more! If we can't tie in Eddie Morrison, this will all have been for nothing. We bust this one little guy, Eddie will fold up shop in this area and disappear."

"I need to see my son!" snapped Whelan.

"I get it, Tom! I haven't seen my son Jack in almost a year! You missed Christmas with Connor? I missed *all* the holidays *and* Jack's birthday! He's five now and probably won't even remember his old man if this drags on much longer. But I keep thinking of all the lives I'm going to save, all the drugs I'll keep off the streets, the guns out of the cities and hands of gang members, the young girls I'll prevent from becoming lost in a world of prostitution."

Pierson collapsed on his bed. "Focus on the positives. Then after this is over, go back to your normal life. Get a desk job if you want more time with your kid. I'm sacrificing my time for my kid's future. I want a safer world for him to grow up in. Don't you want that for yours?"

Whelan sat on the edge of his bed. "Of course."

He lay down and bore his gaze into the ceiling. "I just couldn't fathom the cost before."

Pierson stretched out and stared up as well. "No one can. That's why I never bothered trying to explain it. We sacrifice to protect our country and provide a world our kids can grow up in, safe from some of the nightmares."

"There will be other nightmares to face," said Whelan.

"Yes. Always. So we focus on one and do our jobs. But if we can take down Eddie Morrison, we'll end a much larger plague than just Lil' Baby."

Whelan shut his lamp off. "I need this to end sooner than later."

"I know. I'm working on it."

Pierson flicked the switch on his lamp, and both men lay in the dark, fully clothed and exhausted.

After a few minutes, Whelan whispered, "You awake?"

"Yep."

"Tell me more about your son."

Chapter 9

By the time Whelan finished his recollection of Lil' Baby to Cannon and Garrity, they were also finished with their chowder in the diner.

"So when did you finally meet Eddie?" asked Garrity.

"That's another story. We need to get going. If Connor's here, we've got to start asking questions around the town."

The waitress dropped off their check. When Whelan took out his wallet, she spotted his badge attached to his belt at his side.

"You a cop?" she asked.

"Federal agent."

"Oh, I never knew. Were you back then? You were part of that big takedown, weren't you?"

"I might have played a role there, yes."

"So, why are you back here now?" she asked.

"Well, Gretchen," said Whelan, reading her nametag, "Eddie Morrison escaped prison, and we believe he might have returned to Cumberland."

"I saw his escape on the news. It isn't often Cumberland's mentioned on CNN, but our little town was in the headlines for a day when he got away. That was several months ago. You boys been hunting him this long? And still haven't caught him? Hmm. I don't envy your jobs."

The men contemplated her statement.

"You've got a decent memory," said Whelan. "Do you remember what Eddie looked like from all the news footage?

"I think so."

"Any chance you've seen him around here lately? Past few weeks or months?"

"No, sorry."

The agents all scooted out of the booth. Whelan threw some cash down to cover their bill and handed the waitress a twenty, along with his business card.

"Keep your eyes open the next few days. If you see any sign he's back in the area, call me immediately, day or night. I'll make sure you get some reward money."

"Sure," she responded. "Thanks."

The men took their leave, but she tugged on Whelan's shoulder before he could get out the door. "Sorry, I'm a bit slow on the uptake," she started. "So if you were a 'fed' back then, was the little fellow you used to come in with an agent too?"

"Little fellow?"

"The midget."

"No, why?"

"'Cause he was in here two days ago, for the first time in three years. He sat at the counter, stuffing his face with pork chops, extra gravy."

The air in Whelan's lungs expanded and held tightly as he brought out his phone. He flashed a photo of Lil' Baby to Gretchen. "*This* little fellow?" he breathed.

"That's him. He's dying his hair black now, but I'd recognize the little guy anywhere."

"Anyone with him?"

"Yeah, two men. Never saw them before, though."

"And that was the first time? Since three years ago?"

"Yes."

Whelan called Cannon and Garrity back inside, and they spent five minutes getting detailed descriptions of the other men and the blue BMW they drove.

"Sorry I didn't catch the plate," Gretchen offered. "Didn't occur to me they might be involved in a crime. Well, at least not currently. When I saw you come in today, I thought maybe he was getting his old gang back together. I'm glad you're law enforcement. We don't need any more trouble here. Took us over a year to move on the last time."

"Move on?"

"It was all the town could talk about. Didn't help it was on the news every night. We're a small community. People here know each other. All of a sudden, we were all suspicious of one another. Whenever someone lost their dog, or a kid misplaced his bicycle, neighbors started treating each other like they were hardened criminals."

Whelan was still holding up his phone. "But you're sure it was him? Lil' Baby?"

She took a second peek. "Yeah, it's him. Not many midgets in Cumberland."

"Little people," Cannon politically corrected before he could stop himself.

Whelan squinted at him before thanking Gretchen again. He tipped her another twenty and ensured she'd call him with any sign of Lil' Baby or anyone else in his gang from three years ago or the men from two days ago.

Inside their SUV, Whelan started thinking aloud. "So, odds are, Lil' Baby has spoken with Morrison, and they're going to hook up here. Maybe already have. Where would Morrison hide out? Cacapon Mountain's too risky."

"Maybe he's luring you there?" suggested Garrity. "But won't he know you'll come with backup?"

"He's not there," said Whelan. "I'd be notified if any motion sensors set a camera off in the area."

"He's not a deer," said Cannon. "I'll bet he's smart enough to figure out a workaround for those or disable them altogether. Or hell, the snowstorm could have covered them in a drift."

"I'll go check it out then," said Whelan. "It's about a forty-five-minute drive. You two stay here and canvas all the hotels. Pretty much the whole town will have noticed Lil' Baby if he's still in the area. It shouldn't take long to track him down, and he has an active arrest warrant. If you find him, take him to the local police station and hold him till I return."

"Not a chance," said Cannon. "I'm coming with you. Let's get the local PD on the hunt for Lil' Baby. Garrity can lead it. No way you're heading into the woods alone."

Whelan wanted to argue with him but knew he was right. He wasn't thinking clearly with his son on the line.

They dropped Garrity off in front of the Cumberland Police Department.

"By the time you return," he said, "we will be holding Lil' Baby, assuming he's still in town. Good luck."

Whelan nodded. He and Cannon hopped into their vehicle and raced east out of town to check out Eddie's cabin on the side of Cacapon Mountain.

Eddie Morrison grunted at Connor Whelan, who he'd tied to a rocking chair. "Look, kid, I don't care if I give you to your daddy alive or if I hand him your skeleton. But I promise you, this soup's not poisoned. You should eat."

Connor picked up the coffee cup with his one free hand. It was filled with tomato soup, a can of Campbell's, diluted with water. Eddie didn't have any milk to mix it with like his mother did. It seemed odd this way. But it was hot, and he was freezing. The thin blanket Eddie draped over his shoulders when they arrived at the cabin on Cacapon Mountain did little to ease the chill. He was still wearing his t-shirt and sweatpants from last night. Thankfully, he'd put his sneakers on to take the trash out, but no coat.

He took a sip. "So, you're going to kill my dad when he gets here, and then you'll kill me. I'm alive so he can see me for a second and then you blast him away?"

Eddie nodded.

"And this is all because you want to deal *drugs*?" continued Connor. "They make you wads of money to live the high life, huh?"

Connor moved his eyes around the cabin. It was sparse. Two chairs, his rocker at a small table, and a rumpled mattress were all it held besides the kitchen appliances.

"It was beautiful at one point," mumbled Eddie defensively. "Quite grand. They sold off all my shit when I went to prison. There was at least a million dollars' worth of stuff here."

"A *million* dollars? In guns?"

Eddie gazed coldly into Connor's eyes. "*Besides* the guns. I happen to appreciate art. And I had exquisite furnishings, tasteful, all high-end. A professional decorator did up the whole place. You'd have liked it."

A large rainbow trout mounted on a plaque still hanging on the south wall hadn't been "high-end" enough to confiscate, apparently. It drew Eddie's attention. "Have you ever been trout fishing? The river fishing in the summer is outstanding."

Connor's eyes widened. "You planning to keep me here till summer?"

Sixteen inches of snow on the ground was visible from the side window. The late-season storm dumped much more here than over in Washington. Summer seemed years away.

Eddie sneered. "God, I hope not. Your dad's smart. I'm sure he's on his way."

An alarm started beeping on Eddie Morrison's phone.

"I'll bet that's him now," he said, glancing at his screen.

Eddie pushed a button on the application, and a video played. "Nope, not him. It's our other_guest. Sit tight, kid," he said as he walked out the front door, shutting it behind him.

Connor had little choice. He finished his soup and soon heard voices talking outside on the large porch overlooking the Cacapon River two-hundred yards down the sloped property.

He couldn't see any figures through the window. From the few words here and there he could pick up, it sounded like he wouldn't be here long. The discussion outside was growing heated. His index finger worked quickly, pressing onto the table above his soup cup. When he finished, he dipped it into the bottom, then drew a thin line from his cup to the invisible message.

A gunshot rang out into the cold air from the porch. He glanced at the window again, but still no one. Then another shot passed through the window, breaking the glass out of one pane.

He instinctively tried to duck under the small table, forgetting he was bound to his chair. His feet were cable-tied to the legs, as was his left arm. He gave a strong rock forward and managed to stand, then wobble himself and the chair to the other side of the room, away from the window.

Another bullet broke more glass, and this time he heard it whizzing through the air. It struck the distant wall.

Whomever Eddie's guest was, the relationship had quickly gone off the rails.

Connor tripped, and when he hit the ground, one of the legs broke off the chair. He quickly broke the other one and moved them free of his legs. The one his arm was tied to wasn't breaking. He held it and the rest of the chair up, then smashed it against the wall. It all fell apart, the bottom half of the arm splintered into a sharp section about ten inches long. It scratched his arm deeply, and blood poured across the floor.

He ignored it and grabbed a razored piece of chair leg, holding it like a dagger, prepared to cut anyone who came through the door.

Two more shots rang out, followed by thirty seconds of silence.

Shit, they heard me wrecking this chair!

He positioned himself on the side of the door frame, ready to pounce on Eddie Morrison and run him through with his new weapon.

When the door flew open, Connor was shocked to find a dwarf running into the middle of the room. He froze, unsure what to do. Was he being rescued?

The dwarf turned around and landed his eyes on Connor, who was attempting to hide the rest of his body behind the opened door.

The little person was still holding a gun. "I'm Angel, kid. I'm here to save you."

"I thought Angels were bigger," squeaked Connor.

Lil' Baby grinned. "Not the cherubs."

Connor was still confused. "And you're here to *save* me?"

"I'm here to save us both."

Chapter 10

As Whelan and Cannon drove deeper into the forested area between Cumberland and Cacapon Mountain, the roads became more slick and dangerous with a mix of snow over a layer of ice.

"If you want to save your son, you need to get there in one piece," said Cannon when they rounded yet another curve at fifty miles an hour. Their back tires skidded to within a foot of the steep drop-off on the road's left edge as they climbed higher and higher through the foothills.

"The road sign says thirty-five miles per hour," continued Cannon. "And they mean in *normal* weather!"

Whelan slammed the brakes without warning and whipped the car over to the right side. He jumped out of the car and walked around to the passenger door, yanking it open.

Before he said anything, Whelan took a deep breath and counted to ten. The meditation skills he'd been working on last year were difficult to adhere to in recent weeks as they drew closer to catching Eddie Morrison.

Cannon was still sitting in the passenger seat with his eyebrows high on his forehead.

"You drive," said Whelan.

Cannon hopped out and ran around to the driver's side. They were quickly on their way at a safer speed.

"You don't genuinely think we're going to find Eddie and Connor at this cabin, do you?" asked Cannon after a few more minutes of silence. "I mean, what are the odds?"

"I have no idea," said Whelan. "*You're* the one who suggested we rule it out. I can't even think right now. Phil, I'm tired, and I'm stressed. He's got my boy."

Whelan watched the passing trees and began processing that Eddie Morrison took his son.

Cannon could offer no comforting words. He felt the same way. Over the past year, events bonded the Whelans to him like family. This felt personal to him too. He knew it was tearing Tom apart inside. Usually, the bureau wouldn't allow an agent to lead an investigation when his own family was involved, but these were extenuating circumstances.

The navigation screen on the SUV was indicating a turn in a quarter mile.

The road was barely visible under the snow. There was no mailbox or other marker, but the GPS clearly showed this was the way. At least two sets of tire tracks ran up the path before them.

They wound through the forest, barren of leaves on all the oaks, poplars, and hickory trees. Branches glistened with a coating of ice capped with snow. The white pines were thick in this section and hung heavily with the shiny drapes of winter.

Cannon stopped the car. The two men gaped at the beautiful landscape in front of them. It was like a postcard.

"I guess spring hasn't hit Cacapon yet."

He studied the navigation screen on the display before them.

"We're about 800 feet from the cabin. If I get any closer, he'll see us coming, assuming he's still here. Can't tell for sure, but I think the overlapping set of tracks there," Cannon pointed through the windshield to the road before them, "is heading back down the road. It's hugging that side more."

"We're not going to get much cover from the woods this time of year," said Whelan.

"Agreed. You take the wheel from here. I'll walk up through the trees and try to stay out of sight behind the pines. If he's distracted watching you come up the road, maybe he won't see me coming in from the side on foot."

"Okay. Be careful. He's not alone."

"I'm always careful," said Cannon before heading out into the forest.

Whelan got behind the wheel and drove the remaining distance. An old pickup truck was parked beside the cabin. No other vehicles were present, but there was a small pool of blood on the matted, dirty snow, where another truck or SUV had clearly been.

Sticking his fingers into it, Whelan rubbed it and felt the viscosity, trying to get a sense of how old it was. The freezing temperature made it harder to tell, but he guessed not more than thirty minutes.

He pulled out his firearm, a Glock 19 he carried since his rookie year. The trail of blood led up the steps to the front porch. He followed it, his gun leading the way. Multiple tracks of footprints went up and down the steps. He couldn't discern much from them.

The cabin was large, at least thirty-five feet long. The door was halfway down, but even from the corner, when he arrived at the porch top, he could see it was wide open.

This was Whelan's first time here. He couldn't bring himself to come after the big bust of Eddie's original operation. His old partner, Jay Pierson, was gunned down not four hundred yards away in a clearing on the forest edge near the river. Whelan witnessed it from a few feet away and was forced to sacrifice Jay's body to save himself. He regretted that decision daily for the past three years.

His trained eyes roved quickly around the area. He was about to step inside when his peripheral vision detected a tiny tripwire running across the entryway. He froze, leaning his head through and

EDDIE MORRISON

jerking it back quickly. No one shot at him. It wasn't necessarily a confidence booster.

"Connor?" he said at low volume. *He's not here. No one is here. Shit. We missed him.*

He carefully stepped over the wire and saw the block of C-4 explosive it led to on the bottom of the inside door frame. It was large enough to take out the front half of the cabin. The rest would be incinerated from the ensuing fire.

Eddie's never coming back here.

Whelan surveilled the room, an ample open space with living and kitchen combined. There were two doors at the back, presumably to a bedroom and bathroom. It was professionally built and could be considered an upscale vacation home with the right furnishings. But with most of those seized, and after a year of being shut up, the interior was dingy. Dust and cobwebs made themselves at home.

He came further into the room. There was another large pool of blood near the small table in the kitchen area. A path of red smeared the floor from the table to the first closed door on the back wall.

"Whelan?" Cannon's voice could be heard on the front porch.

Whelan spun around. "Cannon, freeze! The door's wired with explosive. There's a trip wire six inches off the floor, ankle height."

Cannon stepped over the wire and joined his partner, his SIG P226 already drawn and aiming before him.

Whelan signaled with his eyes. Cannon approached the door with the blood path, standing to the side. He reached across to open it. Whelan's head bobbed, and the door flew open. He stepped inside and swung his gun around. It was a bathroom.

Sitting on the counter alongside the sink, with its water still running, was Lil' Baby. His vacant eyes were open to the ceiling. A towel, soaked from his own blood, protruded from a bullet hole in his gut. His right hand was clasping at a second hole in his chest.

There was blood all over the toilet. Presumably, he'd climbed it to get up to the counter.

Whelan released a breath he hadn't realized he'd been holding.

Thank you, God. It wasn't his son sitting there, dead from blood loss.

He heard Cannon's voice, seemingly distant, yell, "Clear!" from the next room.

Soon he felt a hand on his shoulder. He turned to find Cannon shaking him. His mind watched him in slow motion before racing back to normal speed, and he snapped back to the present.

"Lil' Baby?" asked Cannon.

"Yes. That's him. Eddie wasn't only luring *me* to this cabin. There's more going on here than we know."

Chapter 11

The other door at the back of the cabin led to an abandoned bedroom. The two agents searched the main room. It didn't take them long to find the empty coffee cup with dried tomato soup on the bottom.

Whelan had grabbed some extra print-dusting kits before they left D.C., given the message from Connor at Ms. Roffler's home. Sure enough, when he straightened up over the table now covered in black powder, two words were spelled out in little fingerprints: MIAMI and SHEILA S.

"Connor *was* here," exhaled Whelan.

"Who the hell is Sheila S.?" asked Cannon.

"I'm not sure," said Whelan. He stood staring at the dust for a minute. "The last few months before I captured Eddie, there was word about a new player in Miami, Sheila Sanchez. She was stepping on some of Eddie's territory. No one had her on their radar before then. Since she wasn't part of Eddie's operation, I didn't follow up on it. My hands were full, plus I had a one-track mind back then. If I could get my mind working at all."

"Tom, any time we begin talking about your experience in Miami, you either shut down or change the subject. If this Sheila Sanchez is involved now with your son, maybe it's time you told me what went down there."

Whelan ignored him. They finished their search, then called the Baltimore office for an Evidence Response Team to come out and investigate properly, hopefully revealing a lead. Eddie's DNA was on file, and Whelan wanted to know if he killed Lil' Baby or if it was someone else. How many people were here? What kind of car did the second set of tracks outside belong to? What should they be searching for?

They also arranged for a bomb squad to come and defuse the detonator attached to the C-4. The local county sheriff was called to come and babysit the cabin so no one else could get hurt before the feds could arrive.

"I bet that trip wire was intended for you," commented Cannon as they made their way to the car.

"Possibly."

Once a deputy showed up, Cannon climbed behind the wheel, and the agents made their way back to Cumberland. On the way, Whelan called Garrity so he could quit harassing the locals about seeing any dwarfs in town.

"The massage parlor said they saw seven, but I'd have to pay to get all their names. Then they started giggling and hung up on me," said Garrity over the phone.

"Start flashing Eddie's picture around instead. Focus on him. And ask people if they know of anyone named Sheila, possibly Sheila Sanchez. The job's still the same. Hit all the motels, hotels, and B&Bs. But now it's Eddie and Sheila instead of Lil' Baby."

"Got it," he mumbled and closed the call.

"He sounded disappointed," said Cannon.

"Yeah, well, this FBI shit isn't always glamorous. Man's got to pay his dues."

"Have I paid mine?" asked Cannon.

"Definitely."

"Then tell me about Miami. It seems we're heading there."

Whelan studied the younger version of himself, still considered a rookie by some accounts. *His* rookie year, nearly ten years ago at the young age of twenty-four, was more exciting, saving a family from another bad guy, as his son would say. That family was in Grand Cayman now.

What he'd never shared with anyone in detail was his final three months working for Eddie Morrison in Miami. He was undercover, still gathering evidence to bring down Eddie's entire operation, as his old partner, Jay Pierson, wanted.

"I knew when I stayed in Cumberland after Jay was killed, Eddie didn't connect *my* alias to the feds, or I would have been killed the first week. Jay slipped up. He thought he was just going to scout out Eddie's cabin, here on Cacapon. But he wasn't invited and tripped some alarms. Eddie sort of had a policy of shoot first and ask questions later. Jay ran. He should have stayed and bluffed his way through Eddie's interrogation. But just the fact he ran was proof of his guilt, in Eddie's mind.

"I stayed undercover. 'Tommy McMurphy,' I was known by. I don't know if Lil' Baby ever realized Jay was the one who was killed by Eddie on the mountain that day or not. We'd never met Eddie, and he trusted Lil' Baby, so when he vouched for me, Eddie didn't question it. I made up a story that Jay took off for Brazil to handle a personal situation. We'd proven ourselves. Lil' Baby never had reason to question me. For the next two months, I lived every second braced for a bullet to the head.

"When I realized that bullet wasn't coming, I told Lil' Baby I was ready for more responsibility and could use some sunshine. He recommended me for Miami at my request."

Cannon let Whelan talk, taking it all in.

"Now, they weren't going to let me waltz into a city like that and start running the show. I would be the number three man. I answered to a guy named Isaac, and he answered to Eddie."

"Isaac Friedman," interrupted Cannon. "I remember his name in your report."

"Yes," said Whelan. "Isaac ran Miami like an accountant—everything on the up-and-up and with detailed records. I knew if I could get those, we'd be able to throw the book at Eddie. But until then, I needed to prove myself to yet another criminal. All while missing my son," he choked.

Whelan paused his story, engrossed by the passing woods.

Cannon let him work through his emotions.

"So I'm helping move girls," Whelan continued, "from Cuba, from Asia, South America—all coming through Miami and being shipped off to other cities—by train, some by truck, hell, some by boat. Many were eighteen and over, but many weren't. I kept telling myself this would be happening with someone else, if not me. And at least I showed them some dignity and wasn't constantly trying to rape them. Some nights I convinced myself pretty well, even slept okay. But most nights, I was so sick over it, I vomited myself to sleep. I was already thin. No one noticed.

"Then one day, with zero warning, Isaac walks a man into my office and says, 'Tommy, I want you to meet Eddie Morrison,' like it was no big deal. But it was. I nearly shit myself. I turned slowly, ready to see the barrel of a gun. I knew he'd already seen photos of me, videos. The whole place was on camera. I figured he finally remembered me from the day he shot Jay right in front of me, ten feet from the tree line. But he didn't. I was backlit that night by the setting sun and in the shadow of my SUV.

"So, Eddie walks in and shakes my hand, and he's not the beast I'd imagined him to be. I'd seen a couple of bad photos and his face was locked into my head from that fateful day in these woods. But I'd never *seen* him. He was normal. Normal height, normal build, balding but still some hair, nearing sixty but pretty fit. Normal. I had contorted his appearance in my head to reflect the monster I knew him to be. But he could have been any guy sitting at any bar in

America, drinking a beer and watching the game on the big screen while chomping on bar mix."

Whelan paused again, his eyes glazed, staring at the road before them but focused twelve-hundred miles away.

"He tells me they're having a war with a competing sex trafficking operation," continued Whelan. "This was about three months before the big bust. Eddie wanted me to go undercover for *him*, pretending to be a buyer of girls from Chicago. He'd already set up an alias for me, Thomas Billingsly, with a fake passport and Illinois license, and gave me a background story. He'd been working on putting me in this position for a while, and I couldn't refuse if I wanted to continue with his organization—or remain alive.

"Up to this point, I'd stayed pretty clean, but now, I'd have to do unspeakable things." Whelan disappeared into the past as he shared his nightmare memories.

Fourteen months ago, Whelan approached a man at the door of an adult video arcade in Hialeah, a city in greater Miami.

"You're Thomas Billingsly?" the man asked.

It was a smoky hole in the middle of a run-down strip center in the part of town no one respectable went to after 9:00 p.m.

"Yes," said Whelan. "I'm Billingsly. Where's Jorge? I was told he'd show me the merchandise."

He was guided to a door in the back.

Inside was a parlor unlike anything Whelan had ever seen outside the movies. It was part Turkish and part Moroccan with a touch of West India thrown in. There were four casino gaming tables to the left. Two were filled with men playing poker. A large bar was in the back, trimmed in polished bronze, with red-leather stools lining the front. The wall was full of premium liquors. Turkish chandeliers hung everywhere, illuminating the lounge in warm, colorful light.

The right half of the room was set up with padded, stadium style seating facing a small stage on the right wall. Dozens of pillows lined the seatbacks. A curtain was pulled across the performance area, in bright reds and indigos, with gold fringe tying it to the rest of the décor throughout.

Men were scattered around the pillowed seating, casually drinking. Whelan got the impression they were waiting on a show.

A Latino man approached Whelan and stuck out his hand warmly. "Billingsly, I'm Jorge Ruiz. You can call me George. Welcome to The Harem."

He was exceptionally fit and attractive, well groomed, and wore designer clothes costing the equivalent of Whelan's past two paychecks.

After the formalities, Whelan was instructed to make himself at home. The girls he was purchasing wouldn't be arriving until tomorrow. Until then, he would be Jorge's guest. "Enjoy the show. Enjoy the girls. These aren't yours. *Yours* are better. I've seen the photos. You have a $50,000 credit at the tables, or you can grab a girl and have some fun. There are private rooms through there," he pointed to another door in the back left corner. "Party favors come out at eight."

Whelan grabbed a Maker's Mark and took a seat at the poker table. The other players eyeballed him.

"Tommy Billingsly, Chicago," he mumbled.

The dealer shoved over exactly $50,000 in chips. His arrival wasn't a surprise.

The men were generally quiet, occasionally swearing softly when they lost a hand or snickering when they won a large pot, especially if they'd been bluffing.

EDDIE MORRISON

Music started playing from overhead speakers at 7:45 p.m., from Turkey, Whelan believed, *or possibly Egypt?* The house lights dimmed, and a steady line of girls clad in negligees poured in from behind the curtain on stage and dispersed themselves, two to a man, fawning over them and rubbing them in all the right spots.

"Excuse me, gentlemen," said Whelan, standing. He motioned for the dealer to cash him out. He was $23,000 ahead. For a brief flash, he wondered how to collect the actual cash profit and send it home to his ex-wife to bank for Connor's college fund.

Two girls escorted him to a pillow and blatantly offered their services.

"I'm on business, ladies," he jested. "I'm relaxing—not participating—until I can get my pre-arranged delivery."

"How will you know if you want them if you don't try them on for size first?" said one of the girls. Whelan thought she couldn't have been older than fourteen.

Another man joined them. "You don't want them? I'll take them," he said.

Whelan was unsure where the man came from, but he was obviously eavesdropping.

The girls got on each side of the man and began undressing him, kissing each newly-bare inch of skin along the way.

Whelan wanted to leave, but Jorge Ruiz, the owner, was watching him from near the entrance to The Harem.

I'm being sized up. He needs to make sure I'm not some sort of cop or federal agent.

Somewhere, a gong rang. He hadn't seen one earlier. The noise reverberated around the room's insulated walls. His watch read 8:00 p.m.

Trays were passed around with an offering of pills, cocaine, and heroin.

Don't show your shock, Whelan told himself. Jorge was still watching, observing. Thankfully, he recognized most of the pills and grabbed a couple he believed were relatively mild speed. He popped them and washed them down with a swig of whisky.

The show starting onstage saved him from watching the exhibition next to him. A spotlight hit the curtain, and two more girls came out, naked except for thigh-high boots and long gloves running up their arms. They were dancing with a boa constrictor, allowing it to entwine their bodies.

Saved!

Whelan got up and headed to Jorge Ruiz at the door. "I don't do snakes," he said. "I'm going to head to my hotel. You can text me at this number tomorrow when my merchandise is ready."

"Nonsense, friend. You just arrived. Sit and have another drink. The following show will be snake-free, guaranteed."

Whelan detected an aggressive tone in Jorge's voice.

"Fine," he conceded. He was growing foggy, and his body heated. He was beginning to feel like he took ecstasy instead of simple speed. He grabbed another one off a passing tray and held it up to Jorge.

"What is this?" he snapped.

Jorge smirked. "A special recipe. The Harem Molly, exclusive to my guests."

"I thought it was a simple amphetamine."

"You insult me, friend. I would never serve my guests anything 'simple.'"

"Of course. I didn't mean to offend," apologized Whelan. "I'm feeling strange. I normally stick to alcohol."

"Well, when in Rome," said the club owner, wrapping his arm around Whelan's shoulder and leading him back to the bar. He hooked Whelan up with another drink and guided him to the tiered pillow seating.

"You shouldn't be behind the wheel right now," said Jorge, squeezing Whelan's thin shoulders. "Stay. Play."

The drugs were beginning to affect other patrons as well, and soon, half the men were up on their feet dancing or sitting on their asses with a girl straddling them.

A petite young woman, who Whelan was certain must be at least twenty, started flirting with him. The drug in his bloodstream was potent. This was definitely not normal X. She was cute and her makeup was tasteful. She was dressed like a college girl attending an all-night slumber party with the boys of a frat house during Rush week.

Whelan allowed her to kiss him. A steady beat took over in the music overhead.

Thump, thump, thump.

It was a thrustful rhythm accompanied by other percussion and the wailing of a woman who could have been from any Middle Eastern country.

The snake girls were still on stage, so he averted his eyes to the woman in front of him. Her hands were all over him. Her lips were too. Before he knew it, she freed him from his belt and the zipper of his pants.

Thump, thump, thump.

She straddled him as he gave in to his role as Thomas Billingsly, buyer of sex for hire. His head fell back, and his eyes caught Jorge still observing his actions. He gave a nod to the man before bringing his head back to—whatever her name was. She absolutely beamed. Her teeth were straight. Her hair smelled like lilac. The merchandise was high-end. These weren't downtown hookers. These girls were two-to-five-thousand dollar a night money-makers for the disturbed ultra-wealthy a city like Miami could draw in. They'd be able to make a ton in Chicago.

Except *his* delivery wasn't going to Chicago. They were staying here to work for Eddie Morrison. Seven weeks later, Agent Tom Whelan—Tommy McMurphy to Eddie—was promoted to co-run Eddie's Miami outfit in anticipation of Isaac's retirement. He'd proved himself to Jorge Ruiz, and after becoming a regular patron, he soon learned where Jorge bought the girls from. Once enough intel was collected to expand his cosmopolitan prostitution ring, Morrison tracked Ruiz one night to a dark alley and personally plugged three rounds into the guy.

Thump. Thump. Thump.

Chapter 12

"That's pretty intense," said Cannon when Whelan finished his story.

He wheeled into the parking lot of the police station in Cumberland. "I heard the whole experience left you messed up. I mean, it was certainly a culture shock for you, but it didn't sound as awful as I imagined."

Whelan was reminded that, while three years separated his protégé in age, nine more years' field experience was under his belt.

"I shared the 'glamour' and spared you all the gory details," said Whelan. "I was trapped in The Harem for over sixty hours straight that first visit. Jorge captured me, essentially, testing me, making sure I wasn't DEA or with some other agency. No federal agent is authorized to do what I did, not for sixty hours, and not for seven weeks. I wasn't going to let three years go down the drain. And I wasn't going to let Jay's death be in vain. So I played along.

"I snorted, I boozed, I fucked—at least a half-dozen drugs and twice as many girls. I was in there from Friday night until Monday morning, and I wasn't the only one. The Harem runs non-stop all weekend. My first weekend and for the next six, I saw men and girls vomiting, sometimes in the toilets, sometimes, well, they couldn't make it. I saw fourteen to seventeen-year-olds being statutorily raped, slapped around violently, strangled—one of whom died—so old men with fat wallets could get their jollies. I saw five coronaries from overdoses over seven weeks—men and girls quickly rolled up in a tarp, taken out back, and stuffed in a van to be disposed of under a downtown bridge. I witnessed bestiality, pedophilia, sadomasochism—in many forms—every sexual kink and alternate deviancy you can imagine. My 'wholesome' Midwestern brain and Christian sensibilities couldn't cope, so I kept shoveling in the drugs. Of course, I wrote in my reports it was all under control. Told them I wasn't using like I was or becoming addicted to anything."

Whelan rolled his sleeve up past his elbow and pointed to a couple of faint red dots on his arm. "I ended up doing heroin. It's an awful, beautiful, disastrous, magical thing. Merely a few times, but if I hadn't gotten away from it all when I did, I don't know if I could have ever come back from spiraling. Thankfully, the 'big bust' of Eddie's outfit went down four weeks later. There was enough on him to make it stick—on all of them."

Cannon peered closely at the inside of Whelan's elbow. The scars were so light and small no one would ever recognize them against his naturally freckly skin.

For Whelan, they were a much more prominent reminder of how close he had walked the line.

He stared at the little specks, his branded shame. "I always tried to hit the same two spots. Last thing I needed was for my SAC to call me in and see a bunch of track marks down my arm."

He quickly rolled his sleeve down.

Cannon stayed quiet and wide-eyed.

"Over a year ago now, and sometimes, Phil, I think I could still give in to it. Eddie has my son!" Whelan hissed. "And I went to bed last night, on my *ex-wife's sofa*, thinking how nice it would be to simply shoot up and obliterate all memory of it."

Cannon put his hand on Whelan's shoulder. "But you didn't. Because you're *not* an addict. And if you ever start down that road, you *call* me, you understand? I don't care what time of day or night, you pick up the phone, and we'll talk it out. Have you given in to it, ever, since the bust?"

"No. Somehow, I hung in there through the last few cases. I managed okay. But now I'm dying inside. Not even twenty-four hours yet, and I'm dying inside. That bastard ruined me, and now he has Connor."

"Tom, you're stronger than you know. Eddie didn't ruin you. You ruined him. And now he wants revenge. But you have me and the full power of the FBI behind you. We're going to figure out his master plan here, with Lil' Baby, with this 'Sheila' character in Miami, and with Connor, and we'll get him back. I swear to you. Nothing will stop us from getting him back."

Whelan took a deep breath and counted to ten. "Thank you, Phil. I know we will. Let's get inside and see if Garrity has managed to get any answers."

The men entered the precinct. Whelan picked up on a familiar scent hanging in the air near the front desk.

"Took you boys long enough," said a recognizable voice. "Phil must have driven."

They turned to find Assistant Special Agent in Charge of the Kansas City Field Office, Miranda Jones, sitting on a bench beside the front wall of the Cumberland, Maryland, police station.

"Jones! How are you here?" asked Whelan.

She gave one of her generous, glowing smiles. "I had some time off coming. I took it."

Whelan went in for a deep hug then held her shoulders when he tore away, melting into her beautiful face. "Thank you, Miranda."

Her head cocked to the right as she detected something was off with her dear friend and fellow agent. "Of course. It's you. It's Connor."

She gave him another hug, then did the same with Phil Cannon. "Wonderful to see you. Now, let's get to work. Where are we at?"

It was her way of asking for a full update. They had been under her immediate supervision for over a year and a half, and past cases brought her closer than a superior should be toward those under her command. Her own boss, SAC Alan Kendrick, who she was also tight with, reminded her of it constantly.

They filled her in.

"Does Kendrick know you're here?" asked Whelan, "On 'vacation?'" He made finger quotes in the air.

"Off the record, yes. And he sends his hopes and prayers. What's our next step?"

"We check in with Agent Garrity from Baltimore."

"I've done that," said Jones. "He's still in the field. Three local officers are also out, door knocking, flashing Eddie's photo. So far, nothing. Is it enough, or should we be out there too?"

"I don't know. This town can't have that many locations to stay," said Whelan. "After what we unearthed at the cabin, it's a safe bet Morrison is taking my son to Miami sooner than later."

Whelan and Cannon filled in Jones on their discovery at the cabin on Cacapon Mountain.

Jones was puzzled. "I thought Cumberland and the cabin in the woods was the best bet to trap you alone. Sounds like he's not ready for you yet. I wonder why. What do you suppose he's planning?"

"I'm not sure, but my gut is telling me he's not in charge any longer. We need to find out who the hell this Sheila S. is. Connor wouldn't have written her name and the word 'Miami' if it wasn't important."

"If it is this Sheila Sanchez," suggested Cannon, "what is she doing with Eddie Morrison? You said she was his competitor?

Eighteen months ago? You think he's desperate enough to join forces with her?"

"He's desperate enough to do anything at this point. He must be out of funds. We've had him on the run so long he's burned through all his IOUs, and now, who knows? I'll call the SAC of the Miami office and see what they have on Sheila Sanchez—let him know we're headed his way."

"I'll phone Captain Vicente Mansilla," said Jones. "Sometimes the local P.D. doesn't share all their intel with the feds. But we bonded pretty well during the 12 Pills investigation. I think he'll let me in on any news."

"I'll check in with Garrity," said Cannon. He turned toward the sound of the door opening as Garrity walked in with one of the local officers.

"Well, my job's done," said Cannon.

"Two officers are still pounding pavement, but we haven't caught a break all day," reported Garrity. "I need to call Baltimore with an update. What am I telling them?"

Whelan gave him a quick summary.

A loose plan was formed, pending additional information from the Evidence Response Team at Morrison's cabin.

At 6:27 p.m., the call came in. Whelan put it on speakerphone.

"Eddie Morrison was here," they said. "We believe the tracks on his vehicle belong to a 2020 Chevy Tahoe. A BOLO was issued ten minutes ago. If any of those are seen on the highways between here and the Georgia border with only one man and a boy, it will be pulled over and questioned. Best we can do without a tag or car color."

"I'm sure he's already switched cars," said Whelan. "It's part of his M.O."

"We understand. An Amber Alert went out for the entire East Coast. Connor's face is making its way around Facebook and Instagram. People will call."

"Got it."

"Agent Whelan," the man continued. "Eddie Morrison's wounded. The blood beside the parking space *was* his, and it was a fair amount. We brought a portable DNA sequencer. We tested blood throughout the property. Much of it's Angel Baylor's, quite a bit is Morrison's, and there's a third. Not enough to be life-threatening, we believe. We ran it through the national database. It's your son's. We took it by the broken rocking chair, close to the wall. Probably a small wound, nothing serious, or there would have been more volume."

Whelan's eyes closed, and he whispered, "Please, God."

When they flew open again, he snapped, "What else?"

The man on the phone continued. "There are no other fresh fingerprints anywhere on the property. Again, we found Morrison's, Baylor's, and your son's. The detonator and the C-4 were removed, and we've installed new locks on the door. We set up another set of cameras to monitor it all, but it's doubtful he'll ever return.

"Agent Whelan, we did find a tiny bunker about seventy yards up the hill from his cabin, dug out from the ground and lined with concrete. It was about four feet square. Not large enough to house a man, but it could have held plenty of weapons and supplies. No doubt an emergency stash."

"Interesting. Did we miss it the first time, or is it new?"

"We can't be one-hundred percent sure, but I expect it was there for several years. The concrete was dry, possibly waterproofed on the exterior, as no water intrusion was observed inside. We didn't dig the entire thing out, but that's my guess."

"So this is something they failed to discover when they first raided the mountain a year ago?"

"Yes, sir. It's not on the report. Honestly, it's blind luck we hit upon it this time. If it wasn't exposed by his recent entry, we'd have walked right over it. The snow was thick, and below it, the leaves made for efficient cover."

Whelan digested his statement, then asked, "What's being done with Lil' Baby? Angel Baylor."

"Baylor's body left for the morgue. We're sending it back to Baltimore. It will be under our care until we figure out who to release it to."

"Thank you," said Whelan. "Call me if anyone tries to claim it." He hung up the phone and turned toward his fellow agents, his friends, hopelessness filling his eyes.

"I'm sure Connor's fine," said Cannon. "That blood spot next to the busted chair *was* pretty small."

"So," said Jones, "we driving or flying?"

"I don't think we're going to catch up to him on the highway," said Whelan. "By now, he could be driving anything. He'll have changed vehicles at the first opportunity. I think we should catch the first flight out of Dulles and get a jump on finding this Sheila."

"Captain Mansilla gave me a place to start," said Jones.

Whelan nodded gratefully. "Miami, here we come."

Garrity chimed in. "I've never been to Miami. I can't wait to get out of this cold."

"You're coming?" asked Whelan.

"Have to. I'm under orders, remember? To keep my eyes on you? Director Commerson's already signed the transfer to your unit. Don't worry, I won't get in your way. I already let you go to Cacapon without me. But if I let you go to Miami and I'm not reporting in daily on your ability to objectively function as the lead on this case,

I'll be in hot water. Use me. I can be an asset. I've been a Special Agent for two years. I have a doctorate in psychology. I read people well. Use me."

Whelan glanced at Jones and Cannon. They shrugged. It was his call.

"Welcome to the team."

Chapter 13

Eddie swapped cars three times in Virginia. Connor heard a gunshot before he climbed from one car to another during the last swap, but he'd been half asleep and wasn't sure what happened.

When Eddie vacated the car to fill up at a gas station before moving into South Carolina, Connor saw a significant pool of blood in the driver's seat. Eddie had ridden in it for 172 miles.

Is that Eddie's or the previous driver's?

Connor knew of at least two gunshots Eddie was nursing, one in the left leg and one in the left shoulder. While Eddie's body and face revealed he'd lost a ton of blood, he still seemed capable of driving and stealing cars. He was using his belt as a tourniquet for his leg, releasing it every hour for several minutes to get blood flow to his foot, though his wound was bleeding much less now. He'd stuffed his shoulder wound with paper towels. Some nurse was going to have a field day cleaning it later.

Those bullets must not have hit anything important. Connor sighed.

The digital clock on the dashboard read 1:07. *In the morning. We're going to be driving all night. I guess I should be grateful we're not killing another person to save forty dollars on a tank of gas.*

The gas pump was twenty feet from the restroom door on the side of the building.

"Go pee, shit, whatever you need to do in there," said Eddie. "If you're not out in two minutes, I'll come in and drag you out. I'll have eyes on that door the whole time. Don't be stupid."

Eddie didn't anticipate the bathroom had two stalls and wasn't vacant.

"Please help me!" Connor whispered to the man coming out of the second stall. "I've been kidnapped! A bad man out there with a gun has killed at least three people so far tonight. We're heading to Miami."

The man glowered at him, thinking he was a problematic kid fabricating a story for attention.

Connor's eyes were filled with terror. "Please! I'm not joking. My dad is Thomas Whelan with the FBI. He's been chasing this man for six months. And now he's come after me! He's using me to get my dad!"

The man slowly retrieved his phone and dialed.

"911, what's your emergency?" the woman on the other end asked.

"Yeah, I've got a young man here who says he's been kidnapped. We're at the Sunoco in Cana off the Fancy Gap Highway. His name is—what's your name?"

"Connor Whelan."

"His name is—" It would be the last words he ever spoke.

A bullet struck the back of his skull and ripped through the front, taking much of his forehead with it. Blood sprayed across Connor's face. He stood horrified until instinct kicked in, and he bolted for the door. But Eddie was between him and freedom, and took him down with a punch to the face. He nearly lost consciousness but managed to stay awake.

Before he realized what was happening, Eddie was shoving him into the back seat of the other car at the pump—presumably the dead man's.

Connor struggled, but his head was spinning. He managed to kick Eddie's left leg close to his bullet wound before the door slammed against his foot.

The scream was worth it.

"Fucking kids," Eddie mumbled as he turned the key.

They took off flying down the highway. Five minutes later, they turned into the parking lot of a storage facility.

A man was unloading some bags from his Toyota, which he'd foolishly left on between trips inside the building. It saved his life. He never saw the outlaw who stole it or knew he was forcing a twelve-year-old kid to join him.

They altered their route, moving farther west before resuming their southbound trek toward Miami on a new highway.

Eddie stayed off the grid as best he could and used a U.S. Road Atlas as a guide. Connor had never seen anything but Google Maps on his phone and was amused as Eddie fumbled through the pages trying to figure out a fast but obscure pathway.

Around 2:00 a.m., Connor saw a "Welcome to South Carolina" sign.

Eddie was making favorable time despite staying off the interstate. They were southbound on Highway 15. He allowed the boy to ride up front in the passenger seat again since the roads were nearly empty. And it made the kid easier to punch should he get out of line again.

Connor held a cup of ice against his cheek. It helped with the swelling and pain from being struck by Eddie Morrison's knuckles an hour ago. He'd been hit by a boy in school last year. It wasn't nearly as painful as this.

Eddie wore a ring. It was a gaudy piece, overly large, with a deep red tourmaline stone. It was a showpiece and tore open some of Connor's skin.

As he rolled the cup around, trying to find the coldest side, he thought about what his dad said about men who drive extra-large trucks for show. They were compensating for their small penises. He supposed the same must be true for rings.

Suddenly he was aware his crotch was damp. His entire right leg was covered in urine. His bladder decided to empty itself when he was struck in the restroom, though sadly, not into a toilet.

Awesome.

He kept staring at the blood on Eddie's right hand. It was dry and smeared in long lines. It wasn't his. It was the poor man's from the gas station. *Oh shit.*

Connor lowered the visor in front of him. It housed a light-up mirror. He clearly saw his face for the first time. It was spattered in drops of dried blood, except for the left cheek, which Eddie had cleaned with his fist. He leaned closer. Some of the spots contained small protrusions, like the finest ground beef you might find on a chili dog at the drive-in.

What is that? Oh God.

It wasn't just the poor man's blood on his face.

It's bits of brain.

"I'm going to be sick," Connor managed to voice. "Pull over."

"Not now, kid. You gotta vomit, you do it here."

Connor turned to Eddie, who wasn't bothered by sitting in blood for two hours. He would hardly be bothered by a touch of vomit.

The backseat held some old T-shirts. Connor took one and began wiping down his face. It was wet from the sweat on the cup of ice he'd been using to cool down his cheek. Everything was soon clean. Once white, the jersey cotton in his hands was now streaked with the contents of someone's noggin.

Before he could stop himself, he vomited into the shirt. It held the bulk of it without leaking. He rolled the window down and threw it out. If any splashed the side of the car on its way to the shoulder, he didn't notice or care.

Closing his eyes, Connor tilted his head toward the cold night air. It was fresh and comforting. Eddie was stoically quiet at the wheel, so he peered out toward the passing trees silhouetted against the sky by a low quarter-moon. He was exhausted and longed for sleep, but his mind was roused.

I feel completely awake.

He shot Eddie a scowl of growing animosity. A small glimpse of what his dad spent two years of his life dealing with to catch this man the first time came into focus. Not yet a teenager, Connor Whelan knew what it meant to truly hate for the first time in his life.

He felt more wetness on his face. He grabbed another t-shirt from the backseat and flipped down the visor to see what spots on his cheeks he'd missed. There weren't any. Blood was replaced with tears he didn't realize he was shedding. Wiping them away, he disappeared mentally into the tree line again as the pair drove southward in thunderous silence.

Chapter 14

By 7:30 a.m., Agents Whelan, Jones, Cannon, and Garrity were finishing breakfast at their Miami International Airport hotel.

"You look like shit," said Jones to Whelan.

"I tried to sleep. It didn't take. I was on the phone with his mother till three a.m. She cried a lot. Screamed a lot. Blamed me for all of it, and of course, it truly is my fault. I let her vent."

They all stayed quiet. No words of comfort came to them.

"I got a call around six this morning," continued Whelan, "from the FBI field office in Charlotte, North Carolina. A 911 call came into Cana, about an hour north of them, around one a.m. A man was killed in the bathroom of a gas station. Supposedly, this guy was reporting that a kid in the bathroom was telling him he was kidnapped. A gunshot went off when he was about to give the kid's name. The 911 operator thought it was a prank, but after they sent a patrol car over and saw the body, they replayed the audio, tweaking it in their software. Faintly, in the background, you can make out Connor's voice, telling the man his name."

"Oh, Whelan, I'm sorry. I'm sure it was traumatic for him," said Jones.

"Thank you. I told them to check for stolen automobile reports, and sure enough, there were two. They're jumping cars often. There's a BOLO out for the last one we know of, but I'm sure Eddie's in another vehicle by now. He's smart. He'll know *we* know where he was as of one o'clock."

"*And* that he's heading south. No doubt Miami," said Cannon.

"How far is Charlotte from Miami?" asked Garrity.

Jones whipped out her phone and asked Google. "Ten and a half hours. But he'll be staying off the interstate, no doubt, using smaller highways. Add another two to three hours?"

"So that puts him in Miami around?"

"Two to four p.m.," said Whelan. "Assuming they push straight through."

"Nothing like murdering someone to wake you up at one a.m.," said Garrity.

"Eddie's killed so many by now, I don't think it's an adrenaline rush for him any longer," said Whelan. "We've got six hours to figure out where he's taking my son."

He hung his head and disappeared into his oatmeal.

"Hey," Cannon shook his shoulder, "we know Connor's alive. And he's trying to escape. He's smart."

Whelan thought about the confusion and terror his son must be experiencing. He was screaming inside. *He's twelve! He's scared! He's innocent!*

Cannon's eyes poured with compassion. What else could he have said?

"Yes, he is," said Whelan. "Thank you, Phil."

Forty minutes later, they were sitting inside the office of Captain Mansilla of the Miami Police.

"Agent Whelan, I'm sorry to hear about your son," said Mansilla.

"Thank you. What can you tell us about Sheila Sanchez?"

"Not much, I'm afraid. No one has ever seen her. She keeps in the shadows. We captured video footage twice, but it's blurry. She's in large sunglasses, and her hair changed from blonde to black. Either or both of those could have been a wig. Facial rec isn't hitting on anything. We have nothing on her for an arrest, so we can't get a warrant. The members we've interviewed—who patronize her private club—swear no one under twenty-one is inside. All her licenses are legit and up to date. Not a single crime has been reported since she came on the scene over a year ago."

"Word on the street is she's running girls. No evidence of prostitution?"

"None. Drinks and dancing."

"What about her private residence?" asked Jones.

"Can't find anything under her name. Either she's renting, or it's under some trust or LLC we can't attach her to yet," said Mansilla.

"So, how do we get invited inside this private club of hers?"

"*We* don't. But I'll make sure my boys are busy elsewhere if you guys happen to stop by unannounced."

"I like dancing," said Jones.

"I like drinking," said Whelan.

"And I like keeping the two of you out of trouble," said Cannon.

Garrity kept his mouth shut.

"Off the record," began Captain Mansilla, "I hear there's a doorman who's been known to pocket a bill or two to let someone slip in for an evening. A lot of out-of-towners patronize the club, and I doubt they all have memberships. The doorman's got a nightly guest list."

"What about during the day?" asked Whelan.

"Shut up tight. And no, I can't look the other way if you break and enter. Place opens at seven p.m."

"By seven p.m., my son will be here and in her hands already, assuming Eddie's bringing him to her, *and* we've got the right Sheila. I need access *now*."

"Did you file a warrant?"

"I tried on the way over. It's like you said, not enough evidence. My son didn't give us a last name. We're guessing it's this Sanchez woman. She's the only Sheila we know of connected to Eddie Morrison. Sources said she was stepping on his turf before he was busted, stealing some of his girls and setting up a competing operation. It wasn't my case at the time. I was focused on Morrison, and she never came into play."

Mansilla pursed his lips in thought. "Let me make a call. There's bound to be a fire alarm. Perhaps a faulty signal requiring immediate entry? I know the fire chief presiding over that jurisdiction."

Mansilla started dialing on his cell phone. "Should be beautiful. It looks over the water and back toward Brickell Island. At night, those buildings are lit up like Christmas year 'round."

"Brickell?" asked Whelan.

"Yes, didn't I mention? The club is on the top two floors of a thirty-two-story high-rise in Brickell's business district. Plus, the roof."

"The roof? Of course. It's Miami."

"Yes," said Mansilla. "Prime real estate in a city full of high-rises. There's a pool, an outdoor bar, and two hot tubs."

"What's her club called?" asked Cannon.

"The Lemon Drop," answered Mansilla. "It's positioned to have stunning nightly views of the sun setting over the western horizon."

"Dropping like a lemon," mumbled Whelan.

"Top two floors—and the roof—of a building in Brickell? Then she's renting. Who's the landlord? Or the property management company?" asked Jones.

"I've been working on this since you called me yesterday. Again, everything's been by the book with that outfit, so I haven't exactly had a reason before now to check into all this. I'm sorry I don't know more. As soon as we track anything down, I'll text you. We're working on it."

Mansilla wrote the address down on a slip of paper and handed it to Whelan. "Here, get on over there. I'll have the fire chief meet you there."

He spoke into his phone. "Hello? Joe? It's Vicente. I need a favor."

The federal agents were waiting out in front of the high-rise full of primarily office space when a white and red SUV drove up and parked in the fire lane.

"I'm Joe Peters, fire chief for this district. Vicente filled me in. I understand we're investigating a fire alarm going off on the thirty-first floor?"

"Yes," said Whelan. "And maybe on the thirty-second as well. We'll need to confirm there's no one in immediate physical danger."

Jones opened the hatch on their rental SUV and retrieved a battering ram.

Whelan's eyebrows shot up. "You happen to keep one of those in your purse for emergencies?"

She laughed. "It's on loan from Mansilla. I don't expect there will be an easy lock for you to pick. It's all secured with keycards."

"Oooh, fancy," he mumbled.

Jones paused in front of the entrance to the club. There was a logo on the door of the Miami skyline with a setting "lemon" sun in between the buildings. *The Lemon Drop* was written above it.

"Cute," she mumbled before letting the ram fly. The door to the club gave way on her second swing.

It was high-end, tastefully decorated, with magnificent water views. This floor mainly held lounge seating with small, bistro-style tables near the windows. One bar was on this level. A wide, spiral staircase led to the second level, where they discovered a massive dance floor, two more bars, and significantly more square footage. From here, you could see in all directions.

Another set of stairs led to a double-wide door with access to the roof. It was also locked, so Jones let loose with another swing of the ram.

"She's enjoying that," commented Garrity.

"Damn straight," said Whelan. "It's part of her yoga routine."

Jones came back down after a minute. "Roof's clear. We can start digging. You know, I half expected to see a bunch of tiny rooms with beds and massage tables in them."

"That would be too easy," said Cannon.

"I don't get something. The first level occupies *half* the building," said Jones.

"The permit says otherwise," argued Whelan. "She's leasing the entire floor. Let's check it out."

He returned to the floor below and found a door behind the bar, hidden by a small curtain. It led to commercial office space. Three were large, and shared a standard bathroom in the hall, but the one farthest back was enormous. It came with its own private bathroom with a shower, a large sitting area with sofas, a wet bar with an espresso machine, and behind the slick metal and glass desk were floor-to-ceiling views of Brickell Island.

"This must be Sheila's office," Whelan commented to Cannon as he wandered in.

"Impressive," he said, testing filing cabinets in the built-in on one wall. He tried yanking on a desk drawer. "All locked. How are we going to explain busting these open for a fire alarm?"

Whelan smirked. "Who said we have to bust them? Watch the door."

He pulled out his lock pick set and unfolded it across the desktop. Drawers popped open within seconds.

"You see Fire Chief Joe coming down the hall, let me know. He'll need plausible deniability. I don't want this to be traced back to him or Mansilla."

"Gotcha. What about Jones?"

"What about Jones?" asked Agent Jones, stepping inside the room.

"Where's Garrity?" asked Whelan.

"I told him to start with the roof and the top floor and go over each fire alarm and monitor with Chief Peters, and if he 'happened' upon any useful paperwork, to text me."

"Perfect. I'm starting with the desk. Why don't you start with the cabinet there," he said, pointing to a four-drawer on the wall.

Twenty minutes later, Whelan set about re-locking the drawers in the office. "Nothing," he sighed.

"Liquor orders, rent payments, maintenance bills," mumbled Jones. "It all seems legit. I didn't see any membership lists with names, no clientele for us to follow up with."

"I took some notes of two LLCs listed as the recipients for rental payments. I don't see Sheila Sanchez listed as a managing or board member of either of them on Sunbiz. There are two addresses, however. We need to check on them. Can Mansilla loan us a car? We need to split up, save time."

"We can requisition one from the bureau."

"Miramar's forty-five minutes from here. Mansilla's office is two miles away."

"I'll make the call," said Jones.

They collected Garrity and thanked Chief Peters.

Captain Vicente Mansilla met them in the parking lot with a set of keys. "Take mine. I won't have to explain this on paper and wait for approvals."

Whelan gave him a warm handshake. "Gracias, Vicente."

He ordered Cannon and Garrity to check out an office in South Miami.

Garrity paused. "I should be riding with you, Agent Whelan."

"I know," said Whelan. "Keeping your eyes on me. Agent Garrity, you can report back to Baltimore—and Director Commerson—whatever you need to. But right now, we'll cover more ground if we split up, and I'm relying on you to do your job as an agent more than my personal babysitter. Are you okay with that?"

"Yes, sir." Garrity recovered his backbone. "Agent Cannon, I'm with you." He climbed into the passenger seat of Mansilla's car and began texting an update on the situation.

Cannon raised his eyebrows. "He doesn't do anything without reporting in and getting feedback."

"He's under orders. He's new to our team. I get it," said Whelan. "You want me to send him home? I'm happy to if he's just in your way."

"No. We'll be fine. The more we have working to find Connor, the better. Good hunting," Cannon said to Whelan.

When they drove away, Mansilla started chuckling. "Agent Whelan, you ever get tired of the FBI, I'll always have a position open for you." He started walking away, then threw over his shoulder, "You too, Miranda!"

Whelan stared at her. "You know he's got a huge crush on you."

She peeked back over her shoulder, staring a little too long at the man now opening the door to the police station.

"I do like Miami," she mumbled to Whelan. "So, where are *we* headed?"

"Star Island."

"Star Island? Is it full of celebrities?"

"In fact, it is. The Shaq, Gloria Estefan, J-Lo."

"No shit?"

"No shit. At least at some point. I haven't exactly been keeping up with their recent sales activity."

The homes did not disappoint. Ranging from thirty to over a hundred million dollars, the mansions were sprawled out on a literal island directly across from Dodge Island, better known as the Port of Miami, the largest passenger ship port in the world.

When they went over the MacArthur Causeway Bridge, Whelan whistled and pointed at one of the many cruise ships docked. "That's the new one from Kittimer Cruise Lines, their flagship. I think it's the biggest on record now. I can't watch twenty minutes of TV without seeing their ad."

"It's enormous," said Jones. She read the name of the ship off its side. "*Kittimer Journey*."

Whelan quoted the tagline from the newest commercials he'd seen advertising the behemoth. "Because it's not just about the destination. It's about the journey."

"Sounds like fun. You could use a vacation after this last year. Why don't you take a week and go on that once this is all over?"

"You know I love the ocean, but I'd rather be alone in a fishing boat for a week. I don't need all the fancy crap—casinos, nightclubs, stage shows. I'm good."

"I disagree. Tom, you're young. You've got so much life ahead of you still. Quit isolating yourself from the world and start participating in it. Take Connor. Nothing like a cruise to reunite you two."

"His mother would never allow it. Not after this," he said.

"Well, maybe not right away. But *you* should definitely go. Do you a world of good. Take Cannon."

"I've already spent too many nights in a room with that man this year. I'm ready to either marry him, or divorce him."

Jones laughed.

"But seriously, Miranda, if we don't bring Connor home from this...."

"We will, Tom. Whatever this Sheila Sanchez has to do with this, we'll find out, and Eddie Morrison is going down. Permanently."

Whelan knew she meant her words. "Thanks, partner. You know," he paused, choking up.

Jones let him finish his thought.

"When we thought this was all about Eddie using him to get to me, I thought the world made sense. This doesn't make sense. Why is Eddie bringing Connor here? Is he bringing him to Sheila? He could have had me on Cacapon Mountain. What's his endgame? Who is this Sheila to him, and why would *she* want my son? And what did Lil' Baby have to do with all this? Why did Eddie kill him? He used to be Eddie's top man."

"Clearly, they had a falling out." Jones gave him a pat on the leg. "We don't have all the answers yet, Tom, but we'll get them. And we'll get Connor."

They crossed the bridge onto Star Island and flashed their credentials to the guard at the gate. In another minute they were in the home's driveway. Zillow estimated the value at around ninety-million dollars.

Jones read from her phone's screen. "Nine bedrooms, thirteen bathrooms. Over twelve-thousand feet, under air. Swimming pool. Boat dock. You think if we combined our salaries?"

"For a thousand years?" asked Whelan.

They flashed badges to the man answering the door.

"I'm Arnold. I run the home. You obviously aren't expected. Do you have a warrant?"

"No," said Whelan. "But we have an emergency. I need a few questions answered by the owner, Mr. Leon Bergman, and then we'll be on our way."

Arnold handed him a business card. "Make an appointment."

He attempted to shut the door, but Whelan blocked it. "Arnold, I don't have time for this bullshit. Tell Mr. Bergman it won't be pretty if I have to get a warrant. I'll make sure every cabinet, drawer, closet, and cubby hole in here is tossed so badly it will take housekeeping a month to put it back together. And here we are, in the height of 'season.'"

Arnold raised one eyebrow. "Wait here."

After three minutes, Whelan started pacing the front porch.

"Did I threaten enough?" he legitimately asked Jones.

"*I* wouldn't want to be in charge of housekeeping after that. Best you could do."

She turned her head to the side, pointing her ear toward the edge of the home. "Wait here. I think I heard a noise out back."

Jones didn't offer him an explanation. She walked around the side of the home and down a pathway toward the backyard. When she came into view of the boat dock, there was a locked gate, hindering her from going farther.

An enormous yacht was tied up to the pier. It was the starting of the engine she'd heard on the home's front steps. A woman raced on board, wearing a bright yellow one-piece swimsuit with a sheer, light pink cover-up. Oversized sunglasses and a yellow straw hat hid her face from view. Brown wavy hair fell halfway down her back.

Jones whipped her phone out to shoot a photo, but the woman was already below deck before she could get her first shot off. She zoomed in on the yacht and snapped a couple, but after a few more seconds, it zipped away, taking off to the north.

Whelan was still waiting in front when she returned. She showed him the photo and relayed what she'd seen.

"I think we're in the right place," she said.

"How do you know?"

Zooming in on the photo, she pointed to some markings on the back of the yacht. "Because the name of *this* boat is *Sheila's Sunshine*."

Chapter 15

Arnold returned after another minute and allowed them entrance into the home.

"Wait here," he instructed.

The foyer was grand, as expected. The mansion sprawled out in three directions with gleaming white marble floors leading the way. A contemporary, chrome-bannistered staircase swept up to the second floor in grand utilitarian style. Decoration was sparse but felt expensive, purchased certainly to complement the contemporary industrial design of the home.

Arnold reappeared and escorted them to the lanai out back. A man stood to greet them.

"I was about to tackle errands," said Arnold to him. "Should I wait until this business is finished?"

"No, thank you, Arnold. I know you've got a full afternoon scheduled. Thank you for coming in this morning. I'll be fine. See you at eight tomorrow morning."

"Very good, sir. Have a splendid evening."

Arnold strutted past the agents and disappeared inside the home.

"I'm Mr. Bergman," the man said. "How may I help you?"

Jones gave him a quick once-over. He was mid-sixties with thick salt-and-pepper hair and a large belly overhanging his bathing trunks by a considerable amount. A ton of gray chest hair filled the valley between his man boobs. He was physically soft, like most men with money who hire all menial labor done on their behalf.

"I'm Special Agent Jones with the FBI. This is Special Agent Whelan," she began. She intentionally didn't use her Assistant

Special Agent in Charge title. "Was that Sheila Sanchez who took off on that yacht?"

"My guest's information is private. Why are you here?"

"We're looking for Sheila," said Whelan. "We understand she pays rent to an LLC located at this address. You own the LLC *and* this property. We need to know what Sheila pays you for, specifically. We have reason to believe she's connected to an active kidnapping, among other crimes."

"Never heard of her," said Bergman.

Jones showed him the photo of the yacht on her phone. "*Sheila's Sunshine*? Pretty coincidental, wouldn't you agree?"

Bergman pretended to glimpse the photo. "Yep. Coincidental."

"Sheila is your *guest*? Not your tenant? She doesn't live here?"

"I don't know who you're talking about," said Bergman.

Whelan was scouring. "Right. What do you do, Mr. Bergman? For a living?"

"I'm retired."

"What *did* you do?"

"A little of this, a little of that."

Jones snapped at the man. "Mr. Bergman, do you know Eddie Morrison?"

"Nope."

"Do you have any ownership stake in The Lemon Drop?"

"I don't know what that is. So, I'm going to have to say no." His tone was condescending.

"I don't have a problem arresting you for obstructing an active criminal investigation," threatened Whelan.

"I'm not obstructing anything. I've allowed you to come inside my home, and I'm answering your questions."

"You're lying. That's obstruction."

"Fine, arrest me. My attorney will have it dismissed before we even arrive at the station."

Whelan's face was red. The early spring sun was hot in Miami, and Whelan was growing hotter.

He attempted to plead to any morality this man might have. "Mr. Bergman, my son has been kidnapped. This isn't some random, unknown kid you see on the eleven o'clock news. This is *my* boy. Do you have kids?"

"Two, both grown. They've got kids of their own now."

"What if you knew your grandchild was in trouble? What wouldn't you do to save them?"

"A number of things. They're ungrateful little snots who could use a few harsh lessons."

"Mr. Bergman," interrupted Jones, "we need answers. We need them today. This man's son is arriving in Miami sometime in the next few hours. We need to rescue him before anything worse happens, or there will be hell to pay, unlike any you've ever experienced. I'll have the FBI, the DEA, and the IRS scope through your life, your properties, your family—until you're so deep in attorney fees you'll have no choice but to sell this home to pay them all. I'll be a stick in your ass until all of your crimes cling to you like flies on molasses. I'll make it my life's mission."

She practically spit on him with her growing exasperation.

Leon Bergman took a step back from the agents. He clearly wanted to retort something equally hateful, but thought better of it, then walked over to the pool and down the steps until he was waist-deep. "Contact my attorney."

Whelan took off his suit coat and handed it to Jones. He proceeded to do the same with his shirt. He leaned over and untied his shoes, slipping them off one by one, then his socks. Lastly, he dropped his pants and folded them in half over her extended arm.

He took a deep breath, hoping his chest would fill and appear larger than the size thirty-eight coat he wore. He couldn't do anything about his size thirty waist. At least his boxers gave his white freckly body a few ounces of color. They were even clean today.

Marching over to the pool steps, he went down them, slowly, intently, focusing the scariest crazed expression on his face he could gather toward Leon Bergman.

Leon was definitely freaked out. "What the fuck is he doing?" he screamed at Jones. "Is he mad?"

"You could say that," she muttered.

"Stop!" he yelled at Whelan. "Don't you touch me!"

Whelan's voice was eerily soft and rational. "Does Sheila live here?"

"Get the fuck away from me, you weirdo!"

"Where is Sheila going now? Where would she run and hide right now?"

"Help! Help!" Bergman called. There was no one to hear his pleas.

He backed up into the side wall of the pool.

"Are you a religious man?" asked Whelan. "Have you atoned recently?"

"For what?" Bergman asked. "I have nothing to atone for."

"Did you participate in Teshuvah last Rosh Hashanah?"

And then Whelan was on him. He grabbed Bergman's shoulders and pushed him until his head was underwater.

"Help!" Bergman gargled on his way in.

He tried to fight Whelan, but didn't have any strength compared to the insane young FBI agent above him.

Whelan let him rise after a few seconds to take a breath. "Where's Sheila?" he shouted.

Without giving him time to answer, he shoved Leon Bergman beneath the surface again. He counted to thirty this time.

When Bergman came out, he managed to spit out, "Fuck you!"

Under he went again, this time for forty-five seconds.

Jones laid Whelan's clothes across a chaise lounge nearby and walked to the pool's edge. She wasn't sure how far Whelan would go but wasn't prepared to let him kill this man. More because she didn't want to see him go to prison than she was worried about saving the scum in the pond.

On his next breath of air, Bergman spit out, "I know where's she at!"

Jones couldn't tell if Whelan heard the man or not when he pushed him back down again. "Whelan," she started.

"Yeah, okay," he grunted and let the man surface.

After gasping and choking up water, Bergman hoarsely whispered, "Sheila's gone to her private condo. It's on Belle Isle. I can give you the address."

"Where's my son!" Whelan belted five inches from Bergman's face.

"I don't know your son. I don't know what Sheila's involved in. She stays here some weekends and throws private parties, usually when I'm out of town on business."

"I thought you were retired," said Jones, towering above the pair in the water.

"When you have my kind of money, you're never *really* retired. Not unless you want to see some pea-brain swindle you out of all your assets and life's work. Money requires managing, and nobody manages your money like you do."

"I'll remember that when I win the lottery."

"Usually?" asked Whelan. "What about when you're in town?"

"Then I stay and enjoy the party."

"And the girls?"

"What girls?" asked Leon.

Whelan grabbed his shoulders again, ready to push him under.

"Yes! And I enjoy a girl or two."

"As many as your Viagra will let you?" snarled Jones.

The man was utterly defeated. "Let me out of this water, and I'll tell you everything."

Chapter 16

Five minutes later, Whelan put his pants and shirt back on as Leon Bergman recovered in a chair with a towel around his shoulders and a bourbon in his hand.

Jones wished she could have one as well. She'd never seen Whelan snap entirely. She thought she'd seen all sides of the man, but there was still more. She was emotionally somewhere between troubled and impressed by his actions.

She moved her eyes from Leon's rocks glass to his face. "So these private parties, how often are they?"

"Twice a month, and sometimes for special holidays."

"And what's it cost to come to one of these private parties?"

"I wouldn't know. I don't have to pay."

"Zillow says this house has nine bedrooms. I'm guessing they are occupied on and off throughout the evening?"

Bergman nodded, taking a sip. "I have the master bedroom, of course, and it's off limits to anyone but me, but the rest of the home? Safe to say I pay my housekeeping staff plenty of bonuses."

"And what do *you* make? For all this? What's your take?"

"My take?" He seemed genuinely confused.

Whelan found his voice. "You do realize she's running a whore house? These girls are all prostitutes."

"What? No, they're just girls partying in Miami like girls do, having a fabulous time. We drink, we dance, we powder our noses a little."

"You haven't noticed many of the girls seem very young?"

"I'm old," said Leon. "Everyone seems young."

"Those girls are often minors. Some not even teenagers!" snapped Whelan. "Sheila's trafficking young girls for sex, many against their will."

"No." Leon was in denial. "They're *parties*. There are both men and women on the guest list, and Sheila doesn't just have girls." He focused his eyes on the ground after his statement, contemplating what the agents were telling him.

"What does that mean?" asked Jones. "She has boys too?"

"Sheila has guest lists. Some are old, some are young. There's plenty of gender fluidity. Guests can mix with the opposite sex or with the same. There's something for each guest's taste, and no one's judging. It's usually young folks partying it up with older rich folks who can treat them to an evening unlike any they've ever experienced. And if people wind up getting their rocks off in a bedroom before the night's end, well, that's considered one hell of a party!"

"I assure you," Whelan said through gritted teeth, "those girls aren't getting their rocks off. They're frightened children, thrown or trapped into a world of prostitution and drug addiction, unlike anything you've ever seen in the movies. They're victims!"

He stood up and slapped the glass out of Bergman's hand, sending it flying across the lanai. Before Jones could stop him, Whelan was behind Leon Bergman. He whipped the towel from Leon's shoulders and wrapped it around his neck, squeezing tightly.

"Where's my son?" he yelled into Bergman's left ear.

"I don't know your son. I don't know anything about him, I swear! If Sheila has your boy, I don't know anything about it!" he squeaked out before his voice box was cut off.

"Whelan," said Jones. She shook her head.

He never could resist her when she looked at him that way. He let go of the towel and walked over to the side of the property, staring into the water of Biscayne Bay below him.

"Mr. Bergman," said Jones. "Where's Eddie Morrison? I'm giving you one last chance to answer before we have you arrested."

"Arrested? For what? I answered all your questions! I don't know who this Eddie guy is, I told you. Sheila's business is *hers*. I run my own. I attend her parties once in a while. That's it."

"How long have you known Sheila? Who is she?" asked Jones.

"Sheila Sanchez? She owns a club in Brickell. I met her about a year ago. We've shared this living arrangement for six months. She's satisfying company, and she keeps the house in pristine condition. The parties are a fringe benefit."

"Yeah? Well, your partying has made you an accessory to sex trafficking."

"Sex trafficking! What are you talking about? Those girls and boys come to revel in the festivities. They're not slaves. They're not stolen from China. Most are pretty little Latin things—Cuba, South America."

"They're not *things*!" Jones barked. "They're human beings! And that's more than I can say for you."

She picked up her phone and started dialing the bureau. After identifying herself, she was transferred to the Miami Field Office. The special agent in charge was on the phone shortly and she filled him in.

When she hung up, Leon was staring at her.

"Get some pants on, Mr. Bergman. There's a team on the way to take you in. A warrant will be here within the hour to search your home. I will escort you to your bedroom so you don't think about escaping. And if you try anything, you should know I'm armed."

She drew her weapon from the rear of her waistband. "Come on, let's go."

He begrudgingly moved his way inside.

"Whelan, help's on the way. I'm going to escort this jerk upstairs for a few minutes. You okay?"

"I'm fine," he said, turning to her. "Thanks, Miranda."

"As soon as they get here, we'll go grab that bitch. Or better yet, call Cannon and get him and Garrity to pick her up now before she can get away." She walked inside the home.

Whelan yanked the piece of paper with the condo address written on it out of his pocket. He dialed Cannon and updated him on the situation at Star Island.

"Well, thank God," said Cannon. "We're getting somewhere. Whelan, we need to use her. If Eddie's on his way here to meet her and give her Connor, we should let that play out. We'll have Connor back before the night's over!"

"Shit, you're right. I don't know if the SAC of the Miami office is going to see it the same way."

"This is *your* show still. No one has told *me* any differently."

Whelan's whole demeanor lit up like a lightbulb with the flick of a switch. "Cannon, get over there and watch her until Jones and I can meet you there. Don't let her out of your sight, but try to keep your distance. She'll call off her meeting with Eddie if she suspects she's being watched. Hopefully, our arrival here today didn't already change those plans."

"I don't know why it would," said Cannon. "You think she realized it was you at the front door?"

"I have no idea. Maybe. Or it's possible she fled when the doorbell rang. She doesn't like to be seen. She could have flown out of here to avoid a nosy neighbor."

"Why don't you go make sure from Mr. Bergman? It might affect how we play this out. In the meantime, we'll get over to Belle Isle."

Whelan was full of renewed hope—of catching Eddie and getting his son back. He opened the slider door to the home as a loud gunshot came from the second floor.

"Miranda!"

Chapter 17

"I'm hungry," said Connor, as he and Eddie passed a sign for Cracker Barrel on the side of the highway.

They were forty minutes west of Orlando, Florida, on Highway 27.

"You've got to be hungry, too," Connor continued. "I promise to behave. Wouldn't you like some fried eggs and biscuits?"

Eddie Morrison stayed silent as they passed the exit for the restaurant.

"God, fried eggs sound amazing," Connor mumbled.

He peeked at the gas gauge. "You need to fill up. Can we at least get a cinnamon roll from the gas station?"

"Why? Do you want another man's death on your hands?"

Connor's heart fell from his chest. He fixated on the floorboard for over a minute until his grumbling stomach drew his attention.

"I swear I'll keep my mouth shut. Can we go through a drive-through? Seriously, I haven't eaten for two days except for your can of tomato soup. You won't get any ransom money for me if I'm dead."

Eddie jerked the car off the road onto the shoulder and came to an abrupt stop. He glared at the boy, then brutally slapped his face. It was the same side he'd punched the night before. The spot of skin Eddie's ring previously broke open, tore again, pouring blood down Connor's cheek and neck.

Connor didn't bother wiping it away. He shrank farther into his seat and focused his attention out the window. There were cows in the fields on his side, so he started counting them to occupy the minutes as they resumed their route.

Fifteen minutes ticked off the clock. Suddenly, Eddie jerked the car onto the shoulder again.

A man was selling fruits on the side of the road from the back of his truck. He offered oranges, grapefruit, guava, papaya, and assorted vegetables.

"If you open your mouth or that car door, I'll kill this man, same as the others," Eddie threatened.

The farmer appeared old and tired.

"I won't move a muscle," said Connor.

"The others" tallied sixteen now, lives Eddie took since snatching Connor from his home. Lives snuffed for no reason except they were an inconvenience or a means to an end. Lives taken with no consideration or remorse.

Eddie lectured Connor each time he shot someone as though he was giving lessons. "Now listen, kid, when you pop someone, make sure you get them in the head before you walk away. You know, say your first shot is the leg or the gut—even the heart—make sure you pop'em in the head before you leave. People survive all kinds of crazy shit, but they don't survive a shot to the head. Or if they do, they'll be a worthless vegetable. Remember that, kid. Pop'em in the head to make sure they're dead."

Eddie exited the car and spoke with the man operating the fruit stand. He returned with a basket of oranges and a sack of roasted peanuts.

As they merged back onto the highway, Connor's eyes stayed on the fruit vendor. He was about to mouth the word 'help' but didn't want to risk the man's life.

The peanuts were warm. He cracked one open and threw the nut down his throat, barely taking the time to chew it. They needed salt, but he'd take it. He ripped into an orange. Not the sweetest or ripest he'd ever eaten, but to get oranges at all in March was a pleasant surprise.

"Hand me one of those," said Eddie.

Connor obliged. He also placed the bag of peanuts on the armrest between them without having to be told.

Before long, a highway sign read "Miami 210 miles".

They weren't making the best time any longer. After the sun came up, Eddie stayed on more obscure highways. The clock read 10:04. Highway 27 was better than the interstates, but there wasn't much alternative at this point between them and their destination.

He briefly thought about locking the boy in the trunk. Then he could hop on I-75, but he was already delivering damaged goods as it was.

He was scheduled to meet Sheila at 7:00 p.m. They should make Miami by 5:00 at the latest. That would give him two hours to clean up and prepare.

He turned onto a dirt road when the gas tank registered less than an eighth full. They traveled over a mile before he said, "There."

A small farmhouse was on the right. A truck was out front. When they turned onto the property, a woman opened the screen door on the home and waved, smiling.

Eddie screeched to a stop beside her truck.

Connor assumed the pair knew each other, but when Eddie hopped out and shot the woman between the eyes, he realized she'd just been a friendly sort. She probably smiled and waved at everyone.

By now, he knew the routine. He gathered the oranges, peanuts, and the ice cooler with the last four bottles of water from the 12-pack they'd started with and moved them all over to the truck's cabin. This one didn't even need hotwiring. The keys were on the console below the dashboard.

The tank read three-quarters. They might have to kill one more person to make it to Miami. One more would make eighteen. It cost eighteen lives to get from Cumberland to Miami.

As they nearly ran over the dead woman beside them, Connor offered another prayer. He was renewing his religion on this trip, at least. *Eighteen… Forgive me, God. I hope I'm worth it.*

"Miranda?" Whelan shouted again, bounding up the stairs of Leon Bergman's home on Star Island. He flung open doors until he saw her.

She was standing over Leon's body, a shot to his head spilling blood onto marble flooring.

"Shit, shit, shit," she was repeating as Whelan entered. "It wasn't me. I turned my back for five seconds to check out the view from his balcony. He must have had that .44 in his bureau. I guess I'm lucky he took his own life instead of mine. He was a coward, through and through. Shit, Whelan, I'm so sorry. We're not going to get anything else from him now."

Whelan stared at the dead man on the floor. "I was going to ask him if Sheila knew it was me at the door before she took off or if she thought I was some random stranger or neighbor. Cannon believes we can catch her when she meets up with Eddie. No reason to think she won't still keep her appointment. Hopefully, she wasn't supposed to check in with Leon before then."

"I hope not," said Jones. "I tended to believe Leon here when he said he didn't know about your son. It's possible he was just a landlord to the whorehouse and didn't have any further involvement."

"Would you take *your* own life if you had no further involvement?" asked Whelan.

Jones pursed her lips together in thought.

"Uh-huh," said Whelan. He took a long breath, closing his eyes and forcing his shoulders to relax.

"You're counting, aren't you?" asked Jones. "Getting your anger under control?"

"And, ten," he answered. "Learned from the best."

"Well, you can count to twenty, but it won't bring this bastard back. Let me call this in." She started to dial on her phone.

"Wait!" said Whelan. "This entire home is covered in cameras, except for Leon's bedroom. She'll know the jig is up if we have agents roving around. We need to wait until we have Connor."

"Then let's hope she doesn't rewind the footage from the camera overlooking the pool area."

"Let's get out of here. If she takes a peek and sees nothing, she might assume things are fine and Leon simply went out."

"I hope you're right."

"Do you have a better idea?"

"No. This is your show. I'm on vacation, remember? I'm not even here."

"I owe you a real vacation when this is over."

"I'm going to take you up on that," said Jones as they headed out to the car.

The pair made their way over to Belle Isle. Two minutes by boat became fifteen by car for only three miles of roadway in the Miami traffic. As they drove into the parking lot of the address for Sheila's building, they dialed Agent Cannon. His voicemail picked up.

"Must not be able to talk," said Whelan.

A minute later, a text came in from Cannon. *Meet me in the stairwell on the 18th floor.*

Whelan and Jones took the elevator to the seventeenth floor, then located the stairwell and climbed one level.

Cannon was on the landing, propping the door to the hallway open with his fingers and keeping his eyes on Sheila's door.

"Garrity suggested we stop and get a pizza to deliver to Sheila's condo," relayed Cannon. "If she opens the door, we ensure she's in there, then walk away and keep an eye on the place. We were going to tell her we had the wrong unit. That was the plan."

"Well, I didn't have more casual clothes with me, but Garrity brought a bag. He slips on jeans and takes off his dress shirt, so he's in a V-neck tee and some Calvin Klein's. I thought it was a decent plan. Sheila opens the door and damned if she isn't still in dark sunglasses and wearing a ridiculously large floppy hat. And get this. She says, 'Oh, that was fast. Come in. Let me get my wallet.' The woman actually *ordered* a pizza!"

"So, what did Garrity do?" asked Jones.

"He went in! That was right before you got here. He's still inside!"

Chapter 18

It was another three minutes before Agent Luke Garrity exited Sheila's unit. He glanced at the cracked doorway to the stairwell as he walked by but continued to make his way to the elevator and hit the down button.

Sixty seconds later, he raced up the stairs from the floor below.

He spoke in a fast whisper. "Oh my God! I thought I was busted. I thought she'd realize our pizza didn't come from where she ordered, but she seemed oblivious."

"What took so long?" asked Cannon. "You were in there for eight minutes."

"She couldn't find her wallet. Said she'd just gotten in, and the condo was a mess. She was tossing open drawers in the kitchen and dug through three purses. She disappeared in the bedroom for a while, and I'm thinking she's going to come out and fill me with bullets, and my hand's on my SIG in my pocket, ready to shoot back, but instead, she comes out waving a hundred-dollar bill at me, and apologizes for not being able to find anything smaller and tells me to keep the change since I was patiently waiting on her."

Garrity sheepishly held up the bill. "So I guess dinner's on her tonight."

Whelan's brow furrowed. "Were there any other entrances to her unit?"

"No, only the front door. We can definitely see if she leaves here."

"Any signs of anyone else living there?" asked Cannon. "Photos on the wall or tables? Any clothes that weren't hers? Men's or children's?"

"No. Not that I saw. I didn't go in the bedroom. I'm sorry, the place was huge. The furniture was all expensive. There were liquor and wine bottles on the table. I think she must have recently gone shopping and didn't have a chance to put some things away yet. There were papers and mail on the table. I was afraid I'd get caught rifling through them, but the name on the address was Sheila Sanchez. The address was this condo, not the home on Star Island."

"Okay," said Whelan, "that's helpful. What else?"

"What *else*? I had two minutes to myself, and she was in the same room with me the rest of the time. There is nothing else, Agent Whelan. If you expected her to have a full dossier on your son lying on the coffee table with his photo stapled to the front, I'm sorry, it wasn't there."

"What did she look like?" asked Jones.

"She kept those damned sunglasses on the whole time, and I think she might have been wearing a wig. It didn't seem to fit her quite right. Probably smooshed it on in her rush to get away on that boat. I'd guess her around five-foot-six? She seemed pretty fit—nice arms and legs—late thirties to mid-forties."

Whelan turned to Jones. "What do you think? We keep hidden and track her? Or do we hold her until the meet-up and hope Eddie still shows according to their schedule?"

"What if Eddie places Connor with someone else to hold while he meets Sheila? Maybe *that's* the plan. Maybe she's supposed to call with some signal first, and we mess it up? Until we know more, I think we should chance staying put and following her when she leaves."

"But if she's suspicious, if she knows about Leon Bergman, or gets a wild hair up her ass, one call to Eddie could cancel the whole evening."

"If she was suspicious enough to cancel, that call's already been made. Best we can do now is stick to her for the rest of the day."

They took turns watching her door through the crack of the stairwell access. Thirty minutes later, a pizza delivery guy exited the elevator and approached her door.

"Shit," mumbled Jones.

She put one foot in the hall and did her loudest "Pssst!"

The man turned, startled, as she motioned him forward with the hundred in her hand. He entered the stairwell and froze when he saw the three men staring at him like he was a wanted criminal.

Jones showed her badge and federal credentials so he would come to his senses. "Here." She handed him the hundred. "Go down one floor, and then you can catch the elevator on that level. You never saw us. Understand?"

The man's head bounced up and down, his eyes wide.

"Keep the change. Now get going, and if anyone asks, you delivered the pizza to that unit."

He took off, and they heard the door to the seventeenth-floor close below him.

Jones opened the pizza box. "Vegetarian."

She grabbed a slice and handed it off to the men, who proceeded to ravage it.

Two hours passed like two days. The stairwell was permeated with a musty concrete odor. It was eighty-one degrees outside, but with no air conditioning inside the confines of the emergency staircase, it felt like it was approaching one hundred.

Garrity was sweating, even in his t-shirt. He passed the time by texting and surfing the internet. Whelan and Cannon kept their dress shirts on, but the ties and jackets came off.

Whelan was studying Garrity. "Who do you keep texting?"

The man paused his cell phone activity. "My SAC. I'm supposed to report in to him regularly. Give updates. Receive any new orders."

"Make sure I'm not losing it with my personal involvement in the case?" asked Whelan. "And what if I do? He's going to sideline me?"

"Not him. Director Commerson. They're close. Even play golf some weekends. You know this order came directly from him."

"Uh-huh. You mentioned that. And how am I scoring?"

"One hundred percent so far."

"I suppose I should thank you," said Whelan.

"I don't relish being in this position, Agent Whelan. I'm just doing my job here, like you."

At 5:10 p.m., Sheila Sanchez entered the hallway outside her unit and approached the elevator.

"We're on!" whispered Cannon, who was on hall duty.

Jones took off down the stairs as fast as she quietly could and entered the hallway one floor down.

The agents were microphoned and wired for discreet communication.

"She's entering," said Cannon.

"On it," said Jones over the tiny speaker in everyone's ear.

After a minute, Jones said in Spanish, "Hello. Oh, what a pretty dress."

A woman's voice answered her. "Gracias."

Whelan and Cannon turned to Garrity, eyebrows high on their foreheads.

"That's her," he acknowledged.

The three men began racing down seventeen flights of stairs.

"Hello," repeated Jones in the elevator, putting on a thick Cuban accent. "Oh, I don't know anyone on the twelfth floor. I'm Maria Suárez, from the seventeenth."

Two women introduced themselves, and soon the earpieces were abuzz with the Spanish chatter of three women discussing the beautiful weather. Sheila Sanchez stayed out of the conversation.

As the men rounded the corner to the third level, Jones said, "Well, enjoy your day," to the women and presumably to Sheila Sanchez, still in Spanish, "And you too! Whoever you're meeting in that gorgeous outfit is a lucky man."

Sheila mumbled another simple, "Gracias."

After a few seconds, Jones' voice came over the earpieces. "We're in the parking garage, level P-2."

"Meet me on the street level as soon as you can," said Whelan.

He turned to Garrity and Cannon. They were all out of breath but holding up. "Get to your car. We can't lose her. Jones, what's she driving?"

Jones whispered, "I can't see yet! Hold on."

"Vintage Mercedes," she finally answered. "I can't make out the model—four doors, black, heavily tinted windows. I'm snapping a photo of the plate. Got it. She's on her way. I'm in the stairwell."

By the time she made it to Whelan's car, Sheila was long gone.

"We have her!" came Cannon's voice over the earpiece. "We're heading west on the Venetian Causeway. Traffic's a mess. Rush hour. You've got time to catch us."

"We're on an island with more homes," said Garrity. "Okay, it's behind us, but here comes another island."

He counted each time the bridge made landfall. It connected a series of islands across the bay, each full of residential condominiums or single family homes. "Here comes island number five."

"I see you!" said Whelan. "I'm three cars behind you now."

"We're about five behind Sanchez, but I've got her in my sights," said Cannon. "Oh shit. Oh no!"

"What?" screamed Whelan.

"Drawbridge! The light came on, and the cars are slowing. I'm not sure if we'll make it!"

He honked at the car in front, but little could be done. "She's got to stop. The gate's coming down. One more went through, one more... Fuck! She made it over!"

Cannon watched as another car made it behind Sheila, but the rest of them stopped and honored the traffic control signal. They were stuck, watching Sheila's tail lights disappear behind the rising steel bridge in front of them.

Chapter 19

Sheila Sanchez was filling up at a gas station on the mainland. She answered an incoming call as she squeezed the pump handle.

"Eddie? You on track?"

"I'm here," said Eddie from the other end.

"Do you have the child?"

"I got 'em. You have what you promised me?"

"Of course. Passport, travel money, and your wire is ready. Tomorrow, you'll be sipping beer on the beach with two million in an offshore account."

"Perfect. And you'll kill the father?" asked Eddie. "That's more important than the money."

"Eddie, you disappoint me. We have an arrangement, and these details were already discussed. Where's your trust?"

"You robbed it along with four dozen of my best girls."

"I simply offered better pay and a retirement plan. It *is* still a free country," said Sheila.

"Well, for some," she corrected, snickering.

"Right," said Eddie. "I'll see you at seven." He ended the call.

Sheila dialed another number. "We're on. I'll have the boy by seven-thirty. Make sure my *Sunshine* is ready to embark before then."

"His passport is already in your cabin," said a man on the other end. "It's first-rate. He'll be in the Columbian's servitude by week's end."

"Marvelous. Alejandro knows how to break in young boys. Connor Whelan will be working for me next summer."

"I hope the price was worth it."

"It didn't cost too much. Eddie Morrison's done most of the work. And the fool actually thinks I'm paying him for all this."

At 5:30 p.m., Eddie Morrison drove up to a parked food truck in a heavily industrialized area. A pretty Hispanic woman was dishing up tacos and empanadas. He waited until all her other customers left.

"Remember, you do or say anything, and this slut is dead. Understand?"

Connor nodded.

They were on the outskirts of Miami in Hialeah Gardens.

Eddie came back with a sack full of food. Connor opened up the first taco wrapped in paper. It was chicken. He devoured it in less than a minute. Thankfully, Eddie bought six of them.

He opened one up for his kidnapper and handed it to him. "You want hot sauce? There's a little Styrofoam cup with some red sauce in it. Smells like hot sauce."

"Sure, kid."

Connor poured a heavy dose over the top of the taco. As expected, it was soon dripping down the front of Eddie's shirt. He didn't seem to care. What was a little more red on a shirt soaked in dried blood?

"So, you're going to sell me off to this Sheila?" asked Connor.

"Yep."

"I thought you and I were getting along pretty well," he lied.

Connor heard his dad say more than once, *"The enemy you know is better than the one you don't."*

"Sheila's all right. You'll like her. She'll take care of you."

"What does she want with me? Is *she* after my dad too?"

Eddie observed the young man, not yet a teenager. He seemed older than his age. Or perhaps kids were growing up faster these days. "Kid, if you cooperate the rest of the day and don't give me any more shit or try to escape again, I'll let your dad live."

"So you *were* planning to kill him," mumbled Connor. "But not now?"

"Not if you're on your best behavior."

Connor thought about Eddie's offer. He doubted the man was telling the truth. *I may be a kid, but I'm no dummy. You want me to go along instead of finding my opportunity to escape. I bet there's going to be one soon.*

He wasn't sure how to respond without sounding dubious, so he gave a thumbs up.

Eddie was watching the small industrial park across the street. At 6:00 p.m., the last car crept outside the fenced area and stopped. A man jumped out and locked the gate behind him before leaving. The food truck had no more customers and quickly shut down its walls and took out. By 6:10, the whole area was a ghost town.

Eddie started the car and crossed the road. He pushed through the gate of the industrial park, then hopped out and rigged it to stay shut behind him. He wheeled the car around the back of the building and parked by a dumpster. A Florida canal was behind them.

Connor thought it was about as secluded as they could get.

Too secluded. This spot is perfect for killing someone unnoticed. He lied to me. Eddie's going to kill me here and dump my body in that canal. I wonder why he buttered me up with tacos first?

"Hop out," said Eddie.

Connor thought the man would shoot him the second he stepped out, but he obliged, bracing himself the best he could. His body tensed reactively, and his mind flashed images of his mother's face, his recent winning game, and the last Christmas morning he woke to find both his parents waiting for him by the tree.

No bullet came.

"Help me find one of these that's open," said Eddie.

The building featured roll-up doors on the backside, one per bay. It took three tries to find one that gave when he jerked up on the handle. The inside was full of chemicals in bottles, and the walls were covered in boxes with more chemicals and supplies. The tenant manufactured some kind of cleaning solvent.

Connor unboxed a case with the finished product inside. "Spray Away," he read from a twenty-two-ounce spray bottle label. He wondered if it would spray Eddie away if he doused him in it.

Eddie slipped out to the car and retrieved a bag from the trunk. "Come on, kid, let's get cleaned up. We want to be all pretty for our date tonight."

Connor relaxed with a deep breath and a sigh. *Guess I get to live a few more hours at least.*

Eddie grabbed his arm and walked him to the middle of the bay, where there was a small restroom.

Inside, he closed the door and began stripping off his clothes. Even Eddie's underwear was soaked in his blood, so off those came as well.

Connor inspected Eddie's wounds. "You look like you're auditioning for a Jordan Peele horror movie."

Eddie saw himself in the mirror and turned a full 360. His entire left side was covered front and back in various shades of red to brown from all the blood he lost. He'd felt weaker throughout the day but wasn't about to admit it to the boy. He guessed he was down by a pint and a half. The leg wound was starting to fester and pus. The bullet from Angel Baylor was still in there. At least the one in the shoulder went clean through.

He brought out a brand-new first-aid kit from his bag. "Unwrap this," he ordered.

Connor took the shrink wrap off the little kit while Eddie started sponge bathing in the sink. When Eddie finished, he poked through the supplies and grabbed some alcohol swabs and Neosporin.

"So," started Connor, "it seems like you were prepared to get shot?"

"Always be prepared, kid."

Eddie cleaned his wounds as best he could, packing fresh paper towels around his shoulder wounds. "Hold this a second."

"Sure."

Connor stood and held the wad to Eddie's back while he wrapped an ACE bandage around his shoulder and chest as tightly as he could. He clipped it, then worked on his leg for a minute until it was bandaged.

"Your turn," he said to Connor. "Strip."

"You're not going to rape me or anything, are you?"

"*I'm* not," mumbled Eddie.

He confirmed there was no possible way Connor could escape the bathroom if left alone. "I'll give you some privacy. Clean all the blood off you and leave the bloody clothes on the floor. Doctor any injuries."

He whiffed the air. "And sponge those armpits. You're giving off an odor."

"You're sure that's *me*?" Connor mumbled, mocking Eddie's attempt at scary snarkiness. He'd heard his rape remark but chose to ignore it outwardly. Inside he was panicking. *He's turning me over to someone who wants to* rape *me? I've got to find my move.*

Eddie pulled out some clean clothes from the bag for himself. "There's a set in there for you too. Put them on when you're done."

He left Connor alone. Dressing slowly, Eddie winced when putting his left shoulder through the button-down shirt he'd taken from Mrs. Roffler's home. Soon, he was as fit and presentable for his meeting with Sheila Sanchez as he could get.

Rapping on the bathroom door, he asked politely, "You ready, kid?"

Connor opened the door. "Almost."

He was attending to his wound from Eddie's fist and ring. It wouldn't stay closed with a regular bandage, so he grabbed two butterfly bandages from the kit. He was applying the second one now. He hoped Eddie would feel remorse at seeing him trying to doctor the injury inflicted by him.

Eddie's face registered nothing.

Connor was in a dress shirt also, with a green sweater vest and a pair of Dockers, all of which were too small, but he'd managed to button. "The shoes won't go on at all."

Eddie saw the little black loafers on the floor. "So leave 'em. Wear your sneakers." He stepped inside and checked out his reflection in the mirror. He combed his hair, then turned to Connor and ran it through his mane. They both could use a shampooing, but it would have to do.

"Let's go, kid."

They piled back inside the car and headed out of the area.

As they turned onto the street, Connor wondered if anyone would ever see his fingerprints on the mirror, spelling out, "911 - Connor Whelan."

Chapter 20

It took over twenty-five minutes for the agents to get to the mainland after being stuck at the drawbridge on the Venetian Causeway. Captain Mansilla's precinct was nearby, and by 6:15, they were filling up on coffee in his office.

"Any hits on the BOLO for her car?" Whelan asked Captain Mansilla.

"Not yet. They know to follow her only, if they do spot her."

"I can't believe we lost her," said Whelan. "We had her, then we lost her. It's my fault. I made the call."

"It wouldn't have been beneficial to take her before we have Connor back," said Jones.

"Agreed," said Cannon. "Whelan, we'll get him back."

"How?" Whelan screamed at his younger partner and friend. "Just how is that going to happen in a city the size of Miami? Where are we supposed to search *now*?"

Captain Vicente Mansilla stood up. "Well, for starters, I've got two undercover agents ready to go into her club on Brickell, *The Lemon Drop*. I've got Miami Vice's finest monitoring her condo and her yacht, *Sheila's Sunshine*. If anyone shows up there, they have orders to take them for questioning. I've got officers stationed near Star Island. They're ready to thoroughly search the property once you give the word. They've been holding off because you're concerned about her monitoring video footage, but the sooner we get in there and start tossing the place, the sooner we might have information opening up other locations where she might be. Same with her condo, frankly. I've got warrants in hand for both, and if she returns to Star Island, we'll be watching by road and from a boat on the water.

"Oh, and in case it all goes sideways, I've alerted the Coast Guard, and they're keeping an eye on all traffic coming and going out of the inlet around Virginia Key and Key Biscayne. Anything bigger than a fishing boat not registered to someone known and identifiable will be stopped for questioning tonight. They'll do the best they can. Not too many coming and going after dark, and they told me all available response boats would be on top of it tonight."

Whelan rose to his feet, his eyes opening wide toward Captain Mansilla. Without warning, he leaned in and gave the man a firm hug. When he backed away, his eyes were wet, but he contained his emotion.

"Thank you, Vicente."

"It's my pleasure," Captain Mansilla said. "And my job. Right now, I'm delighted I'm exceptional at it."

He shot Jones a smile.

She returned it and mouthed, "Thank you."

Garrity couldn't take the following minute of silence any longer. "Okay, so what's *our* next move?"

Whelan was smart enough to know he was not at the top of his game. He raised his eyebrows to Jones in defeat.

"With no fresh leads and the clock ticking," she started, "I'd say it's time to start ransacking her condo. I doubt she kept many files at the Star Island home, but there's a chance she's got guest lists there. We need names, and we've got to start interviewing people. Find out who knows her best, where she might go when not at home or the club, and if she has any other properties in the area."

"I'll make the calls," said Mansilla.

Cannon repeated Garrity's question to Whelan. "And us? Where do you want us?"

"Get back over to the condo. Supervise the search. You know what we're looking for."

"You got it." He patted Garrity's arm and motioned him to follow.

Jones caught Whelan's eyes. "You hold strong. We'll find him."

Whelan nodded. "I've got to call his mother with an update."

He stepped out of the office, then continued out of the building. He found a sidewalk bench out front. High-rises surrounded the precinct. You couldn't see the bay from here, but he knew he was a few blocks away. *Connor would love Miami under normal circumstances. We should plan a trip. Maybe take that cruise.*

Whelan sighed pulling out his phone to call his ex-wife, Georgia.

She answered in one ring. "You have him?"

"Not yet. We're in Miami. We have leads. We'll get him." It was the best he could manage.

She was silent for a few seconds before spitting out, "I hate you right now."

"I know," he said. He ended the call. *I hate myself right now.*

His phone rang, and he answered without checking the screen. "For what it's worth, I still love you."

"You're going to love me even more," said Jones on the other end.

"Miranda? Sorry, I thought you were Georgi, calling me back. What's happened?"

"*Sheila's Sunshine* is on the move. Vice is following it discreetly. I've ordered the searches on the condo and the home at Star Island to stand down until we see how this plays out. I got in touch with them before they entered. If she is monitoring those locations, there is no reason she'd be tipped off yet.

"Whelan, she didn't make it back on board. They're likely on the way to pick her up. Eddie should be in town by now with Connor.

125

This is our best bet if he's meeting up with Sheila Sanchez. I'm heading out. We must be ready to go when we know where it's heading. I'll meet you at the car. Cannon and Garrity are heading back this way."

The call came in at 6:45. The radio speaker for the police dispatch cracked over Jones' cell phone speaker. "It turned south and went under A1A. It's going through the cruise ship turning basin. It might be heading to Dodge Island, where the cruise ships depart. They've all sailed already. Stand by."

Whelan and Jones were both tense, waiting helplessly for a stranger's voice to guide them.

"It went under Port Boulevard," came the update. "We're waiting to see if it docks at Miamarina, at Bayside."

Jones drove their rental SUV slowly down US1. "Should we turn into Bayside? There's a garage."

"No," said Whelan. "It won't be here. It's too busy, too public."

The radio voice agreed. "*Sheila's Sunshine* is continuing south along the coast. It's heading toward Brickell Island."

Jones hit the gas.

"Cut over to Second Avenue here," said Whelan. "Cannon, you on the call?"

"I'm here. We're seven minutes behind you. I've got the map up on Mansilla's navigation screen."

"I'm here too," said Mansilla. "I've got three cars and a SWAT unit all heading south."

Whelan and Jones crossed the bridge over the Miami River and headed into the Brickell Business District.

"Is she going to her club?" asked Jones. "It's two blocks ahead."

"Doubtful. Too many witnesses. Small marinas and individual docks are lining the coast for another mile, between here and the

Rickenbacker Causeway. If her boat goes past there, she will likely board in Key Biscayne."

"The office buildings are giving way to condos."

"We're heading into the residential district."

Jones pulled the car over to the side and waited for an update.

The radio clicked. "The *Sunshine* is slowing. We believe it's headed for a private marina in front of one of the condominium buildings."

"Which one?" asked Jones.

"Hold on."

Whelan was staring up through the windshield. "These condo buildings are massive, thirty to fifty stories."

"Do you think Sheila Sanchez is already here? If we arrive too early, she might see us."

"Too late and we might miss her."

The update squawked over the radio. "1601. *The Commander* Building. *Sheila's Sunshine* is docking alongside the end of the northmost pier. The Coast Guard is standing by. They're waiting two minutes out, so they won't draw attention. Vice is moving into a slip on the south end. They're in *The Valor*. It's unmarked, otherwise. Four officers are on board. We're all listening and waiting for your orders, Agent Whelan."

Chapter 21

Whelan shrugged. "Let's pull in."

They parked on the main level in a "short-term" visitor parking spot. There were six. Otherwise, you needed to valet or self-park in the garage if you were a resident with a bar code on your window. Three of the other short-term spaces were occupied.

They questioned the valet, pointing to the other cars. "Were any of those drivers or passengers a middle-aged Hispanic woman with long brunette or blonde hair, a hat, and big sunglasses?" asked Jones.

The valet's face scrunched. "I don't know. Maybe?"

She scowled at the young man. "Have you valeted anyone with that description in the past hour?"

"No."

Whelan showed him a picture of Connor on his phone. "What about this boy? Has he been through here? Valet or these parking spots?"

"Uhmm, I don't *think* so, but I can't be sure, sorry. I'm the only one here. If I were retrieving someone's car from the garage, I wouldn't even see anyone who parked in the guest spaces up top. But I don't think I valeted anyone with a kid since lunchtime."

Whelan locked eyes with Jones.

"It's your call," she said.

He pressed the radio call button. "Everyone stand by, out of sight. But stay close. We're going in to check things out."

"If anyone comes or goes in the next few minutes, we were never here. Do you understand?" he threatened the valet. "You do your job and forget anything we've asked you about."

The young man's eyebrows reached his hairline. "Am I in danger?"

"Not at all. Just be your friendly self, and all will be fine."

The valet resumed his post, forlorn and frightened, despite the agent's attempt to soothe him.

Whelan and Jones entered the lobby. It was spacious, with a concierge desk off to one side and an information desk on the other wall, staffed by an attractive young woman.

"May I help you?" she asked.

The agents presented their IDs.

"We're going to give the property a once-over. There might be some suspicious activity. Please continue monitoring this desk as usual, and should anyone ask, we're the Parkers. We live on the thirty-fifth floor. Though I doubt anyone will inquire."

"Parkers. Thirty-fifth. Got it. The rear doors leading to the pool and boat slips lock up at ten. After that, you'll need a fob." The woman was collected, as if covering for federal agents was in her everyday job description.

It was 7:02, according to Whelan's watch. "We won't be here that long."

The lobby was three stories high, with a grand chandelier overhanging a fountain in the middle. There was plush seating arranged in groups throughout. Toward the back was a bar. Barstool seating lined an inside countertop, and a massive set of sliders on the adjacent side was open to the pool area. Here was another long bar top, with at least ten people socializing over drinks in the perfect late March weather of Miami.

Kids could be heard shouting in the pool.

Whelan raced through the back door and stopped short of diving in until his eyes landed on the little screamers. *Not Connor.*

They were simply children horseplaying and teasing one another as kids do.

His eyes directed Jones to go left as he took the right path around the pool. Large planters were filled with small palms and flowers. Giant royal palms and other landscaping, all illuminated with brilliant warm lighting, created a haven for the residents.

Benches lined the path, some filled with people watching their kids or stealing a kiss under the stars. Another fifteen people were scattered about on chaise lounges or seated at small tables sipping on cocktails. Chatter and cachinnations filled the remaining space.

"This is much busier than I thought it would be," muttered Jones when they connected on the other side near the pier leading to the boat slips.

Whelan studied the back of the building. "Over forty stories, and I'm guessing sixteen to twenty units per floor. There's got to be over six or seven-hundred units here."

"And it's still season," said Jones. "The snowbirds haven't flown home yet."

She put her arm around his waist, catching him off guard.

"Blend in, husband," she ordered.

He put his arm around her shoulders, and they turned toward Biscayne Bay and the boats in front of them.

Twelve vessels of varying sizes were docked at the little marina. They noted *The Valor* at the far end. It was quiet. The police were keeping a low profile.

Sheila's Sunshine was a few yards away.

"That's one hell of a yacht," mumbled Whelan. "Someone's making a load of money."

It was four decks, counting the bridge, and 146 feet long.

"She probably carries a mortgage," Jones offered, to make him feel better. "High interest rates. Costs her a *ton* in maintenance."

Whelan sighed but played along. "And gas isn't cheap. It couldn't get more than one mile per gallon."

Jones' face grew serious. "You know, I doubt it's truly hers. I bet we find out Leon Bergman holds title. That prick was in this a hell of a lot deeper than he wanted us to think."

They retreated toward the pool area and took an empty bench with some foliage secluding them yet still allowing a view of the marina.

"Anyone approached the *Sunshine*?" Whelan asked into the radio.

"The crew of *The Valor* says no," came the response seconds later. "And no one's left."

"Okay, hold position."

Whelan peered through a low hibiscus hedge at a boy walking by the pool. He stood up so he could see him better, without obstruction. It wasn't his son. He sat back down before he drew attention to himself.

Perfect. Now I'm stalking children in Miami.

"What if we're all wrong?" he asked Jones. "What if this Sheila Sanchez is the wrong Sheila? What if we've got everyone standing by to arrest an innocent woman who just wants to go out for an evening on the bay?"

"Sheila Sanchez isn't an innocent woman. We have Leon Bergman's dying confession she held sex parties on Star Island with a slew of girls."

"And boys," Whelan spit out. "But we didn't truly get a confession. He was expressing his innocence of her operation till the end."

"To *his* end, which he *ended* himself. Whelan, Leon wouldn't have killed himself if he was innocent. His kind of money could hire lawyers who would have freed him in no time unless he was in pretty deep. He shot himself because he didn't want to go to prison. Guys like Leon don't do well in prison."

"Agreed."

"We've got the right Sheila."

Jones was watching for people coming down the path toward the marina while Whelan kept his eyes on the *Sunshine*. They pondered the day's events, replaying their decisions, and planning their next moves.

Without warning, Jones turned to Whelan, threw her arms around his neck, and pressed her lips to his. He tried to back away, shocked by her action, but she locked his neck with her hands.

He'd wanted to kiss her since the day he met her nearly two years ago. Improper thoughts of a relationship with her crept into his mind at least once a month still, though it was no longer daily.

Thank God.

He was about to give in to desire and genuinely kiss her in return when his left eye spotted a woman approaching along the path from the building. She had long, brunette hair, smashed down by a wide-brimmed straw hat, and oversized, dark sunglasses covered her eyes.

Whelan turned, so from the woman's perspective, all she would see was the back of Jones' large mop of curly hair.

She wore flats and was moving briskly, passing them without cause for attention.

Whelan parted his lip lock and peered at Jones. She nodded confirmation. It was Sheila Sanchez.

He raised his radio, speaking softly. "Sanchez has arrived. She's heading toward her yacht. Stay alert."

A voice cracked over the speaker, "Confirmed. *The Valor* has her in their sights. She's boarding. No sign of Connor Whelan yet."

"If the *Sunshine* so much as casts off a single line from that dock, I want everyone to move in. Make sure the Coast Guard is close."

"They are. They're ready."

Three minutes passed.

"Where's Connor?" Whelan asked Jones.

"I don't know. Eddie may be running late. Maybe he didn't make it to Miami? There's been no word yet from FHP. No sign of them. Maybe we got lucky, and he succumbed to his wounds."

"Connor would have called me. Unless..." Whelan's eyes widened.

Jones put her hand on his shoulder. "I'm sure he's fine. They'll be here. This has to be where he's headed."

"Does it? We're assuming they're meeting tonight. Maybe they're meeting tomorrow. Maybe Sheila Sanchez is taking the yacht to another meeting point—Key Biscayne, Key Largo, Key West? What if Eddie's five hours south of us?"

"Quit speculating."

Whelan raised his eyebrows. "It's my job. I think it literally says that in the description. 'Speculating, for long, unthankable hours, in shit motels, with an allowance barely covering the vending machine.'"

"*I* thank you all the time. And you *love* Cheetos." Jones flashed her killer smile at him.

It worked to bring a chuckle and ease some tension.

She spun her head to check the path before wheeling it back to face him again. Her magical scent carried over to him once more. He inhaled, losing himself in her copper eyes. They hadn't worked side-by-side in the field since her promotion last year. He missed it. He missed her, being in his daily life.

Whelan sighed. His sole focus was on bringing his son home safely to his mother. Thoughts of his ex-wife, Georgia, sitting there waiting for news, filled his head. He would always love her, and there were times when he wished he could return to her and try to make it work.

Would I do it all differently had I known then?

He didn't think he would. Being an FBI agent was in his nature. He operated on a different frequency than her. They all did. Miranda Jones understood him. She was wired the same way. *Maybe...*

A piercing scream came from the top of *Sheila's Sunshine*. Both agents jumped up and began running toward the pier. An adolescent, dressed only in underwear, was running along the side toward the aft end of the boat, closest to shore.

"Help me!" she screamed.

A burly man chased her halfway down, then paused and shot her in the back. His weapon had a silencer, but Whelan's trained ear heard the whisp.

The girl fell overboard with a splash.

Whelan shouted into his radio. "Everybody, move in!"

Chapter 22

Jones tapped his shoulder as they ran down the pier. "I've got the girl. Get onboard!"

Whelan heard her splash into the water as he ran up the small gangplank and onto the *Sunshine*. His head wheeled in each direction once inside the main salon. No one was in sight. There was one full deck above him, two below. He was unfamiliar with the layout of a mega-yacht. He was still near the aft of the vessel, so he started working his way forward, with his weapon leading his steps.

The same man he saw shoot the girl ran into the hall before him. He was startled and drew his weapon.

Whelan fired first, into the man's shoulder, causing him to spin.

The injured man returned fire as his body twisted, missing Whelan and putting two holes into a cabinet behind and above him.

Whelan fired again, this time into the man's chest. It put him down on the floor.

"FBI!" Whelan shouted at the man. "Drop your weapon."

The assailant lifted his gun.

Whelan put another bullet into his chest. "Where's Sheila Sanchez?" he shouted at him.

A gargled mutter came from the floor. "Fuck you."

Whelan kicked the gun out of his hand as the guy's last breath wheezed into silence.

"Sheila Sanchez!" Whelan shouted. "FBI! Come out with your hands up!"

She failed to show.

Where the hell is she?

He made his way forward through the galley. A sound behind him alerted him to someone's presence. He turned in time to dodge a stock pot being thrown at his head by a woman wearing a chef's hat.

She screamed at him in Croatian, then picked up a large skillet and hurled it toward him.

He ducked again and shouted in English. "FBI! Where's Sheila Sanchez?"

The woman took off down the corridor toward the aft of the ship. He debated following her but proceeded forward. When he reached a stairwell, he heard screams from the lower decks.

Racing down the steps, he paused on the next deck. Another girl, fifteen possibly, was running away from him. Someone grabbed her arm as she passed a bedroom, yanking her out of the corridor. She screamed.

Whelan started to go after her when more screams echoed up the stairwell from the lower deck. He reversed his decision and ran down the last flight, his weapon ready.

"Sheila Sanchez, we've got you surrounded! Come out with your hands in the air!"

He braced himself for a bullet and turned into a hallway. It was clear. Proceeding forward, the screams kept coming.

This deck held the engine room, water processing, storage, and crew quarters. The first cabin on his right held empty bunk beds. To the left, the door was locked. He jiggled the handle. The screams were further up. When he was confident he'd found the right cabin, he shot the locked knob, then kicked in the door.

It was another room with bunk beds, but thirteen girls were in this one, ranging in age from eleven to seventeen, plus two boys in their early teens.

Not Connor. Where the hell is he?

The girls all froze in terror.

"FBI!" he shouted. "What's going on here?"

They began shouting at him in multiple languages. It was deafening.

"Stop! Quiet!" he yelled.

Pointing to one older girl, he said, "You."

She began chattering in Spanish. He understood much of what she explained. They were being held against their wills. Promises of a beautiful life in America and being cared for by rich and powerful men lured her into service. She was supposed to work her first night this weekend but changed her mind. She was still in Honduras two weeks prior, and the "party" got out of hand. She was raped and beaten when she tried to complain.

Ten other girls and two boys confirmed their stories were similar. Columbia, Mexico, Dominica, Argentina, Venezuela, Honduras, Brazil, Chile—it was a veritable pot luck of Caribbean, Central and South American countries. All of them were threatened and abused.

"What happened just now?" asked Agent Whelan. His Spanish was shaky, but well enough for them to understand. "Who was the girl running up on deck?"

"She made it!" exclaimed the Honduran girl. "That was Fernanda. She's from Brazil. I don't speak Portuguese. We haven't been able to understand each other. We've been trapped in this cabin for five days now. The last time I saw the sky, we were in Trujillo. She stood up to Señora Sanchez a few minutes ago, striking her, then ran out of the cabin. We were locked inside again by one of her men. He said if any of us tried to escape, we'd be killed. We were too afraid."

"You did the right thing," comforted Whelan. "Fernanda was shot up on deck. I don't know if she survived. We have many officers—police—swarming over this boat by now. We'll make sure you're all safe and get you back to your homes."

The girls and boys all began speaking at once in ecstatic garble.

Whelan brought out his phone and tapped on Connor's photo. "Have any of you seen this boy?" He waved it around, repeating himself in English.

The gist of his question was understood, even by those who didn't speak either language, and they all shook their heads, quieting again.

A voice from the hallway rang out. "Agent Whelan?"

"Here!" he replied.

He chanced a peak into the hallway. A man was racing toward him, dressed casually and leading his way with a gun.

"Miami Vice," he introduced himself as he approached. "Four of us are onboard now. SWAT should be here within two minutes."

"Have we found Sheila Sanchez?"

"Not yet. We're still searching. We—" he was interrupted by the sound of gunfire up on deck, possibly on the pier. They weren't shielded by silencers. And one might have been a rifle.

"Shots fired! Shots fired!" came a yell from Agent Jones over the radio. "At least five, maybe six men jumped on the dock and are running for shore! I'm in pursuit!"

Whelan ordered the officer. "Stay here. Guard these kids!"

He took off down the hall toward the stairwell.

On deck three, he located a door opening to the outside. The pier was now four feet below him, an easy jump. He raced toward the condominium building, careful to check behind him. No one else from the yacht was following him.

More shots could be heard near the pool area. New screams erupted, this time from residents and guests of *The Commander* building. As he approached the pool, he saw kids and parents ducking behind trees and garbage cans or trying to hide underneath tables.

Two men with pistols and a third with a rifle were positioned behind overturned tables, firing toward the slew of police and SWAT officers on the other side of the pool near the building. A shootout ensued. Thankfully, none of Sheila's goons held any hostages. One of them was making his way between rounds toward a three-year-old girl separated from her parents. She was hiding unsuccessfully behind a bench, clutching a Sponge Bob inflatable.

Whelan aimed and fired. He never liked shooting a man in the back, but his approach from the rear gave him the element of surprise and the shot. He took it. The man fell. He was about to go and take the girl to safety when Jones swooped in from his left flank and snatched her up. She gave a little wave before taking the girl safely deeper into the foliage and disappeared.

She's safe! Whelan paused, raising his eyes to the heavens. "Thank you," he mumbled.

A bullet whizzed by his ear close enough for him to hear, and he dove for cover behind a nearby palm tree. After a few seconds, he jutted his head out and fired three shots, winging the rifleman in the arm. It was enough to stop his assault, and he lay on the ground voluntarily, pushing his assault rifle out in front.

"You don't get to surrender!" shouted one of the other gunmen. He put two rounds into the rifleman's head, then wheeled around to shoot Whelan.

Whelan ducked behind the palm tree again as the bullets continued. When they stopped, he took a peek. The man was lying face down, and blood was pouring from the side of his head above the ear. Captain Vicente Mansilla stood across the pool and found Whelan's eye. He gave a quick "you're welcome" nod, indicating he'd been the one to put the man down.

SWAT worked their way forward over the next few minutes, and then it was over. Five of Sheila's gunmen were dead. Another was wounded and taken alive.

Multiple officers were soon boarding *Sheila's Sunshine*. Jones located the little girl's parents and reunited them before joining Whelan in boarding the yacht.

A gunshot or two was sporadically heard. Eventually, silence settled in. It lasted nearly five minutes until the girls in hiding realized it was over and began shrieking, crying for help.

Whelan made his way to the crew quarters again to check on the cluster of girls and boys being trafficked. He passed the first locked room from earlier and jerked the handle. It still didn't open.

He motioned to Jones with his head, and she stood back as he fired at the lock and kicked the door.

Nine women were in the room. They shouted initially but quieted when they confirmed they were being rescued. This group was in their early twenties to forties. They had stayed silent earlier out of fear. All they could hear from the room down the hall were screams and didn't realize those girls were being rescued. They chose to remain silent in case their captors won the gunfight.

"There are more cabins up the hall," muttered Jones. Her firearm was drawn again, and she inspected the remaining rooms. They were unlocked and empty of people. Presumably, they were for the crew, most of whom were now dead, save three onboard who turned themselves in.

The girls and boys he'd saved earlier were gone—already escorted by Miami's finest out of the boat.

Whelan stepped back inside the room with the nine newly discovered women. "Okay, it's clear. You're all safe. The police have the ship contained. You're free."

He scanned their faces, hoping to find at least one who might speak English, given his rusty Spanish. A familiar face moved toward him, catching the light from the high hat in the ceiling above her. "Agent Whelan? Thomas Whelan?"

"Yes. Do I know you?" He came close, within a foot of her, in the crowded room as the other women zigged around them to exit.

"Cliburgh?" he asked. "Joyce Cliburgh!"

"It's me," she said.

She was one of Jay Pierson's original team who went undercover to infiltrate Eddie Morrison's outfit. She'd been sent to Miami to investigate his sex trafficking operation and was presumed dead in a raid that went wrong three years ago.

"What are you doing here?" asked Whelan. "I'd heard you were killed."

"I've continued working undercover," she said. "Agent Whelan, we've much to discuss, but your bust was premature. We were headed to Columbia, so I could take down the ringleader of this trafficking operation, Hector Valencia. In addition to Brazil and half of Central America, we discovered he was moving a large supply of girls to the U.S. from Chile and Argentina through Panama. The Panamanians are cooperating with us. We have our players in place. You cost us the best chance we've had to bust this guy, not to mention twenty months of work!"

"The FBI thinks you're dead! Who's *we*?"

"The CIA. I was recruited shortly after arriving in Miami. My death was staged. The director is aware of all this."

Jones entered the room behind Whelan and again drew her sidearm, pointing it directly at Joyce Cliburgh's face.

"Jones, lower your weapon. She's a friendly," said Whelan.

"Friendly?" she asked. "Whelan, this is Sheila Sanchez!"

KIRK BURRIS

Chapter 23

When the last few shots around the pool were fired, Eddie Morrison was driving by the front of *The Commander* building on Brickell Avenue.

The driveway and short-term parking were full of police cars, and a SWAT BearCat Armored Vehicle was parked outside.

Eddie shoved his gun deep into the side of Connor Whelan, sitting in the passenger seat.

"Ow, you're hurting me," said Connor.

"Stay quiet if you want to live."

Connor tugged furiously on the door handle. The Buick was locked and wouldn't let him out. He tried to pull up on the lock, but it was receded inside the door. His hand pressed the unlock button on the armrest. They all flew open with a loud clack. His head turned without thought to see if Eddie was witnessing his escape as he tried the handle again.

Eddie was indeed watching. He slammed the butt of his gun into Connor's head, on the side of his left temple.

Connor flew back against the door, losing consciousness. Before he could fall out, Eddie leaned over his body and grabbed the door's armrest, shutting it with a fierce slam.

"Fucking kids," Eddie mumbled as he stared back to *The Commander* building.

He kept driving slowly, away from the crime scene, his evening exchange with Sheila Sanchez ruined.

"Your dad cost me two million dollars tonight," he continued talking, more to himself than the boy. "Someone's going to have to pay."

Whelan drew his firearm and aimed it at Sheila Sanchez's face.

"Where's my son?" he shouted.

"Your son?" she answered. "Agent Whelan, I don't know anything about your son. What are you talking about?"

"Eddie Morrison! He's bringing my son to you. He has Connor!"

Joyce Cliburgh, a.k.a. Sheila Sanchez, stepped back and adopted a soothing tone. "Agent Whelan, I'm sorry, but I know nothing about your son. I haven't been updated on Eddie Morrison in over a month. Last I heard, he was on the run in Oklahoma. Did he take your son? I've been arranging safe transport for the women and children on this boat. We plan to make a pit stop in Panama, where they'll be released to diplomats, ready to take them home. I'm also picking up additional CIA agents. When we get to Columbia, I'll have an entire team ready to sweep in and take down the head of this operation."

Jones failed to make sense of her statement. "If you're with the CIA and these women are safe, why did one try to flee and get shot by your men? Why the shootout up above? Families were put in harm's way."

"Were any injured?" asked Cliburgh.

"Yes. And the girl who was first shot is heading to the emergency room in critical condition."

"Shit. Agent—Jones—was it? Agent Jones, those men aren't mine. They're Hector Valencia's. They keep tabs on me and report directly back to him while I continue proving myself in the Miami market. He'll be suspicious when he learns they've all been killed, yet somehow I survived."

"Three people onboard are safe. A cook, the pilot, and one more man. They're being held for questioning. There's also a survivor in the pool area. Why don't we go get some answers?"

"They can't know who I am—that I'm undercover," said Cliburgh. "Eventually, it would get back to Hector and ruin all our work. Agent Whelan, we're so close to taking him down."

"How were you planning to release these girls in Panama if his men are watching you the whole time?"

"They're watching *me*, not them. They aren't paying any attention to their faces. Hector has conditioned them not to watch the merchandise too closely. 'No touchy.' One of the men on board is mine. Or was, if he's not one of the two men you say survived. He was going to keep the crew busy for fifteen minutes in a meeting while I took the girls out and swapped them with my team."

Jones was wide-eyed during Cliburgh's explanation. "Whose yacht is this?" she asked. "There's no way the CIA is fronting a wad big enough to cover this."

"Of course not. It's Hector's."

"With *your* name on it?"

"Yes, well, that's new. We're becoming 'close,' while I build trust. And any endeavor he endorses is top-notch, all the way. Plus, he uses it personally much of the time."

Jones turned to Whelan. "This sounds pretty far-fetched."

"Agreed. Let's make some calls."

"Agent Whelan," said Cliburgh, "you do that, you'll ruin twenty months of work! This was all culminating on *this* trip! You need to let me finish it."

"Assuming what you've told us is true, how will you explain to Hector Valencia his men were killed, yet *you* got away?"

"Just that. Just that, exactly. *And* I saved the merchandise. That's all he'll care about. Henchmen are replaceable. But the quality of those girls and boys is harder to come by and much more valuable. You've got to let me and the four survivors go. They can vouch for me to him—tell him we escaped."

"And how are you going to swap those girls and boys for your people *now*?" asked Jones.

"I've been working on that. I think it will be easier. The four remaining loyalists won't hesitate to take my orders after being single-handedly saved by me. And with a promise to load up more of Hector's men once we've dropped off this batch, they'll feel safer and more trusting."

Jones's tone heated. "This *batch*? Lady, these girls and boys aren't going anywhere but to the hospital and a counseling center. They'll be under the protection of the FBI until we can reunite them with their loved ones."

She took a photo of Joyce Cliburgh on her smartphone, then headed out of the room, patting Whelan on the shoulder. "I'm going to start those calls."

He nodded.

"Agent Whelan," said Cliburgh with a sigh, "I need to get up top and view the bodies so I know who the surviving men are. If one of them is mine, it will be easier. Otherwise, I might have to bring on a couple more here to help."

"Why not bring them all on here? The women, girls, and boys are already off the ship. They are being given medical exams and food. They'll be taken away for questioning shortly and then put up in accommodations."

"Shit. You fucked this all up."

"What's the problem? If your story checks out, you can make the switch now."

"My team is in *Panama*, Agent Whelan! They're not here! They're trained, updated, and matched to resemble the assortment of nationalities Hector's been briefed on. You have so fucked all this! Twenty months! I need to get up top and see what the hell is going on."

She pushed past Whelan and left the small cabin. He allowed her to go but was quick on her heels.

Once on the pier, Joyce Cliburgh saw the cook and pilot being escorted onto shore. They waved at her. She returned it and gave a comforting nod.

"Agent Whelan, I need you to make it seem like I'm your prisoner as we walk by them. Once we're alone, I can examine the bodies."

He obliged by zip-tying her hands behind her and roughing her, pushing her forward as she pretended not to cooperate.

When they walked by the pair from the ship, she spoke softly to them. "Don't worry, I've got this all under control. Tell them nothing. They're out of their jurisdiction. I'll have us back on board and heading to Columbia by morning."

They were relieved.

Once out of sight, Cliburgh asked, "Where are the other two men? The other survivors?"

"I'm not sure. Perhaps being questioned. This place is a mess."

The pool area of *The Commander* looked like a war zone. Indeed, for a few minutes, it had been. Four residents took stray bullet shots, three minor, one critical. Paramedics were treating victims on site, ensuring they were in shape to move to the hospital. No one bothered to straighten back up any of the tables, chairs, benches, and trash cans toppled and used for shields. Bullet holes riddled everything.

"Holy shit," mumbled Cliburgh. "What the hell did you guys do?"

"*Your* guys," said Whelan. "Or Hector's. They weren't ever going to surrender, and they wanted to take out as many of us as possible on their way down."

"Loyal to the end," she mumbled. "And they weren't going to go to prison. Let me check the building's lobby and see if my guy's there. Can you cut me free now?"

She tried to move from Whelan's grip, but he felt a tap on his shoulder and turned to find Agents Cannon and Garrity standing behind him.

"Where the hell have you been?" he snapped.

"Garrity doesn't know how to read a GPS map," Cannon snarled. "The drawbridge on Brickell was up, according to what he saw on his Maps App, so we went down two blocks to Miami Avenue. Last thing we wanted was to be stuck behind another draw bridge. Well, there was a huge wreck at the other end of the Miami Avenue bridge, and we were stuck in gridlock. We could see the Brickell bridge from where we were, and it was down! Wasn't up the whole time. I'm sorry, Whelan. We got here as fast as we could."

"Okay. You're here now. We had plenty of help from Vicente's men and the Miami Vice squad. Thankfully, no police were shot. We do have civilian injuries."

Cannon looked at Joyce Cliburgh. "And this is?"

"Sheila Sanchez."

"You found her. That's great! Where's Connor?"

"Well, funny you should ask. Sheila Sanchez is a federal agent, undercover. Her real name is Joyce Cliburgh, and she was part of Jay Pierson's original team."

"Come again?" asked Cannon.

"Let's sit, and I'll fill you in."

"Agent Whelan," said Cliburgh. "Please, could you cut off this zip tie? We're out of sight now from Hector's crew. I need to check the lobby. I'm not happy one of my team is missing and unaccounted for."

"I'll have to escort you. Turn around."

He carried a small knife in the lock pick set he always kept in his jacket pocket. He unfolded it and spread her fingers out of the way so he wouldn't accidentally cut her.

"Stop!" yelled Agent Jones from behind the group. She was running from the pier.

They all froze and raised their eyes to her.

"Joyce Cliburgh isn't undercover as Sheila Sanchez. The CIA's never heard of her. I just got off the phone with Director Commerson. He never signed a transfer to them. When he checked his file on her, it showed MIA, presumed dead."

They all turned back to Sheila Sanchez, whose bound wrists were squeezed tighter by Whelan. He spun her around so he could see her. "You're quick with your lies, I'll give you that. Sold it pretty well."

"Fuck you," she said, then spit in his face.

He wiped it away and then violently grasped her shoulders. "WHERE'S MY SON?"

Chapter 24

Eddie Morrison headed north along US1 and Ocean Drive into Fort Lauderdale. The hotels were all high-rises with exorbitant prices, and his cash was running low. There was no credit card he could safely use and no bank account he could withdraw from. He was down to less than two-thousand dollars. That was all the money left in his whole life, this man who once lived high on the hog.

Connor Whelan had a colossal knot growing on the side of his head. His lungs were moving up and down, which was enough for now.

"Kid, you up?" he asked softly.

There was no response. Eddie figured if he were awake, he'd be moaning in pain. The neighborhood grew a little rougher, so he chanced a seedy motel one block off the ocean. Hourly rates were offered at forty dollars or nightly for ninety-five. With tax, one-twentieth of his wealth was gone. There would be little choice but to swap cars in the morning. He could always get more cash from his victims. *Perhaps find me a beamer and some prick with a fat wad of bills in his pocket this time.*

Eddie carried Connor into the room and laid him on one of the two double beds. The goose egg continued to grow on the boy's head, and he started worrying he might not recover. Perhaps he'd wake up a vegetable, unable to communicate or understand his surroundings. He didn't care much, but it would be easier to use a hostage who could still move on his own accord.

Eddie strapped Connor down with some rope he obtained from one of his cars along the way. He bound the boy's mouth with a rubber ball and ACE bandages. *Even if he squeals, the neighbors will think it's a hooker.*

Tired of raiding vending machines and food trucks, Eddie walked three blocks back up the road to a diner and ordered home-cooked take-out. He set it all up in the motel room and tried to wake Connor for dinner.

"Come on, kid, aren't you hungry? It's ten o'clock. You gotta eat."

He wiggled Connor's feet, then his whole body. He slapped his cheeks twice and threw a cup of water on his face.

"Okay, suit yourself. But don't get mad at me when your meatloaf is cold."

After dinner, Eddie showered and hopped into the bed closest to the door. Around midnight, he turned the light off.

"Don't die on me, kid."

Soon, he fell asleep to the sounds of late-night television.

Joyce Cliburgh, a.k.a. Sheila Sanchez, was sitting in an interrogation room in the Miami field office of the FBI.

"Where's Connor Whelan?" asked the Special Agent in Charge, Oscar Bardem.

Agents Whelan, Jones, Cannon, and Garrity were all ordered to sit on the other side of the mirrored window and stay still. Their actions at *The Commander* building were questioned. People were hurt. People were killed.

"People were saved, too," Jones reminded him. "Innocents, whom that bitch had vile, grotesque plans for. Remember that when you speak to Director Commerson."

"I don't know where Connor Whelan is," Joyce Cliburgh told SAC Bardem. "He was supposed to be delivered tonight. Your team interrupted the handoff."

She looked directly into the two-way mirror separating her from Whelan and the others. "If you'd waited a few more minutes, you'd have your son now." She snickered and mumbled inaudibly.

"What was that?" asked Bardem.

Cliburgh cleared her throat. "Nothing. If you want the boy, I need complete immunity. And I wouldn't waste time. There's no telling how desperate Eddie Morrison will become now he's lost out on the two million I guaranteed him."

"For *Connor Whelan?*" asked Bardem. He realized how crass his comment sounded and glanced at the mirror.

Agent Thomas Whelan pushed a button on the wall and spoke into a recessed speaker beside it. "Why did you want my son, Joyce? What was he to you?"

She was distant, her eyes squinting as her mind played God knew what thoughts.

Bardem left her room and entered the other side. He found four pairs of eyes, eagerly staring at him for permission.

"Fine," he said. He pointed at Whelan. "You, and you alone. The rest of you sit tight."

He escorted Whelan back into interrogation and gestured for him to sit opposite Joyce Cliburgh.

Bardem backed up into the corner of the room and leaned against the wall, sipping coffee.

It took everything Thomas Whelan had to control himself, but he held it together for Connor. In the softest voice, he asked again, "Why did you want my son, Joyce?"

"He's a nice-looking boy. He'd fetch a pretty penny in the industry."

"Two million dollars?" asked Whelan.

Cliburgh shrieked. "Please! Like I was ever going to give Eddie any money. The man's a desperate fool."

Whelan shifted gears. "How did you go from Joyce Cliburgh to Sheila Sanchez? What happened to you that you gave up a career in the FBI to run hookers and drugs?"

"I never run drugs!" she snapped. "I run a high-end escort service."

"You traffic children for large profits."

"Nonsense. All my workers are of legal age and work for me of their own free will. They're paid handsomely."

"You imprison them! Brainwash them into submission. I know how this works. It's a long, psychological slide down a dark rabbit hole so deep there's no escape."

Whelan cleared his throat. "Jay Pierson would be ashamed of you, of your betrayal to the agency, and to him. He would have done anything for you."

"No, he wouldn't," she said. "He sent me down here to rot."

"How so?"

Cliburgh fidgeted her fingers on the table. She was chained to a heavy bar running the width of it and mounted to the top. It didn't have enough slack to move her hands to her lap where she preferred. Nervous habits are more comfortable when kept out of sight.

"I asked him twice to reassign me. It was quickly getting dangerous here, and I was over my head. He kept telling me I could handle it."

"How was it dangerous?" asked Whelan.

She fixated on her hands, clasping them. "I need my attorney."

"We left him a voicemail. How was it dangerous?"

"I was supposed to be monitoring Eddie's trafficking operation. I used the credentials the bureau set up for me, but the Miami operation was suspicious. One night I wound up defensively holding two men at gunpoint. I either had to put up or shut up. I'd spent months undercover and didn't want my time and effort wasted. And there was a load of girls I was allowed to relocate on the line. I weighed my sanctity against the lives of a group of strangers.

"Truthfully, I don't think Eddie even ordered them to do it. I don't know. He was busy elsewhere and wasn't monitoring the Miami outfit closely at the time."

"Put up or shut up?" repeated Whelan.

Cliburgh shriveled into her chair as much as possible. "I had to fuck them. Or they said they'd kill me. I'd witnessed two other murders in the operation by then. I believed them. At one point, I changed my mind, but I chose to live. So I turned my gun over to them, and my body."

She closed her eyes as though it could keep them from seeing the horror of her past replayed before her.

"I'm sorry that happened to you, Joyce. Truly, I am. Pierson didn't know, I'm sure, or he would have extracted you."

"*Would* he have? I don't think so. He was determined and too invested to let any ends drop that would help bring down Eddie's entire operation in one swoop. After a month of being raped on a regular basis, hatred grew inside me. For Jay Pierson, for the team— for *you*. I hated all of you!"

Whelan tried to make sense of her path. He was essentially in those same shoes when he was in Miami. But he always remembered himself. It would have been easy for him to succumb to the money, leave the bureau and head up a lifestyle of crime, working for Eddie.

What pushed her *over the edge? What saved me?*

154

"I don't get it," he said. "I understand you experienced a terrible atrocity on behalf of the bureau, but how did you jump to trafficking girls for your own operation? As Sheila Sanchez?"

Joyce Cliburgh's pupils locked onto Whelan's, expanding in size. "I didn't *jump!* It was a long bumpy road, spiraling downhill, and each time I looked up and back, my former life seemed so far away, no longer in reach. I kept drowning, kept fucking, working my way to the top in Eddie's Miami market. The further I sank, the higher I climbed. I learned all the ropes. And each time I thought of leaving and bringing him in, I felt like his goons were watching me. Which, of course, they were. But I was terrified they'd pin me for a fed. So I kept playing along.

"And then one day, I wasn't playing any longer. I was doing it, the job, and being paid handsomely. No one at the FBI seemed to care about me. I'd been all but forgotten. I grew angry and resentful. And then came the shootout. I was injured, and with no real eyes on me from the bureau, it was easy to pass along intel that I'd been killed. I paid off one of Eddie's guys to tell *him* I'd been killed, too. Of course, he didn't care. There's always someone on the ladder ready to step up and take over at the first opportunity."

"And then Sheila Sanchez materialized out of thin air?" asked Whelan.

"And then Sheila Sanchez."

Cliburgh took a drink of water. "My Spanish is perfect. I worked years on it. Of course, people questioned my history, the 'new girl' in town. I created one. I'd been working with Eddie's girls for months. Luring many of them to work for me was easy. They trusted me. I was kinder than all the men. I ensured larger wages with the escort service I was establishing. And I guaranteed none of them would have to put out. If they did, it was their choice, but never a condition."

She sat up straighter in her chair and unfolded her hands. Sheila Sanchez was making an appearance. "I run a professional escort service, Agent Whelan. Nothing more."

"Where do you get your girls from then? A want-ad?"

"Word of mouth. Best advertising and all that shit."

"You think those girls we rescued from your boat will say they were here freely? Not kidnapped and brought here from who knows how many countries? Your word of mouth must be pretty wide if you recruit all the way from Colombia. And one of them is dead now! The girl who was shot escaping? She didn't make it. That's on you, Joyce. All those men who worked for you who chose to die instead of going to prison? On you. And the residents and guests who were shot and injured during tonight's engagement? On you!"

Whelan leaned against the back of his chair, again collecting his calm. The staring match continued, but it was no longer Joyce Cliburgh he was speaking to. It was Sheila Sanchez. Her entire demeanor was different, refined. Her body language shifted, gaining confidence.

This woman suffers from a split personality. Did we do this to her? Or was she like this all along and we missed it?

"I need my attorney," she said. "If mine is unavailable, I'll work with the one appointed to me until mine can be contacted."

Whelan made one last plea. "Joyce, where's my son?"

"Complete immunity or you get nothing."

"People are dead. Women were kidnapped and raped. They're never going to give you a deal. Even if I begged them."

Joyce Cliburgh briefly resurfaced. Her shoulders slumped, and her voice became a whisper. "I know. It's sad, isn't it? It's all so sad."

"Why Connor, Joyce? Why my son?"

Her speech remained faint. "Because that hatred inside me for you never left. My desire to hurt you flourished. You all let me drown—everyone at the bureau, especially Pierson, and you. You were brought on to be the conscience of our little group. Pierson told us you were the only one of us with any morals. You were supposed to guide us to victory. Some morality you have there. You abandoned me same as he did. Same as all of you. And *you're* the last one alive. It was never about your son. It's always been about you, about making you suffer. Like you made me."

She began to straighten in her seat while a smirk formed on her lips. "*You* made me."

"Please, Joyce, where's Connor? Where's my son? Do one last good deed before you rot in prison. Tell me where he is."

"He's with Eddie Morrison. And Eddie, he's gone with the wind."

Chapter 25

Eddie's wind was dwindling. His blood loss stopped, but the wound in the leg was infected, and the bullet lodged there still caused incredible pain. He woke at 2:40 a.m. and checked his phone for messages. There were none. He sat up on the edge of his bed.

Connor Whelan was awake and staring at him. The boy's eyes were wet, and the glare of the television light danced around and reflected back in Eddie's direction.

"What's wrong, kid?"

The boy was still bound and gagged and made no effort to respond.

"I can't take that off unless you swear not to scream. If you scream, I'll have to kill you. I don't have time for horseshit. You understand?"

Connor made no reaction or sounds. His eyes continued to water, the tears racing one another down his cheek.

Eddie took his gag off, and Connor swallowed two large gulps of air.

"My nose is getting stuffy," said Connor. "A few more minutes, and I think I would have died from lack of oxygen."

"You're pretty smart, aren't you, kid? Good thing I woke up, then. How are you feeling? Can you travel?"

"Now?"

"In the morning."

"Yes. My head hurts. Do you have some aspirin or Tylenol?"

Eddie walked around and checked out Connor's head. The goose egg was still there but hadn't grown since he last saw it.

"Sure. I've got something better."

He fetched a pill from his bag, and Connor took it without question. He no longer cared. His prayers shifted from rescue to death. He was on the fence about which way he wanted it to go.

Eddie retrieved the cold food from the table and placed it on the side of Connor's bed. He freed one of the boy's hands.

"Eat, kid. Then sleep some more."

"I think I've slept enough. Where are we?"

"Still in Florida."

"What city?"

"Doesn't matter, kid."

Connor sighed. "I have to pee. And I could use a shower."

"Eat a few bites first."

Eddie watched Connor Whelan for a few minutes. As suspected, his hunger kicked in once he got the first morsel down, and he ate voraciously.

Afterward, Eddie untied him and led him to the bathroom. There was no window for him to escape.

"Remember, kid, scream, and you're dead."

"Promise?"

Eddie took a step back and studied the young man before him. "Hang in there, kid. You keep doing like I say, and I'll let you live."

"After you kill my dad?"

Years of criminal hardening were ingrained in Eddie, but for a single moment, he was unsure if he still wanted that for Thomas Whelan. His own painkillers were working effectively, and his exhaustion was profound. "Shower, kid. Then let's both get some sleep. The pill I gave you will help you relax, and your body still needs rest. Trust me."

"Uh-huh."

Connor spent ten minutes under the warm water and was sound asleep within five minutes of returning to bed.

Eddie observed him a few more minutes to be sure he wasn't faking it. He bound Connor's hands to the headboard again so he couldn't leave. Soon, they were both snoring themselves into oblivion.

Whelan and his team were checking themselves into a hotel at 3:00 a.m. Nothing else helpful was obtained from Joyce Cliburgh. The Miami office would take over her case and assured them they would be the first call if she released any new intel.

"There was no contingency plan between 'Sheila Sanchez' and Eddie Morrison," Whelan commented to Jones before she opened the door to her room. "I believed Joyce when she said Eddie was 'gone' with my son."

Miranda Jones gazed into Whelan's hazel eyes. She put her right hand over his heart. "I did too. We're back to figuring out Eddie's moves."

"I don't think Eddie knows his next move. He undoubtedly thought he was getting money from Sheila for my boy. I wonder if he'll contact *me* for money in exchange for letting him go."

"Letting him *escape*, you mean? Once we catch him, there's no letting him go."

"I can't swear I wouldn't turn my head the other way if he gave me back Connor."

"Whelan, you can't do that. You can't trust anything he tells you."

"I know."

"He wants you dead," said Jones.

"I know!"

The two maintained eye contact for a few seconds in silence.

Whelan became aware for the first time she was touching him. Her hand felt warm against his chest. He took a deep breath through his nose. Even after a long day, he was jolted by her familiar and mesmerizing fragrance.

She patted him, then unlocked her door. "Get some sleep, Whelan. We'll plan to convene at eight for breakfast."

She disappeared into her room.

Thomas Whelan could scarcely move but managed the four yards down the hall to his room. He lay on the bed and was out cold in minutes. For the first time since his son was kidnapped, his dreams didn't start with a nightmare.

Breakfast was a cheap buffet in the hotel lobby. Eggs, bacon, and home fries tasted reheated but satisfied their hunger.

Whelan poured syrup all over his little waffle shaped like a dolphin.

Garrity held his up and studied it. "I guess because we're in Miami? Miami Dolphins?"

"Bingo," said Cannon. He'd stuck with eggs and yogurt. He'd already hit the gym and run two miles on the treadmill before 8:00. Muscles and fitness took work. He wasn't blessed with Whelan's metabolism and naturally thin body.

Jones reminded them all why they were there. "You boys have been on Eddie for months," she said to Cannon and Whelan. "What's his next move?"

"He's out of cash," said Whelan. "He's out of friends. He's out of favors."

"He's on the run," said Cannon, "and he's desperate."

"And with my son," echoed Whelan. "He'll continue to switch up cars, which means more murders are in store. We need to figure out where he's headed before he knows himself. Right now, he's likely holed up in some motel, trying to figure that out."

"And he's injured," offered Garrity. "He left a significant amount of blood at the cabin. He can't seek professional medical help. Maybe he's dying somewhere?"

"I hope not," said Whelan. "That would be dangerous for Connor. If Eddie thinks he won't survive, he'll kill my son as a consolation prize for me."

"He called you in Washington," said Jones. "He'll call you again soon, I'd wager. You're his only bet now."

"That's what I'm counting on."

"So, when he does," said Cannon, "what's the plan? Lure him out? He won't have Connor with him if he wants to meet. He'll lock him up somewhere, and once it's safe, he'll what? Would he release him or run? Let's say we gave him money. A hundred thousand."

"We're not giving him any money," said Jones. "The FBI won't offer a dime at this point, not even for Connor."

She turned her head to Whelan. "Sorry, Tom. I've already been working that since before coming to Cumberland. SAC Kendrick says they won't make any exceptions for him any longer."

"I know. I get it. Eddie can't be trusted. He wouldn't keep his word to free my son. What if I put my own money on the line? Money *will* flush him out. I've got about $70,000 in Connor's college fund. You think he'd show for seventy K?"

"I would," said Cannon. "Especially if I had nothing. It's at least travel money and might buy him a passport."

"And he's traveling to where?" asked Jones.

"Anywhere at this point," said Whelan. "But I don't think he'll leave the country. There's nowhere he could go and renew relationships with his old contacts. Most were arrested, and the rest won't touch him. He's soiled forever. Wherever he goes, he's starting fresh."

"Seventy-thousand isn't enough to start fresh," said Garrity. "Anywhere."

"It does get you farther in Mexico than the U.S., though," offered Cannon. "My bet is Mexico."

"Well, he can't fly there. At least not commercially. And he'd have to drive around the entire Gulf of Mexico if he plans to go by car."

"I've got every traffic camera in the state of Florida scanning for his image," said Jones.

The group ran out of thoughts and finished breakfast in silence.

After checking out, they returned to the Miami field office to borrow a desk and strategize. Around 9:30 a.m., Agent Thomas Whelan received a call from an unknown number. "Whelan," he answered.

A whisper came from the other end. "Dad?"

"Connor! Where are you? Are you okay?" He put it on speakerphone and snapped his fingers at one of the local agents who was ready to trace his phone.

"I don't know where we are. He hit me—hard—knocked me out. I'm not sure if we're still in Miami or even Florida. We're in a motel. It's dark."

"Are you alone?"

"No. He's sleeping. I'm locked to the bed, but I got one hand free and was able to grab his phone. Can you trace this call?"

"Already being worked on. Stay on the phone, don't hang up. We need another thirty seconds. Are you still hurting?"

Whelan ignored all the eyes gathered around his desk, "I'm going to kill Eddie," he mumbled, covering his phone.

"My head hurts," said Connor. "He gave me a pill for pain, but it hurts. There's a big knot on my head."

"Connor, can you get your other hand free?"

"I don't think so. He's got me handcuffed. My wrist is black and blue, but I'll keep trying."

"Is there a phone, son? A *motel* phone? It might have the motel's phone number or address on it. Maybe the name of where you're at."

"It's on the other side of his bed. I can't see it."

"We've got a ping!" said Jones. "They're in Pompano. No GPS signal, but we've got it down to a six-block radius."

"Connor, turn on the phone's GPS! Turn on the internet!" said Whelan.

"It's a burner phone, Dad, not a smartphone. Only makes calls."

Whelan's mind was racing. *Burner phone? What has my son been watching?*

"We've got local police on the way, Connor. And I'm headed your direction. I can be there within an hour, son. Stay put. We'll find you. Don't let Eddie leave with you. Fight him if he tries to move you!"

"Whelan," murmured Jones. "Don't encourage him to go against Eddie. He might get hurt again. Or worse."

"Do your best, Connor," said Whelan, "but stay safe! If he threatens to hurt you again, do what he says."

"I have been. I've been cooperating. I'm...shit! He's up! No! Don't!"

The lifeline to Connor Whelan went dead.

Chapter 26

"Connor? Connor!" Whelan yelled into his phone before closing the screen.

Cannon tapped his shoulder. "Let's go. We're on the move!"

Ninety minutes later, they were part of the fray of FBI agents, Broward County Sheriff's officers, and SWAT members searching a six-block radius around a cell phone tower on the south end of Pompano Beach, Florida.

Each street corner had a patrol car, and the sidewalks were being pounded by officers. Teams of two were canvassing US1 and A1A. The Coast Guard offered a boat, now going south down the Intracoastal Waterway between the mainland and the barrier island on the coast, where much of the action transpired for tourists.

Whelan scratched furiously at his scalp. "This is pointless. The second Eddie woke up and found Connor with his phone, he was out of there. They're long gone."

"Let me explore the possibilities," said Jones.

She tapped away on her smartphone, looking at maps of the area. "Whelan! There's a local airport a half-mile due west of us."

"It's worth a shot. He loves little airports, and enough people are covering these streets."

Ten minutes later, the four agents split up and began interviewing everyone they saw at Pompano Airpark. They drifted between hangars for small aircraft, prop planes, and private jets. There was nothing to lose, and Connor's life on the line. If Eddie hit the highway, he could be halfway to Orlando by now. And yet nothing was picked up by facial recognition software on any traffic camera between here and there.

The small airport had thirty-one hangars of varying sizes, each accommodating six to fifteen planes. It would take hours to visit them all. Luckily, most were hidden behind closed hangar doors, so they focused on what was open. If Eddie had been through here, it was within the past two hours.

A maintenance worker in oil-stained coveralls gave them their first bit of hope.

"Yeah, I spoke to him," he said, staring at the picture Whelan held on his phone. "Didn't see no kid, though. He was trying to find a pilot to take him straight away."

"To where," asked Whelan.

"Didn't tell me. I sent him over to Jeffrey's, hangar 24. Good luck."

The sign on 24 read: *Broward to Bahamas and Beyond.*

Whelan's heart sank. If Eddie managed to take Connor to the Bahamas, they could go anywhere. The airport in Freeport was international. Many private charter captains ignored the lack of a passport when enough cash was flashed before them.

"We're looking for Jeffrey," Whelan announced when they entered the building, flashing IDs and badges.

"Jeffrey isn't here," said the woman behind the desk. "He's on his way back from the Bahamas. We have three other pilots on duty. They don't fly international, however. Jeffrey should be back by eleven. Or Franklin is in at two. They're the only ones who go to the Bahamas."

"Where? In the Bahamas?" asked Jones.

"Freeport or Nassau."

She pushed a price sheet toward them. "We have three seats left on the eleven-thirty to Freeport and two on the two-thirty to Nassau. Those are the next two flights. If all four of you need to travel together, I can see if someone wants to get bumped to the evening schedule. It'll cost you, though. People will switch for money. Usually starting at six hundred per person."

"Wait a minute," said Cannon. "Jeffrey is due back at eleven a.m.?"

"Yes, sir."

"What time did his flight over leave?"

"Eight-thirty."

Cannon wheeled around to Jones, Whelan, and Garrity. "Eddie wasn't on that flight! He was still in his motel here at nine-thirty."

Whelan came to his senses and showed the woman a photo of Eddie Morrison.

"He was here," she said. "Told him the same schedule, so he left."

Hope filled Whelan's chest for the first time this morning.

"Did he say where? Did you suggest another company?"

"No, sorry," she answered. "But I don't think anyone but us flies to the Bahamas. At least, not commercially, for customers."

"What do you mean? Does someone else fly there for another reason?"

"There's a lot of hobbyists flying in and out of Pompano Airpark, who store their single or twin-engine props here, around a hundred and eighty. And some like to go to the Bahamas. Freeport is under an hour for them."

She brought up a page on her browser and clicked around. "No one but us has public flights to the Bahamas today. There would be flight logs filed. Or they're supposed to file them, anyway."

"What *is* filed for today?" asked Garrity.

"Let me see." More clicking ensued. "Six today are filed, but sometimes last-minute flights are added."

"Any in the past hour?" asked Whelan.

"Two. There's one to Tampa and one to Jacksonville."

"Where are they leaving from? Which hangars?" asked Jones.

"Tampa is at thirty-one. Oh," she paused and clicked. "That one left ten minutes ago."

"Is there a manifest? Can you tell who was on it?" asked Cannon.

"Not from here. You need to check with them directly. The other one is scheduled for…now. Out of fourteen."

She pointed the way, and four pairs of legs bolted down the apron alongside the runway in search of fourteen.

"There!" Whelan pointed. A twin-engine prop was taxiing out of the hangar.

As they raced to apprehend it, the plane reached the tarmac and moved into takeoff position.

"There are three aboard," yelled Cannon as they ran. "I can't make out any faces!"

Whelan pulled his gun and fired a warning shot into the air. It went unanswered. The plane began its takeoff. They were all paralyzed, watching it head straight toward them on the runway. Jones thought to move them back a few steps before they were run over.

Connor Whelan's face appeared in the rear window as the plane passed. It now wore a black eye to go with the split lip, busted cheek, and giant knot on his head. He put his hand on the glass and pounded, before being yanked away, out of sight.

Whelan focused on his team. "We need someone here to take us to Jacksonville."

They split up, maintaining radio contact. Twelve minutes later, Cannon's voice came over the earpiece. "Hangar 18. He can be ready in a few minutes, but it's a tiny plane. He can only take two of us."

EDDIE MORRISON

Chapter 27

Jones and Whelan were soon airborne and on their way to Jacksonville, Florida.

There was no choice but to leave Cannon and Garrity behind. They would make their way to the Fort Lauderdale airport and catch the next commercial flight out.

Jones notified the Jacksonville FBI office. Agents were ready to catch and hold Eddie Morrison, and rescue Connor, at Craig Municipal Airport, the destination filed by the pilot of the twin-engine that got away.

When they landed, they were greeted by Assistant Special Agent in Charge of the Jacksonville bureau office, Li Chen.

"I'm sorry," she said, "but they never landed here. We've been on top of all the flights, and I put two agents at JAX, Jacksonville International Airport, with eyes on any twin-engine prop landing. So far, nothing. I've got agents on their way to Cecil and Herlong—two local airports—but if your guy rerouted there, he will have a twenty-five-minute jump on them. At least we'll know."

"Thank you," said Whelan. "Is there any way to get someone to bring up the radar history and follow it from Pompano to here?"

"We can ask."

The answer from the Air Traffic Control Specialist at Craig Municipal was disappointing. "Usually, smaller aircraft aren't equipped with transponders and are unreliable regarding radar detection. And if they stay low enough, there's so much interference from clutter, you'd lose it after a few minutes."

"How far could they fly in a twin-engine prop? On one tank of gas?"

"What kind?"

"I don't know. I didn't catch it," said Whelan. He turned to Jones. "Miranda?"

"I think it was a Cessna, but I'm not sure of the model. I tried to read the tail numbers, but I couldn't see them clearly at the angle we had."

"A newer Cessna could easily go a thousand to twelve-hundred miles on a full tank, depending on wind direction and passenger load."

"So, they could have gone anywhere," said Whelan. He hung his head.

"From Pompano?" the specialist replied. "Yes. Anywhere within twelve-hundred miles."

"That's a lot of country," said ASAC Chen.

"It's a lot of international countries as well," said Whelan.

He was dejected. "Shit, he could have made his pilot go to the Bahamas or any of the Caribbean islands, or...." He paused as his mind fought to accept the dire circumstances.

Jones finished his thought. "Or most of Mexico."

Whelan slammed his fist on a nearby table and collapsed into a chair beside it.

"How do we put out a notification to all the airports for a thousand miles? Is there an emergency broadcast system of some sort?"

"Yes, the FAA has measures, but honestly, the likelihood smaller and local airports are notified in time is hit and miss. Offices aren't always manned twenty-four/seven. And if he left the country? Your odds go down, I'm afraid. Significantly."

"We have to try. Do it anyway," he ordered.

"What's *our* game plan?" Whelan asked Jones as they stepped out of the airport.

"Whelan, I'm sorry, but the ball's back in Eddie's court. We'll do our best with BOLOs from here to Kansas City, Texas, and New York, but we're in a sit-and-hold pattern ourselves until we catch a break."

They thanked the Jacksonville ASAC and headed to JAX to meet up with Cannon and Garrity, who were due to arrive in another hour.

Updates confirmed Eddie Morrison and Connor Whelan didn't land at the other two local airports the Jacksonville teams were investigating.

Two hours later, the four agents silently ate hamburgers at a local joint, each contemplating Eddie's possible moves.

"I still think he's headed to Mexico," said Cannon. "His money will go farther there than in the States. If his goal is to draw out Tom so he can kill him, there's a whole country happy to turn their heads the other way."

"Possibly," mumbled Whelan.

"I think he's headed back to Cacapon Mountain or Cumberland," said Garrity.

The other agents all turned their heads to him.

"Why?" asked Jones.

"The old case file emphasized Morrison's affinity for the area. The history with Agent Whelan is rich. That's where trust was first established. I'm betting, if it's become so personal for him, that will be where he wants to finish it."

Whelan, Jones, and Cannon reflected on the thought from the newest member of their team.

Jones was the first to react. "That's ludicrous! He has to know we were there and the place is being watched."

"It was being watched before," said Garrity. "And it didn't stop him."

"But we're *actively* watching it now, not just some tech guy scrolling through images at one a.m. on fast forward."

"Maybe there's another stash there he didn't have time to grab the other day," said Whelan. "More cash, more weapons. A backup emergency stash."

"A *backup* emergency stash?" questioned Jones. "Whelan, you're reaching. If Eddie is as low on cash as you guys say he must be, he would have taken all he had at the Cacapon cabin when he was there."

Whelan put down his half-eaten burger. "Yes. Of course you're right."

"What do you think he plans to do *now* with Connor?" asked Jones.

Whelan lifted his chin, inhaling deeply. "He didn't get to trade him for a large payment. I imagine he's torn between selling him to someone for whatever he can get or holding him for revenge against me. If I were a gambling man, I'd bet on revenge. But we should have someone start monitoring the calls and movements of all the known child traffickers in the U.S. See if he's approached any with offers. Make it worthwhile for them to tell us."

"We're pretty tapped out on favors from informants, I'm afraid," said Jones. "But I'll try to call in the few I have left."

She stood and went outside to speak without the background noise of a lunch crowd.

Whelan began swirling a cold French fry in and out of his ketchup, making figure eights on his plate.

"I need to step out as well," said Garrity. "Make a report to my supervisor."

When he left, Cannon slid over closer to Whelan. "How do you think Connor's holding up?"

"Not well. He sounded terrified."

"He sounded frustrated to me."

"Frustrated?"

"Yes," said Cannon. "His tone. Scared? Yes. But also frustrated and annoyed. I think he's hardening to Eddie. That might be positive for him, for his psyche."

"Building a mental wall? That has consequences, long-term, which can't be easily measured by a few visits to a PTSD shrink. Eddie's damaging him mentally as much as physically, guaranteed."

Whelan peered directly into his friend's eyes. "Phil, we need to end this before Connor withdrawals so deep no amount of light can ever bring him out."

"What do you have in mind?"

"When Eddie calls me, I'm giving myself up to him. Whatever he asks for. I'm swapping places with Connor, and I need you to let me do it."

"What if a trade isn't what he wants? What if he just wants you *both* dead? Tom, you're exhausted. Your head's not on straight. Let me be your rationale until you can get some sleep and think clearly."

"Sure."

He stood up from the table and threw money down to cover the bill, absently stuffing the receipt into his wallet before marching outside.

Cannon mumbled to himself as he watched him leave. "And I need to be there to make sure the bastard ends up dead no matter what happens."

Chapter 28

Eddie Morrison was staring at Connor Whelan inside the Cessna. He finished the call he was on and directed the pilot to keep heading to New Orleans.

"What's wrong, kid? You look like you've been put through the wringer."

Connor couldn't tell if he was joking, so he opted to sit in silence. He watched the ground below. They weren't flying very high. He could make out cars and even people walking around when they flew over small towns. Soon, the ground gave way to the Gulf of Mexico. After the last beach was out of sight, he lay across two seats as best he could and closed his eyes.

Please let me sleep. I'm so tired.

It wasn't in his cards. He fought restlessness for over an hour. Land was now outside the window, and after another forty minutes, they started descending. He watched New Orleans come and go underneath them, and then they headed north over Lake Pontchartrain.

"We'll land at Saint Tammany Regional Airport. It's practically vacant," said the pilot.

"I thought you were going to Hammond?" asked Eddie.

"It's much busier. I'll have to notify air traffic control, and there will be a ton of eyes on you. It's best we stay unnoticed. You said privacy was a topmost concern."

"Yes. Okay," Eddie conceded.

Connor debated whether or not to speak up. He didn't want to see any more people killed at his expense, but the pilot had the upper hand right now. Perhaps he could encourage him to use it.

"You know he's going to kill you when we land, right?" he shouted to the pilot. "I'd stick to an airport with more witnesses if I was you."

The pilot turned to Connor for the first time since they took off from Pompano Airpark. "Nonsense. We have an arrangement."

"Well, if that involves money, I can tell you, he doesn't have any!"

"Shut up, kid!" shouted Eddie. He tried smacking Connor's face with the back of his hand, but the boy jumped back, and he struck an armrest.

"The kid doesn't know what he's talking about. I showed you the money," he told the pilot.

"You showed me *some* money," the man said. "We agreed on ten thousand. You've got that much, right?"

"Of course."

"Ten thousand?" yelled Connor. "Mister, you know how to count? I'll bet he doesn't have ten *hundred* left in that bag. You're a dead man, for sure. Better land at the busy airport if you want to live."

"Connor! Shut your mouth!" screamed Eddie.

Connor Whelan reacted to Eddie Morrison as though he'd assaulted him again. *I think that's the first time he's ever called me by my name. He's getting desperate, for sure.*

"Let me see the ten thousand," said the pilot.

"I've got it. Now, land the plane."

The pilot pulled on the yoke violently, and the plane began ascending rapidly. "We're not landing until I see the money."

"I've got a thousand now, and I'll get you nine thousand when we land. I can have it wired to your account by 5:00."

"Sounds like horseshit to me," said Connor. "Take his thousand now and get his gun!"

"Gun?" asked the pilot. "What the hell's going on here?"

Eddie didn't have time for questions. He removed his SIG from his pocket and fired a shot into the pilot's leg. He allowed the man to scream for a few seconds before he pointed it at his head.

"Look, I get it," he said quietly to the man. "You've got the control, right? Fine. Either we all live, or we all die. I'm tired, and I don't give much of a fuck right now. So, land the plane, or I'm about to get the shortest lesson in piloting a man ever had."

He turned to Connor. "It's been real, kid. Sorry we couldn't meet up with your dad."

The pilot was frozen in terror.

Eddie put his gun into the pilot's side. It seemed less intimidating somehow than up against the skull. "What's it going to be, all live? Or all die?"

After the past three days, Connor wasn't sure which he preferred either. He hoped to discover a renewed interest in living, but it was evading him. "Better land where he says, mister. He's crazy."

He turned and stared out the window. He was sure he'd just caused this innocent man to lose his life. He'd made a decision and chosen himself over this stranger. *I wonder if he's married? Does he have kids? Someone my age? Maybe we could have been friends.*

"Okay, we're headed down. I'm going to Saint Tammany. When we land, you keep your money and walk away, and I'm going to fly away quietly, and we'll both pretend we never met. Agreed?"

"Peachy," Eddie snarled.

Connor fixated on the pilot as they skidded along the tiny runway. *Kill us, mister. Just kill us all, and let's be done with this.*

They came to a slow taxiing speed, and the pilot turned at the end of the runway. "Okay, you two jump out, and I'm going to fly away as we agreed."

"You want us to jump?" shouted Eddie. "You're nuts. I'm already wounded. How would you like to jump out with that bullet in your leg? Well, I've got one in mine! Stop the fucking plane, or I'll plug you right here."

The pilot began increasing speed.

Eddie shot the man in the gut, then again in the head. Blood sprayed the window. The throttle was released, and the yoke turned to the left, moving them off the runway and toward the one building on the strip. It was a small tin hangar, barely large enough to accommodate even one plane.

Eddie grabbed the control column and tried to steer them away from the building. He failed. They crashed into the corner, and the structure landed on top of the Cessna. At least they were stopped.

No one was inside the structure, but two men from another building a hundred yards back came running to assist.

Eddie got the door open as they arrived.

"Our pilot collapsed," he said. "I'm not sure what happened."

One of the men was about to comment when Eddie shot him in the chest. He blasted the other man in the back as he turned to run.

Eddie took the portable two-step unit out from behind the co-pilot's seat and dropped it on the ground. It toppled to the side and underneath the plane.

"Shit."

Eddie jumped to the ground, trying to put all his weight on his better leg. It crumpled underneath him, forcing him to brace himself with his injured leg. He screamed as the weight of his body hitting the ground from a three-foot drop shot pain through his wounds and traveled all the way up his back. He howled again as his whole body hit the asphalt. His free hand broke the fall, but bits of loose gravel were forced into his palm. He stood, dusted himself off, and released another scream, this one long and as loud as he could manage. It was full of pent-up tension, and he felt better having let it go.

Connor was behind him, still in the doorway of the plane. He understood that third scream and released his own primal roar. It was equally loud and long.

Eddie was startled and whirled his body around with his pistol still up and ready to fire.

The two gazed at one another once Connor stopped yelling like a madman. Eddie was the first to crack a smile, then a chuckle. The release of energy was cathartic for both of them. Connor smiled in return and then began laughing loudly. The two souls met on the same playing field for the first time and boisterously roared the remaining energy out of their bodies.

Eddie walked over to the first man he shot and put another bullet into his head. There was only silence.

Connor watched the second man crawling away on his stomach. He was moaning, possibly crying. He was mumbling imperceptibly.

A prayer?

Whatever sound he made was more like a wounded animal than a man. The next bullet into his head was welcome relief for him, and Connor's ears. He was beginning to tire of people whimpering for their lives.

Eddie looked at Connor and said, "Pop'em in the head to make sure they're dead."

Connor nodded.

They exited the building onto the desolate little runway with no one in sight as far as they could see.

"What now?" asked Connor.

Eddie saw the car parked in front of the building the two men came from. He pointed at it. After retrieving keys and cash from the men's pockets, he pushed the alarm on the matching Ford fob. It worked. They were on their way in a little white Fusion, headed northwest on Highway 36.

Connor was too tired to add the two men to the death toll. It was becoming easier not to think about that number any longer, the number of souls sacrificed by Eddie in the name of revenge and at his expense. *Please, God, let the next one be me.*

Chapter 29

Jones approached Whelan, who clicked away on his laptop in the Jacksonville International Airport, following up on dead-end searches. With no clear direction, they decided the airport was the best spot to "hole up" for the inevitable call from Eddie Morrison and spent the past two hours on the phone or online. They were in the executive lounge for one of the major carriers and had it primarily to themselves.

Whelan held hope in his eyes. "Anything from your informants?"

"Not yet. We've heard responses from three, and I'm waiting on callbacks from four others."

"Okay, thank you."

She placed a hand on his shoulder. "Tom, I need to get back to K.C. There are two different homicide investigations ongoing, and Kendrick needs me."

Whelan stood. "Go. We've got this. Thank you for all you've done. Honestly, Miranda, your being here made all this bearable for me."

"Catch this bastard and come home."

"Yes, Ma'am."

"Where's Cannon?"

"He went in search of a snack."

"There's a perfectly fine fruit bowl on the counter," said Jones, pointing to the reception area. "You'd think it would be right up his alley."

"I think he needed to pace away some of his frustration."

"Okay, whatever works. You still meditating?"

"Not so much this week, but yeah, and it's helping."

"I'll see you soon." She gave him a long hug and then headed out.

Garrity watched Whelan's face when Jones left the room. "You two are pretty close, huh?"

Whelan took his seat and focused on the computer screen. "Sure." His tone was dismissive, causing Garrity to chuckle.

Cannon came running into the room a half hour later. "Whelan! They got a hit on facial rec outside of New Orleans! Eddie's plane crashed into a hangar at a small regional runway. They had cameras! He headed west out of the airport. Might be going into the city. They're trying to track the car he's in. The New Orleans office is four miles from the Lake Pontchartrain Causeway. They've set up a traffic stop on the south end. If he comes across there, we've got him."

"Any word on Connor?"

"There was someone with him in the car, but they couldn't tell who from the camera angle. They were upright and apparently okay. Eddie shot the pilot, though, and left two other men dead at the airport."

"We need to find the first flight to New Orleans."

Cannon was energized. "Gate 12, fifteen minutes."

"My hero!" Whelan jumped up, optimistic for the first time today. He turned to Garrity, who was tapping away on his phone. "Let's go, Garrity."

"Are we sure that one will arrive first? I'm trying to see what flight will land first. Make sure there are no layovers."

"That one will. It's a direct flight," said Cannon. He didn't like having his diligence questioned and it showed in his tone.

"Sorry," mumbled Garrity. "Just trying to be helpful."

The agents landed at Louis Armstrong New Orleans International Airport two hours later.

Special Agent Amber Caulfield from the local field office met them at the gate.

She spoke with the thick, Cajun-Creole accent many southern Louisiana natives carried. "While you were in the air, the Ford Fusion Eddie was last seen in was located in the parking lot of a Comfort Inn up in Covington, on the north side of Lake Pontchartrain. Police confirmed with the manager there were no cameras in the lot. We're working on the assumption Eddie stole another car off the lot, but no one on the property is missing their car yet."

"Address?" asked Cannon.

He put it into Google Maps on his phone. "Shit."

Whelan took his phone from him, pinching and expanding the image, scrolling around the satellite aerial view. "It backs up to a huge residential neighborhood. He'll have taken a car from there. There are apartments, duplexes, single-family homes.... Garrity! Get on that phone of yours and work for me instead of Baltimore for a minute, would you? Call the local police and get as many officers as they can spare to start door-knocking that area. See who's missing a car. Maybe we'll get lucky."

"Yes, sir." He took the number from Agent Caulfield and stepped aside to make the call.

"Okay," she continued. "I have wonderful news, Agent Whelan. The traffic cameras on the Tammany Parkway did pick up your son in the car with him. He's bruised but alert. We think he might have been on the lookout for the cameras. There are several that caught detailed shots of him. We lost him, of course, when they turned into the Comfort Inn lot. But your son's alive. Last seen one-hundred-thirty-five minutes ago."

Whelan took in a long breath and counted to ten in his head on the exhale. He needed to stay focused and not let his emotions cause mistakes. "Thank you, Agent Caulfield. How many agents can New Orleans lend us to help with a search here?"

"I'm not sure. You have me and two in our office—one on traffic cam watch and the other is coordinating with the Covington police department and New Orleans PD. They have jurisdiction over all of Orleans Parish. The minute we get eyes on Mr. Morrison, we'll have the full resources of our office at our disposal."

"Eddie Morrison will be disguised as best he can when they arrive. He'll know New Orleans has a ton of cameras."

"We understand. What about your son? Will he put him in a costume, too?"

Whelan paused, then spit out, "He's likely in the trunk. So the traffic stop on Pontchartrain? Nothing?"

"No. I'm sorry. We're about to call it off. It's a clear day. He should have been across in thirty minutes if he came that way. They gave it two hours. We need to free up the Causeway for rush hour by five. Assuming Morrison is coming to New Orleans, he must have driven around the lake. Oooh, that's a long time to be squashed into a trunk."

SSA Caulfield bowed her head respectfully and threw up a quick prayer for the boy. She reminded Whelan of Agent Miranda Jones in some way. She was about the same size and wore a similar hairstyle, loose and bouncy curls, though cut shorter. The resemblance made him comfortable with her.

"Thanks for the prayer," he said. "I'll take all I can get."

He threw up another prayer of his own. *God, please let this be the end.*

Chapter 30

Connor Whelan blinked his eyes and rubbed at them, forcing them to see again in the daylight after being locked for over three hours in the trunk of a Toyota Camry.

He stood dazed, trying to get some sense of direction, but the sun was high overhead and he couldn't make out which way the shadows were leaning. A small river was on one side of them, a jungle of trees on the other. Spanish moss hung thick from the branches of the trees, largely Bald Cypress and Water Tupelo, both of which gobbled up the banks.

"You brought me to the swamp?" he asked Morrison.

Eddie simpered. "What, did you think we would eat beignets in the French Quarter? Drink chicory and take an afternoon river cruise?"

His statement carried little relevance for Connor. "I thought we were going to New Orleans. This is a jungle."

"You're in the bayou, kid. Think of it as the suburbs."

Connor saw nothing but trees and water in front of him. "There's nothing here. It's a dead end. Are we supposed to pitch a tent?"

"Stand quietly for a minute. Listen."

A low buzz could be heard from the south. It got lost on the breeze at times but grew louder over the following minute.

An old, fourteen-foot, Deep V aluminum Jon boat emerged out of nowhere. An even smaller waterway about a hundred yards south joined the one they stood beside. A woman was piloting a trolling motor and headed straight toward them.

"Get in," said Eddie when she pulled up to their bank.

"In that?" asked Connor. "I think it'll sink with all three of us."

Eddie grabbed his arm tight and shoved him toward the water. "It's the boat or the alligators. I don't have time for games, kid. We've got to get off the grid. You prove more trouble than you're worth, I won't hesitate to feed you to the swamp."

Connor squinted at the man. Each day he feared him a little less. Or perhaps he relished life less. He thought he could outrun Eddie from here and was tempted to try, but the pilot was holding a rifle, and his instinct said she knew how to use it. "Yes, sir."

He climbed aboard and sat on a wood plank rigged as a seat. "I'm not the strongest swimmer," he lied. "Don't you have a lifejacket?"

"Do you *see* a life jacket?" she replied. "I suggest you don't fall out."

Her ebony skin was weathered, and her wifebeater and cargo shorts weren't in much better shape. She was fit for an older woman. "Now, stay quiet, boy!" she shushed him. "Or I'll knock you upside your skull with an oar."

Connor viewed each side of the small boat, where an oar was locked into a little holder mounted to the metal. He turned away from her and faced forward. If they were playing "good cop, bad cop," he'd take the cop he'd come to know over this strange woman with a thick, creole accent.

"Don't pay attention to Jolie, kid. Her bark's worse than her bite. Help me," commanded Eddie as he tried to get his leg over the side and climb in.

Connor stood, lending his shoulder for support, and helped Eddie sit on a bench in front of him, facing himself and the woman. His butt barely hit the seat when she reversed the motor, then headed north with her cargo.

Eddie saw Connor's concern in his eyes. "Just keep doing what you're told, kid, and you'll be all right."

They traveled for over half an hour, rounding one little island, then another, all by trolling motor. The woman eventually started a traditional outboard motor to make better time once they were in deeper, wider water. Four more hours passed. Connor's rear end was getting sore from the bench seat, and his restlessness was felt with each shift of his body weight.

He was trying to keep track of the general direction they were heading. *North for sure, and I think west.*

Sometimes they were on a wide bayou. Sometimes they hoisted the outboard and relied on the trolling motor to barely squeeze the boat between the shorelines. Never once did the woman appear lost.

How many miles have we gone? he wondered. *She's filled that motor three times now with gas.*

He stared at the red five-gallon tank.

They rounded two more sharp turns and motored up to a floating jetty on the side of a rickety pier. The little dock was buoyed to float up and down beside the fixed pier as storm surge and the rain could alter the water level here by well over a foot. A small ladder was attached to the pier's deck, making a three-foot climb up from the dock at the current water level. The wooden pier was more weathered than the woman's face and possibly older.

She hopped off and tied both ends of the boat to secure it. Once on the pier, she marched onto shore toward a storage shed.

Connor stepped onto the dock, then helped Eddie climb out of the boat and onto the ladder. Only the pier attached to the shoreline.

"I'm going to let you loose for a few minutes," said Eddie. "There's literally nowhere to run here. Closest neighbor is upriver two miles, and if you don't get swallowed up by the alligators, the snakes will get you quick. If you see one, assume it's a water moccasin, and they're all poisonous. Water's on all sides of this little patch of dirt. There's a fridge in the cabin, and Jolie usually keeps a ton of potato chips in the pantry. Help yourself if you're hungry. Don't touch anything else, and be respectful to the hired help."

Eddie walked over to Jolie and began speaking in hushed tones.

Connor guessed her to be at least forty-five, "old" to the eyes of a twelve-year-old, though certainly not as ancient as Eddie. He couldn't compare her to the women he knew in D.C. She wasn't wearing a dress and didn't have an ounce of makeup on her face. Given her affinity for snacking on potato chips, he wondered how she stayed in such superb physical shape.

Jolie wasn't overjoyed to see Eddie. That much was obvious. She kept sneaking peeks at Connor and would turn her head back to Eddie each time with sharp words cutting the air through the whispers.

Connor took in his surroundings. It was a small area of dry land approximately a hundred feet long and eighty feet wide. It sat on a waterway he guessed was about thirty feet across. He knew it must be one of the hundreds of distributary bayous and estuary forks bleeding off toward the sea along the southern edge of Louisiana. Many of the more significant, more popular, and well-traveled bayous had names. He doubted this one was wide enough to have one. Geography and Social Studies weren't his favorite subjects, but he'd paid enough attention in school to understand his environment. And he'd seen his share of *Swamp People* episodes.

Something caught the corner of his eye, and he turned toward the water as a jumping fish landed with a large splash. The action caused a disturbance underneath the pier, which was barely holding together after years of no maintenance. He saw the head of an enormous alligator disappear under the surface and then a few bubbles popping up for breath. The giant lizard failed to reappear. It must have taken its lunch back to its nest to feast.

Ten yards from the water's edge, the "cabin" was more of a shack, also needing repairs. Part wood, part tin, with a roof covered in solar panels, Connor feared it would collapse on him as he entered the screen door. Inside, he found the pantry, and at least eight kinds of potato chips, their bags in various stages of fullness. Chip clips held the remains fresh. He saw his favorite, kettle-cooked with jalapeño, and tore into them like he hadn't eaten a large portion of meatloaf less than twelve hours ago.

Inside the refrigerator were cans labeled "Yoo-hoo." It tasted like watered-down chocolate milk but was drinkable and soothed the spiciness of the chips. There was no television, so he settled down on a ratty old sofa full of holes and watched Eddie through the window.

I wish I could read lips.

Eddie waved goodbye to Jolie, who was leaving in the boat they arrived in.

Connor sighed. *We're stranded on this tiny island in the middle of swamp hell.*

Eddie saw Connor staring at him. Instead of coming inside, he walked over to the bayou's edge and looked both directions like he was expecting another visitor by boat.

I wonder who I'm being sold to now?

Connor turned his focus to the refrigerator. *It might be days before I have a chance to eat again.*

The creak of the screen door behind him drew his attention. A man came in, his skin so dark Connor couldn't make out any features as he stood silhouetted against the bright outdoors. He nodded to Connor from beneath a brimmed straw hat, then proceeded to the refrigerator. Not much taller than Connor, he was older than Jolie, much skinnier, and more ragged.

The man dug through plastic storage containers until he uncovered some cold fried chicken. Two pieces were put on a paper plate, and then he approached Connor directly, holding his hand out toward the bag of chips.

Connor leaned it in his direction, and the man took two handfuls. He motioned invitingly with a broad, toothy grin for Connor to help himself to the chicken box he'd left on the counter. Then he was gone, as silently as he came.

There were three pieces of chicken left. He devoured them, not considering even once whether Eddie was hungry. They were seasoned well and hit the spot.

A probe of other cabinets revealed a supply of rat-killing pellets. His first thought was to see if any rats were running around wild. The place certainly looked like it could host a few.

A second thought popped into Connor's head. He glanced out the window to ensure Eddie was still occupying his time by the river. He snatched a large chef's knife and began cutting and mashing the rat poison into powder. He mixed it with water in a small bowl and worked it into a paste. Soon there was at least a quarter cup of sludge. He fished a fresh Yoo-hoo out of the refrigerator and drank a couple of sips before spooning the mix into the can and stirring it well.

He grabbed his own drink and the can of death mix and headed out toward Eddie. The Chicken Man was sitting under a tree at least fifteen yards away. He was curled up tight and reading a paperback between his bites.

Connor focused on Eddie Morrison.

"It's kind of humid. Aren't you thirsty? These were in the fridge. They're not as good as real chocolate milk, but they're cold. Here," he offered up the Yoo-hoo to Eddie.

Eddie took it and read the label. "This shit's for kids. Jolie usually keeps beer on hand. You couldn't have brought me a beer?"

"It's nutrition," said Connor, "and apparently good enough for Jolie. Cheers." He held up his can.

"I prefer to get my nutrition from barley, hops, and malt," said Eddie. He hurled the can across the water, aiming at a turtle banking on a cypress knee. He missed.

"Damn."

Eddie turned and walked toward the shack, presumably in search of beer.

Connor's heart plummeted to his gut.

You can say that again.

Chapter 31

Supervisory Special Agent Amber Caulfield led the team back to the New Orleans bureau office and set up a desk from which to work. The Special Agent in Charge, Carson Orville, came by for a minute to give his "thoughts and prayers" and confirm the visiting agents knew they had the full resources of their office at their disposal. He wasn't terribly sincere, but Whelan appreciated the gesture. He knew the man was busy, and the office was scattered and frenzied as agents ran around putting together solutions for their ongoing cases.

Caulfield had a quiet energy about her, like the whirring fan of an air handler waiting for the compressor to kick on. "Since I've been assigned to you gentlemen, how about catching me up on the case."

They obliged.

She listened to them without interruption.

"All right," she started, "the one thing you lost me on was this Angel Baylor, a.k.a. Lil' Baby? Why did Eddie Morrison kill him? How was he involved in all this to begin with? I read up on your old case, Agent Whelan, and I thought Lil' Baby disappeared into the shadows after your big bust. Why surface now?"

"At last!" said Whelan, to Garrity. "Someone's paying attention."

Garrity raised his brow. "Excuse me?"

"Okay, okay," interrupted Cannon. "We're all tired and on edge. Let's not start."

He turned to Caulfield. "Fantastic question. We've been working on it, and frankly, we aren't sure. Either Eddie contacted Baylor with a job offer, enough to make him risk showing himself back in Cumberland, or Baylor somehow got in touch with Eddie, but that seems unlikely."

"Lil' Baby was smart," said Whelan. "He'd have known Eddie was on the run and likely out of funds. If Eddie promised him a huge payday, he'd have seen through it. We're assuming Eddie offered other compensation for Baylor's help—a stash of weapons perhaps, or easily sellable drugs—and then it all went south for some reason. There's no way to know at this point, and now it doesn't matter. We have to figure out what Eddie's doing in New Orleans."

"Clearly, he thinks someone here can help him," said Caulfield. "Your case file said six known figures escaped the multi-city bust of Eddie's operations. Baylor and his main henchman were two who got away. His guy wasn't mentioned in your last report update. Angel Baylor was discovered alone."

"Presumably, his 'muscle for hire' went his own way long before now. I expect he's a non-issue, though there are still active warrants for his arrest should he ever surface."

"Were any of the other four in New Orleans?" asked Caulfield.

Whelan took a long breath and expelled it slowly as his mind searched. "Not by name."

"The 'Unknown Soldier'?" asked Caulfield.

"You read thoroughly. Yes, ma'am. That's what I named her. Eddie's main operator in New Orleans was busted, and we took over fifteen other people here. But there was rumor of one who got away, an important player. She and her partner worked on the sidelines, always staying low on our radar. An assistant to the top brass but much smarter, I suspect. There was a blurry photo at one point, but it was so lousy, facial rec couldn't get a hit. She was an African American woman with short hair. She ghosted Eddie and the entire operation, I'm sure, to save herself. There's little loyalty in the trafficking business."

"What was she trafficking?" asked Cannon. "Here, in New Orleans?"

"Drugs. Eddie ran tons of drugs through here. He didn't traffick any sex workers that we're aware of, but Louisiana is an easy state to move drugs into the country. Everyone's focused on the Mexican border, and they ignore the rest. They come by boats from the Caribbean or up from Mexico, around the Texas coast, or straight across. He owned a few small pontoon planes as well. They'd land four or five miles offshore. Then, smaller fishing boats would meet them and pick up product, or he'd air-drop them at a floating drop site.

"He was smart and not over-zealous. Shipments were broken down into manageable sizes, even single kilos sometimes, if necessary, to avoid detection. Dozens of bass boats slipped in and out of the bayous and were tough to track. Reports said the Unknown Soldier knew the bayous like no one else. Teams swept the area for over a week. No doubt she was right under their noses the whole time."

"Then it sounds like we're in the wrong area," said Caulfield. "We need to be in the swamp."

"If that's where they're at," said Garrity, "how in the hell are we going to find them if a whole team couldn't find her in an entire week?"

SSA Caulfield stood up. "Because they didn't have *me* in that bust. I was in Georgia at the time. I recently transferred here."

"No offense, ma'am," said Garrity, "but if you're new to the area, what's going to give you a leg up?"

"I'm not new to the area, agent. What I should have said was, 'I recently transferred *home*.' I grew up here, in those very bayous Connor Whelan is likely being held right now. And I got a whole lotta kinfolk who've spent their lives navigating those waterways, too."

She turned to Whelan. "Eddie brought your son to the wrong place. The playing field just evened out."

"We need to narrow down where the Unknown Soldier might be living," said SSA Caulfield.

They were all standing before a large monitor in the bullpen of the New Orleans Field Office. An aerial map of Louisiana, south of New Orleans, was up for view.

"The bayous of southern Louisiana cover an area almost two-hundred miles wide and come inland twenty to seventy miles, on average. Some are tiny, travel a few miles inland, and a few come up hundreds."

She looked at Whelan, "Any of these cities jump out to you? What area was she from?"

Whelan scanned with his eyes. He pinched and pushed on a tablet casting to the monitor, zooming in and out of different areas. "Well, west of the Mississippi, East of Franklin. Thibodaux, Houma. Lafitte. Those towns jump out at me for some reason. Morgan City. I remember those names. They were focusing their search to the south. South of U.S. 90. And this large Bayou, Perot, I remember that. Barataria Bay. Terrebonne Bay. Atchafalaya Wilderness. She's somewhere in here."

He circled an area on the map with his finger.

A tool on the map measured the area as he drew. They all gasped at the number it calculated—5,174 square miles.

"How the hell are we going to find him in over five-thousand square miles?" mumbled Garrity.

Before anyone could retort, Special Agent in Charge for New Orleans, Carson Orville, turned away from the map to a room with fourteen of his agents and analysts. "Listen up! We've got a workable lead. This is on our soil, people. An abducted child of one of our own is in our backyard. You all have the updates and recent photos of the players. Go to work!"

They scrambled, on phones, on computers, scanning camera footage, and chasing leads.

"Thank you, Carson," said Whelan. "I appreciate the support."

"Of course."

SAC Orville motioned Caulfield over to Whelan, Cannon, and Garrity. "Agent Caulfield, until we hear Eddie Morrison or Connor Whelan are no longer in our jurisdiction, this case is your top priority. I'm naming you Supervisory Special Agent on this while it's in our wheelhouse."

"Sir," started Whelan. "With all due respect, I've been working Eddie Morrison for months."

"And you haven't caught him," said SAC Orville. His tone was matter-of-fact, lacking condescension. "I don't know how you managed to convince Director Commerson to let you remain lead on this once Morrison nabbed your boy, but when you're in my territory, you'll do as I say. Caulfield's an exemplary agent, Agent Whelan. You're lucky to have her."

"Sir, yes sir, but I need to be able to make the call on what direction this investigation takes. I *know* Morrison."

"From what I understand, he's out of his element now. You're out of yours. Trust Agent Caulfield. We all want the same thing here."

"Sir," started Whelan.

"It's done. Go to work, people."

Orville left the bullpen to update the mayor of New Orleans on another investigation.

His "support" knocked the wind out of Whelan.

Caulfield stepped in front of him, making eye contact. "Agent Whelan, don't worry. We'll make decisions together on this. We *do* all want the same thing, don't we?"

Whelan pondered her question. Of course, they wanted the same thing—for Connor to come home safe. It was the means to that end he couldn't assure her—the rules he was prepared to break.

She watched his eyes dart back and forth. Whether she was a mind reader or simply intuitive after thirteen years in the field was unclear, but she commented, "And don't worry. I've been known to bend the rules myself on occasion."

SSA Caulfield walked to the bullpen doorway then turned back to the visiting agents. "Agent Whelan?"

"Yes?"

"The final two of the six unaccounted for? Where are they? Do we know who they are?"

"We do. A Mexican and his wife. Last seen in Texas."

"Ah. Not my jurisdiction. Well, let's go. We're traveling, and one of you needs to drive. I've got a boatload of calls to make."

Chapter 32

Eddie Morrison grimaced as the scalpel plunged into his leg. He'd been given a local anesthetic, but pain still shot through his nerves as he was cut open. His wound was infected, and the peroxide bubbled ferociously as it worked its magic.

"Half an inch to the left, and it'd have torn clean through your femoral artery," said the doctor.

After a couple of minutes, a clink was heard as the bullet dropped into an empty beer can.

Connor was in the corner of the shack, watching the doctor work on Eddie, who was sprawled across three pillows on top of the dining table.

"All right, Jolie, sew him up," continued the doctor. "It's as clean as we're gonna get it."

"Are you a nurse?" asked Connor.

"Nope," she mumbled. "And I ain't gettin' paid 'nough for this shit, neither."

The doctor explained, "She's had field training—emergency triage. I'd take her over a real nurse any day. We served together in the war."

"What war?" asked Connor.

"Don't be nosy," snapped Jolie. "It was in another country a long time ago."

The doctor handed Eddie a bottle. "Cephalexin—antibiotic. Two a day for ten days, and if you're lucky, we've done our job, and you'll keep that leg." He chortled with his delivery.

Eddie snorted along, though Connor suspected he wasn't sure of the doc's sense of humor.

After five days, Connor was getting to know his kidnapper more than he'd like to admit.

The doctor gave another bottle to Eddie. "Oxy, for pain. Don't overdo it, that's all I have on me at the moment. If you stick to two a day on those as well, it should last you a week."

Connor hopped up and went to inspect the doc's handiwork. "Looks pretty good for a pig doctor and Not-a-Nurse."

"What?" exclaimed Eddie.

"He's a pig doctor," repeated Connor. "That's what it says on his boat canopy."

He could read it through the window. "'Doc Holiday, Veterinarian. Specializing in swine and bovine. Office visits or house calls by appointment. Servicing Baton Rouge and the Bayou for a fifty-mile radius.'"

Eddie strained his neck around until he could see Jolie. His bare ass flinched each time she went in with another stitch, five inches south of his left cheek. "You brought me a *pig doctor*?"

Connor started laughing uncontrollably, howling so loudly he thought it best he take himself outside before Eddie jumped up and hit him again.

Jolie grinned. "It takes a pig doctor to doctor a pig. And this one won't squeal."

She finished closing his leg and bandaged him up. "Good as new."

Eddie stood, testing the weight on his left leg. It held, and the oxycodone the doctor gave him was still helping to relax him. He went outside to check on the kid.

Connor was down on the dock with the Chicken Man. They both had a fishing line in the water.

"Doc Holiday" packed up, then joined Eddie on the pier. He loaded the last of his tools and looked up at Eddie after boarding his boat. "Jolie covered your tab. If you need more painkillers after a week, she knows how to get hold of me. Keep your wound clean, and don't run any marathons for a couple of weeks. If you're still here then, she can take your stitches out."

He lowered his voice. "Don't tell her I said this, but she did a damned fine job. She missed her calling, that one. You'll be solid as a rock soon."

When he was out of sight, Eddie made sure he had Connor's attention. "Remember what I told you, kid, respect the help. I'll be inside keeping an eye on you."

He left the pair and disappeared behind the screen door.

After an hour, Connor went to the kitchen and fetched himself and the Chicken Man a Yoo-hoo. Eddie was sacked out cold across the sofa.

Jolie watched him as she peeled potatoes. "I wouldn't get no crazy ideas if I was you. I'd stick to fishin' for supper and stay close to the cabin. The Bayou will kill you quick if you don't know what you're doing or where you're going."

"Yes, ma'am."

He returned to the dock. There was enough bass and catfish for dinner. *Perhaps Eddie's planning to stay the whole week?*

He studied the old man beside him. "You got a name? If we're to be your company this week, it'd be nice to know what to call you."

"Why, you tired of Chicken Man?" he replied.

Connor's jaw dropped as the man cackled. "Yeah, I heard you and Eddie earlier. Name's Reevus."

"Reevus?" repeated Connor. "Glad to meet you, Reevus. I'm Connor."

The man nodded.

"You got a last name, Reevus?"

"I do," he said, but failed to tell it.

"So, you're the hired help, according to Eddie," said Connor. "You on his payroll?"

"You might say that."

"Are you and Jolie married?"

"Not legally, but I'm her guy."

"Oh."

Connor thought he'd press his luck and try to get the man on his side. "Does she have 'other guys'? Because I saw her and Eddie getting pretty chummy."

The man's face scowled for the first time all day. "Boy, you're tromping into territory that could get you whipped or killed."

Connor had been joking, but clearly, he hit a nerve. "I'm sorry. I didn't realize it was a sensitive topic. Let's just fish."

He cast his line across the water, reeling it back slowly like he'd been shown earlier.

So, not exactly 'family.' Maybe I can turn them all against one another? One thing's for sure, any one of them is ready and willing to kill me *if need be.*

He thought he might cry but was too tired to muster any tears. *How's my dad going to find me* here?

They fished for some time, and Connor's thoughts drifted. *I wish I was at a ball game right now. I wonder if I'll be home for the next one? I bet Jolie likes baseball. She'd be a good pitcher with those strong arms of hers. How long has she known that doctor? And what war did they need pig doctors in, anyway? I never read about a pig war in school. I bet the battlefield smelled like bacon.*

Connor's line went taught, and his reel started spinning. He put a lock on it and began to crank. The rod bent in a sharp arc. He'd hooked a big one.

"Easy now! Like I showed you," said Reevus. "Give it room to run for a minute, then reel slowly. You got to tire them big ones out."

For over five minutes, Connor worked the line like a professional, with guidance from the Chicken Man. Once they wrestled it below the pier, Reevus pushed a wide net on a long pole into the water to get under it.

When Connor's catch was near the surface, Reevus retrieved the empty net. "We've got the wrong tool."

"Huh?" asked Connor.

He peered into the water as he kept winding. At the end of his line was a four-foot alligator.

Reevus retrieved a large stainless gaff mounted to a six-foot pole. It was clamped onto one of the pilings rising above the deck of the pier.

"That's a little one," he crowed.

He hooked the gator through its bottom jowl. "Come on, boy. He's heavy. Help me get him up."

When they had him on the deck, Reevus grabbed a machete, sitting beside his tackle box. It flew through the air and sliced into the neck of the monster. The blade was drawn out sideways, then quickly attacked again and again. Reevus severed the head completely free of the body in eight seconds.

"You're stronger than you look," muttered Connor.

Reevus beamed, "You're in for a treat now, boy. You ever eat gator tail?"

Connor's face scrunched. "No. What's it taste like?"

"Somewhere between catfish and chicken. I'm gonna have to start calling you Gator Boy! Chicken Man and Gator Boy. We'll be superheroes."

"Sounds more like a stand-up comedy act," said Connor.

Reevus laughed a belly-buster. "Yes, it do."

Then he paused, sobering, and squinted at the boy. "He said you was clever. I'll be sure not to underestimate you."

The Chicken Man patted Connor's head, mussing his hair. "Come on, boy. I'll show you how to clean a gator."

"You've got to be kidding," said Connor.

"Hell nah. You think that meat's gonna jump out of that skin on its own? We don't eat the skin. We wear it."

Reevus stood up as tall as his five-foot-four-inches could muster and showed off his black leather belt.

Connor leaned in closer. It held an alligator pattern, all right. "I'm going to be learning leather tanning, too?"

"Boy, think of this like the cub scouts. And this week, you're gonna earn *all* your badges."

Chapter 33

"What do you mean you aren't the lead agent on the case any longer?" screamed Georgia Whelan over the phone to her ex-husband.

Tom Whelan sighed. "Georgi, there's an agent here with seniority over me, and she knows the swamp. It's best she takes over unless we get word Eddie's moved on again."

"*Moved on*?" she yelled. "Are you planning on letting him escape *again*? And he has my son in a swamp?"

"It's the Louisiana Bayou. It's safe. Lots of kids grow up there."

"In the *swamp*? Tom, this is the fourth night. My heart can't take it any longer. And your mother…."

"Georgi, you didn't."

"Today, Tom. I broke down when she called. Earlier this week, I stayed strong, but today, I lost it. She didn't call you? That was hours ago."

"No. She would know I'm working on it. She wouldn't want to interrupt my thought process, knowing she'd be a distraction. And now she is. Shit. I guess I should call her."

"Wait till tomorrow. She's on a flight here. She's going to stay with me until this is over. Until you bring Connor home."

"That's the plan, Georgi."

They hung on in uncomfortable silence. Eventually, Georgia pushed the "End Call" button.

"Rough one, huh?" asked Phil Cannon. He and Whelan were in the backseats of the SUV.

Garrity was driving, and Caulfield was on the phone non-stop since heading south out of New Orleans.

"Yes," answered Whelan. "Each time harder than the last. The next call might kill her. I pray it doesn't kill us both."

"Amen."

"Oh, and she told Kathryn," said Whelan.

"Ouch," said Cannon. "I forgot to mention, your mother tried calling *me* yesterday. Her message said she'd made loaves of banana bread and I should drop by and pick one up. She didn't phone you?"

"She did. I didn't answer it either."

At 6:00 p.m., they stopped for dinner in Jean Lafitte, *Leona's on the Waterway.* It was a local joint with ten tables and a take-out counter. What they saved on overhead and décor, they made up for in flavor. Serving fresh shrimp, oysters, crawfish, and crabs, plus six kinds of fish, Leona knew what she was doing with seafood.

"I feel guilty having a meal like this when God knows what Connor is being subjected to," said Cannon.

Whelan agreed. "Let's appreciate it. It might be our last decent dinner for a while."

SSA Amber Caulfield was busy working on a fried softshell crab Po'boy. "I told you this place was the bomb."

She jumped up when the door opened. "Here's the first group."

Five large men came in, two of which hugged Caulfield before sitting at a table nearby.

"Édouard," said Caulfield to one of the men. "This here's Agents Garrity, Cannon, and Whelan." She pointed to each man as she introduced them.

"It's Whelan's boy we're searching for. His name is Connor. I texted everyone the recent photos earlier."

"I'm sorry for your situation," the man told Whelan.

"Thank you."

"You boys fill up," continued Caulfield. "We're going to be starting early. Sun's up at six-fifty-five. I want to rendezvous at the Jean Lafitte mouth to Lake Salvador at six-thirty."

"Yes, ma'am."

Over the following thirty minutes, six more groups of three to seven men and women trickled in and took seats. There were thirty-seven total, and she gave the same instructions to all of them.

Whelan was impressed. He had hoped for ten.

"Are all of these your cousins?" he asked SSA Caulfield.

"No. But about twelve of them are. Big family. The rest are their own families or friends."

They annihilated all of poor Leona's menu that evening. Another man entered when they were finishing the last of her pies. He wore a U.S. Marshal's badge proudly on his belt.

Caulfield met him at the door. "Thanks for coming on short notice, Paulie."

"My pleasure, Amber." He kissed her on the cheek, their fondness for each other evident in their eyes. They obviously shared a history.

She introduced him to the FBI agents, then led him to the front of the dining room where they could all see him clearly.

"I hope you all enjoyed your fabulous dinner, courtesy of the FBI." She waved her hand toward Whelan's table and added, "Kansas City office."

Whelan chuckled and bowed his head.

"You all know why you're here. We're searching for Connor Whelan and Eddie Morrison. You have photos of both on your phones by now. Connor's an innocent child. Our goal is to bring him home alive and well. Eddie's a mass murderer who tainted our great state of Louisiana for years by infiltrating our bayous to traffic his drugs. It made him a wealthy man and endangered your children's lives by introducing fentanyl and oxycodone to our streets.

"You're here because you know these waterways better than anyone else. You know how to navigate, search in grid patterns, and communicate your findings. Your boats have the latest radios and tech on board. You're here because you have big hearts, a sense of morality, and display respect for your fellow man. And you're here because, let's face it, most of you will make much more this week than working whatever part-time gig or fishing expedition you're pretending to sacrifice."

Everyone laughed.

Whelan whispered to Cannon, "Damn. I didn't know we had a politician in our midst. She should run for Congress."

Caulfield said, "And now, I'd like to introduce you to U.S. Marshal Paul Pierre-Auguste. He'll be leading your deputation."

The marshal took the room. "She left out, you're here because you all have a significant arsenal of your own rifles and guns. And we can't afford to arm you all."

More laughter ensued. With one statement, he'd won them over. He instructed them all to raise their right hands and swore them in as deputy U.S. marshals. It would be on a temporary basis, for the lesser time of one week or until they located and recovered Connor Whelan and Eddie Morrison. If they weren't located within a week by this task force, then it would be assumed the kidnapper moved on to another area.

The marshal read them a series of rules and regulations on conduct and jurisdiction and made them agree to each as he went. He reviewed weapons, reminding them the inventory they planned to take into the field would have to be recorded and cataloged. He finished with a warm welcome and individually issued them an official, embossed, stamped document, shaking their hands one by one as they came up to register their names. He photographed their state-issued IDs and thanked them in advance for their service to their country. After the red tape was finished, he ended by passing out silver badges. They were round with a star in the middle. DEPUTY U.S. MARSHAL was engraved into each of them.

"Where did he find thirty-seven badges on short notice?" mumbled Whelan.

Caulfield smiled. "A movie prop website. Well, three, to get enough of them. We weren't sure how many we'd have, so we ordered forty. Glad we did. Shipped them same-day air. The shipping cost way more than the knock-offs. But we need them to have it in the field."

Most of the newly formed task force filed out following the swearing-in and badge delivery, but a few returned to their seats to finish their dessert.

Caulfield gave Marshal Pierre-Auguste a warm hug and walked him to his car.

She returned after a couple of minutes.

"Okay, gentlemen, we've got a plan, we've got the manpower and equipment, and we've got daylight at seven tomorrow. The three of you will start with me until the rendezvous. Then we'll split up. They've been instructed there will be a minimum of two people per boat. I haven't received a final count yet, but we'll have at least fourteen craft. How many did the Coast Guard offer?"

Whelan checked the most recent text on his phone. "Two. That's all they can spare from Grand Isle."

"It's okay. We'll take 'em. That's sixteen. Oh, wait, I forgot to count myself. Seventeen."

"All this, and you captain a boat, too?" asked Whelan. "When do you make your senate run? I'm ready to check your box on my ballot."

"I'm shooting for 2028," she said candidly.

He wasn't sure if she was joking so refrained from making any comments.

"I'll pick you up at your hotel at six," she said. "Have your breakfast eaten and be ready to roll. Where are you staying?"

"I thought we'd find a room here, but there doesn't seem to be even a roadside motel," said Cannon.

"No. You'll have to head back up the highway about eight miles to the outskirts of New Orleans. There should be some in Estelle or Woodmere."

"We'll be all right. Thank you, Agent Caulfield. I'll text you the address when we check in."

Whelan stood and shook her hand. "I can't thank you enough for all this. You've gone so much over and beyond. I'm optimistic we'll find him."

"You're welcome, Agent Whelan. You men get some sleep. Tomorrow will be a long day."

Chapter 34

Connor Whelan went camping once, but it wasn't in the bayou of Louisiana. Whenever a bird whistled, a frog croaked, or an unknown animal snorted, he jumped in his cot. At one point, around 2:00 a.m., something growled. Something close.

"Eddie?" he whispered. "Eddie, are you awake?"

Eddie spent the night trying to get comfortable on the lumpy sofa. Jolie and Reevus were in the only bed.

The cabin was essentially one room. The refrigerator in the kitchen area was powered by the solar panels on the roof, and there was a solar storage battery hanging on the wall beside it. Otherwise, there was no electricity or running water. He discovered earlier if he wanted a drink, he would have to pump a well, and if he needed to pee, it was the bushes behind the home. A port-o-potty was also out back for more critical toilet needs.

Connor had never rinsed his shit out of a bucket with hand-pumped well water, but he was a fast learner. He wondered what the scout badge for *that* must look like. So far, he'd earned two.

"Eddie?" he whispered again.

"What, kid?" he murmured back. He was still zonked on painkillers.

"I think there's a lion outside."

With no air conditioning, the windows and front door were opened to let in a breeze, though there wasn't much of one this evening. Thankfully, there were screens to keep the mosquitos out.

"There's no lions in Louisiana, kid."

"Well, I heard a roar. A loud one."

"Probably a bobcat. They like to hunt at night. Chasing himself a tasty meal, no doubt. Snake or a rat, perhaps."

"What if he comes in here? That screen door isn't real secure."

"Well, you're closest to it. I think I'll be fine. But thanks for your concern."

Connor jumped up from his cot. It was an old, stinky canvas model dating back to World War II. Jolie told him it was her granddaddy's when he was in the service. Connor had to build it if he wanted to sleep off the floor. It was encouraged as the better alternative if he didn't wish to get nipped on all night by the rats.

He didn't mean to create such a loud noise, but when he dragged the cot across the room, putting Eddie between him and the door, it made an awful screech.

"Shhh," hissed Eddie.

"Sorry," said Connor. "That bobcat can feast on *you*, now. You're not going to be running with that bum leg anyway."

From the quiet corner of the room where Jolie still managed to sleep, Reevus let out a low, whoop-filled cackle.

It put a smirk on Connor's face, and he managed to drift off. Soon he was dreaming of bobcats and alligators chasing Eddie through the swamp. They caught him and tore him to shreds before feeding on his entrails. It was Connor's turn to whoop and cackle, and he watched the show from the dock with a cold Yoo-hoo in his hand.

"Wake up, Tom, you're having a nightmare," said Phil Cannon, shaking Tom Whelan's shoulder.

Whelan saw the clock on his nightstand. It was 5:00 a.m. "Shit. I just got to sleep an hour ago."

"What were you dreaming?"

"What do you think?" snarled Whelan.

The men showered and headed to the Waffle House next door. They were supposed to meet Garrity there at 5:15, but he failed to show. The men wolfed down a quick breakfast and took coffees to go. At 5:50, they knocked on Garrity's motel door.

He answered in his underwear, rubbing his eyes.

"Rough night, Garrity?" asked Whelan, handing him a coffee.

"I couldn't sleep in that lumpy thing. And something's biting my legs." He scratched his right calf as evidence.

"You haven't been in the field much. If you're not ready in ten, we'll have to leave without you. Hell, I'm not in charge anymore. Why are you still here? Go home to Baltimore. Tell your SAC someone new is leading this now. Oh, wait, you already have, I'm sure."

Garrity was somber. "Agent Whelan, I'm legitimately invested in this. I'm trying to help find your son. I apologize for not being ready. Give me six minutes."

He shut the door and raced through the shower.

Six minutes later, the three men stood beside their rental SUV, waiting on SSA Amber Caulfield.

She arrived with a minute to spare. "Hop in. Leave your vehicle here. Parking is limited at the boat ramp."

Behind her F-150, she towed a trailer with a sixteen-foot Tracker Mod V boat onboard.

"Is that a new toy?" asked Whelan.

"It is," she said proudly.

They drove south for ten minutes then turned into a small parking lot with a boat ramp. She maneuvered it like a pro into the water. They were soon boarded and flying fast downstream. The shiny new bass boat held two seats low behind the steering wheel and two raised high on the deck for fishing, one in front, one in the rear. It was top-notch.

At 6:25 a.m., they turned off toward Lake Salvador. Eight other boats were already waiting, including the two from the Coast Guard and one with U.S. Marshal Paul Pierre-Auguste. By 6:45, the special task force was lined up and ready.

It was an impressive showing.

Whelan expected a rag-tag menagerie of thirty-year-old rust buckets in dire need of repair.

The boats before him were all in fantastic shape, many less than five years old. He hadn't considered they served as the livelihood for these folks. Fishing, tour guiding, and water taxiing were their lifeblood. And they seemed to be lucrative based on the showing in front of him.

SSA Caulfield fished out a bullhorn from a cubby hole on her boat. "Good morning. I trust you all ate a big breakfast and drank plenty of coffee. For those of you with short-wave radios, I'll broadcast updates every two hours, on the even hour. That's two, four, six, eight, et cetera for you non-math majors."

Chuckles ensued, same as the previous evening. Though merely cousins of Amber Caulfield, they were a close-knit bunch.

Whelan was impressed at how jolly they were. *I continue to underestimate the power of happiness—the satisfaction of it. God, please let Connor and me find it again.*

Caulfield continued, "Turn your shortwaves to fifteen megahertz. I have four satellite phones for those who don't have radios. I know three or four of you have your own as well. Please, let's make sure we share with those in need. It's essential each boat can communicate long-range.

"I see the majority of you have your deputy badges on. If you're not wearing yours, please put it on now and keep it on the entire time you're on duty. You're going to be on and off citizens' personal property. If someone approaches you, make sure you identify yourself as Deputy Marshal so-and-so and you are on their property under exigent circumstances. Write that down if you can't remember it—exigent circumstances. Conduct your questions. 'Have you seen this boy, this man?' Show them the photos on your phone.

"Now, and this is important, people, do not, I repeat, DO NOT land at any site where there are structures without having backup! If you spot a houseboat, a cabin, a tent, commercial or personal, *anything* that could be hiding this fugitive and his hostage, you call for backup from the nearest team before stepping ashore or boarding another vessel. Is that clear?"

A few people mumbled, "Yes."

"Are you sleeping, folks? Can you not hear me in the back? I said, IS THAT CLEAR?"

"Yes, ma'am!" they shouted in unison.

"That's better. And, if you find a reason to step ashore, you call it in to me—every time. No one steps off their boat without calling in the GPS coordinates and giving a brief description of what they're approaching. Is *that* clear?"

"Yes, ma'am!"

Caulfield looked pleased. "Okay. Now, I spent all night working out assignments and teams. Please respect this. I've got those with smaller bass or Jon boats, able to tackle the narrower bayous and waterways, separated from those with larger bay boats and bowriders. Henrí, what are you doing with your pontoon? That must be thirty feet. How are you going to get in and out of small water? Our targets will not be drinking beer on a sand bar in the middle of Turtle Bay. They're going to be well hidden."

"Relax, Amber. I'm towing two jet skis. We'll be able to zip in and out where even William's Jon boat can't go," he replied.

"Oh. Well, all right then. Kudos. Marshal Paul is going to start passing out assignments. He'll address any specific questions you have or shout them up to me if he doesn't know. You all know I'm from here. I grew up on these waters, same as you. We're the experts in this arena, and this man trusts us to find his son and bring him home. Good hunting!"

"Yes, ma'am!" they shouted.

SSA Caulfield took her seat. "Well, it's the best we can do."

Whelan felt numb. "I was a fool to ever question your authority here. Thank you."

"Absolutely. These are your assignments." She handed him three envelopes with each of their names written on them. "I'll help you find the right boats."

The sun was up, and folks corralled around one another and jumped from this boat to that one until the right teams were in the proper vessels. Once secure with their contingent and which part of Caulfield's grid they were in charge of, they headed out, west or south, like some odd regatta.

"I'm still getting a cell signal," commented Whelan to his new boat team. "Oh, I'm Special Agent Tom Whelan," he introduced himself, extending his hand.

"You'll get a signal on and off. It's not reliable out there, however. We're Franny and Jaques. And no, we're not married. Everyone asks. They think they know what's better for us than we do."

She was pale with an Alabama accent. He was dark with thin dreadlocks hanging down past his shoulders. They were currently ponytailed behind him. They were both in their mid-forties.

Whelan looked at Jaques, who tilted his head and popped his eyebrows. He kept his mouth shut.

"So, it's your boy we're tryin' to save, huh?" asked Franny. "That must be rough. You have my condolences."

"Thank you," said Whelan. "Hopefully, condolences are premature."

Chapter 35

Connor Whelan woke to the smell of pancakes sizzling in cast iron. The small, propane-powered stove had another pan on the second burner cooking eggs and ham.

"What time is it?" he asked, rubbing his eyes.

"Ten-thirty," said Reevus. He was standing at the stove, turning flapjacks.

"I can't believe it's ten-thirty," Connor mumbled, crawling off the cot.

"You needed your sleep. Now you need food. Eat."

It was more of a command than an offer. Connor took a chair at the little table near the front window.

"What's this?" he asked as Reevus served him a stack of buttery pancakes topped with a berry preserve.

"Dewberries. They grow here in the spring. There are wild patches near here, so Jolie picks 'em and I can 'em. Like my mama taught me, with wild honey for sweetener. After they sit for a few months in the pantry, there's nothing better on flapjacks or biscuits."

Connor took a nibble. They were incredible. "Maybe you could show me how to can berries this spring. You think I'll be here that long? Maybe I could earn another badge."

Reevus shook his head. "Hell, boy, as soon as Eddie can walk without crying, you'll be outta here. Or dead. Now eat up."

"Dead?" Connor put his fork down. "What do you mean, dead? He needs me alive until my dad shows up."

"I believe he's rethinking his moves."

Reevus slapped the back of Connor's neck. It left a sting. "Eat!"

"Okay. Damn."

The pair wandered outside to the dock when the plates were cleaned and put away. There was no sign of Eddie or Jolie. The boat was gone.

"Where'd they go?" asked Connor.

"Supply run. You ate all Jolie's jalapeño chips. And you're making a dent in the Yoo-hoo."

"Oh, well, excuse me. Next time, plan for company when you kidnap someone."

Reevus guffawed like he'd told a joke, but any humor was lost on Connor.

"Isn't Eddie afraid to be seen?" he asked. "And he's not supposed to travel on his leg yet."

"I suspect he had cabin fever and needed to get some air."

"You mean, he needed to take a break from watching me nonstop."

Connor whipped his head around as if he hadn't already inspected the entirety of this patch of land eight times. He frowned at the water before him. *There's no way I'm going to escape without a boat.*

He was an accomplished swimmer but doubted he could outswim the alligators or the snakes. "So, what are *we* doing today?" he asked.

"Fishing."

"We did that yesterday. I thought we caught enough for several days."

Reevus frowned. "Can't never have too much fish. We trade with the folks downriver for shrimp and crab. Usually have a proper seafood boil on the weekend. So, we stock up."

"Oh. I noticed your freezer. It's like a professional market in there. All that brown parchment, neatly labeled. I didn't see the alligator tail from yesterday in there, though."

"It's in the fridge, soaking in buttermilk. Helps to tenderize it. It'll be our dinner tonight."

Connor turned his head to the big tub sitting on the end of the porch. It contained the salted, rolled-up hide of the alligator he'd helped skin the day before. Reevus explained they'd tan it the "old-fashioned" way, as the natives did, without all the fancy chemicals they use today. It would take several weeks, but in the end, they'd have the softest, prettiest leather hide from which to make belts and wallets.

Before this week, Connor would have never been able to handle the blood and guts which came with skinning an alligator. But Eddie Morrison changed all that. After seeing over twenty people shot and killed, having human brains sprayed across his face, and witnessing countless pints of blood spilled from innocent men and women, extracting the innards of essentially a giant lizard didn't seem to faze him.

Sighing, Connor turned back to the water, certain he wouldn't be here to see the fruit of his labor. A part of him was curious to see how that alligator skin tanned, and he was battling the desire to own a belt which he'd worked on himself. Maybe Reevus could ship it to him when it was ready?

Connor snickered to himself. *Like I'll be here. Eddie's going to kill me. He can't let me live. I've seen too much.*

"Reevus?"

"Yeah, boy?"

"You have kids?"

Reevus looked at him and wiped his usually-goofy expression from his face. His eyes narrowed, and the left one glazed over with a tear. "Not anymore."

"What happened?"

"I had a boy, a lifetime ago. Another woman, not Jolie's. Henrietta. She was a beautiful girl from Chicago. She and I took to one another straight away, when we was a little older than you. We were like piano keys all through school. And we made the sweetest music."

"What happened to your son?"

"He drowned."

Connor felt like he should cast his eyes away but instead studied the creases across the face of the older man beside him. A feeling of pity came over him, and he patted the man's knee. "I'm sorry. Was that here, in the bayou?"

The man's eyes shifted left, drifting upward with the memory. "No, boy. It was in a public swimming pool in New Orleans. He was five and hadn't had any lessons yet. Fell in and drowned before the lifeguard even noticed. There were over thirty people in the pool that day, and not one person saw my boy drowning. The townsfolk said it was tragic. I say it was criminal."

"Did the lifeguard go to jail?" asked Connor.

"Nope. Lost his job was all."

"And what happened to Henrietta? Did she blame you? Is that why you're not together?"

"She blamed herself. She was with him that day. I blamed her too."

Reevus lost himself a minute, in the shadows underneath the cypress across the water, searching for a reason which would never come, no matter how many years passed.

"So you left her? Or did she leave you?" asked Connor.

"I suppose you could say she left me. She hung herself eight days later."

He stared directly into Connor's eyes. They were also wet now. For thirty-three seconds, the pair locked sight of each other's souls, both refusing to be the first to let a tear fall.

The silence grew uncomfortable for Reevus. Soon he hopped up and headed inside. "I'm grabbing a glass of tea, boy. You want one?"

"No thanks. I'm fine," said Connor.

He watched the man enter the darkness, and a memory flashed through his head, a lesson his father once tried to teach him. *Life's hard. Make allies when and where you can. Challenges are more easily tackled in numbers.*

Connor Whelan had a challenge before him. And he was confident he'd broken through the first layer of defense in one of his kidnappers. He thought he'd make an ally out of Reevus yet, and they'd take on Eddie Morrison together when the time came.

At least, that was his game plan.

Chapter 36

Caulfield gassed up her boat at one of the marinas on Grand Isle. It was 2:40 in the afternoon, and so far, twenty-eight homes and forty-seven boats were searched with no result. Many houses were abandoned over the years and their shells remained. Half of them were ever scarcely more than a shanty, built by folks eager to be off the grid but never having formal carpentry training.

The bulk of the task force refueled their boats and their bellies over the following two hours, giving Caulfield in-person updates and stories of the day's search thus far.

In turn, she updated Whelan when Franny and Jaques maneuvered their vessel into a slip to wait for a gas pump to open up.

"Agent Whelan, so far, nothing. We've covered a tremendous amount of territory in one morning. We'll get in more with four hours of daylight left."

"Much of what we covered today didn't have trees," said Whelan. "I was picturing more tree cover, more jungle-like. We covered a ton of marshland and sawgrass."

"The 'jungle' is west of where I started you today. I put you on Yankee Canal 'cause you mentioned Lafitte and Barataria. I've got four teams west of U.S.1 today, and by tomorrow, we'll all be nearing, if not inside, Atchafalaya. That's where some of the thickest growth is."

"Then why aren't we starting there?" asked Whelan. "Eddie's smart. He won't be hiding in open water. He'll be wanting more cover."

"For starters, your Unknown Soldier was working south of Houma, which puts us more east. And Atchafalaya is heavily patrolled, both by the state and parish wildlife departments, as well as tourists and locals. I figured if he's staying off the beaten path, he won't be where there're boats going by with fishermen and tour guides all day long. Of course, we took half of those to form this task force."

"I have to defer to your judgment," Whelan said. He stood on a pier alongside Caulfield, watching Franny and Jaques troll their boat over to an empty fuel pump.

"How you liking those two?" asked Caulfield.

"Fine. Quiet. Respectful. He's still passionately in love with her. He's soft in voice but loud in body language."

"Right? I picked up on that too. I don't know why they don't get married."

Whelan gave her a wry smile.

They stood in silence for a few minutes. More boats came and went, a coordinated dance of professionals rotating positions around the fuel dock. Occasionally a laugh would travel across the water, or someone's name would echo around the marina as friends met up with friends to grab a quick lunch at the restaurant inside.

Whelan tapped Caulfield's arm, and allowed his feelings to surface. "I'm grateful for this," he started, choking up. "This is above and beyond my wildest hopes. The more time that passes, the more Eddie will fuck up my son. He knows how to push a man's buttons—mentally. And physically, he won't care if he tortures him to death if it brings him pleasure and hurts me in the process."

"It's become personal to the two of you. You and Eddie, I mean."

"Yes. I believe so."

"Then let's get back to work." She motioned toward Franny and Jaques. They were heading back to pick him up.

Whelan whispered another "Thank you."

"You're welcome, Agent Whelan."

By nightfall, there was still no sign of Eddie Morrison or Connor Whelan. There were no witnesses who reported seeing them.

Whelan, Cannon, and Garrity were dropped off at the boat launch where Caulfield started the morning. Her truck was still there. They arrived fifteen minutes apart. Whelan had an LED flashlight with a lantern mode. He and Cannon sat on the boat trailer, waiting patiently for Caulfield while Garrity paced back and forth, staring into his phone.

"I still don't have a signal here," Garrity mumbled to himself. "Last night, there was a signal here. Why don't I have a signal?"

Cannon asked Whelan with a whisper, "Does he have a family? Is he trying to get in touch with his kids to say goodnight? Cause he sure never mentioned them to me if he does."

"Wasn't in his file," answered Whelan. "I think he's wound tight. His sense of duty tells him to follow through on his orders, which were primarily to keep an eye on me. Must be killing him that he can't get a signal so his SAC can get an update on my sanity. But I don't give a rat's ass any longer. The more eyes to help me scan this swamp for Connor, the better. I'm surprised he wanted to stay and help. I thought he'd run back to Baltimore when Caulfield took over. Hey, speak of the devil. Here she is."

"Can one of you back my trailer down the ramp?" she hollered from her boat on the waterway.

Whelan walked toward her. "Throw me your keys."

"They're under the mat on the floorboard. Door's open."

"That's trusting," said Garrity.

"Yeah, well, anyone who'd steal that old truck might be doing me a favor, as much insurance as I pay."

They loaded her boat and stopped by *Leona's on the Waterway* again for a quick dinner.

Several recruits were back as well, grazing and sharing stories of the day.

"So, Agent Cannon," said Caulfield, after they ordered, "you had a more productive day than the others. Thirteen homes, two boats, and two commercial structures you searched today."

"Yes. Sadly, none of them revealed anything to help us."

"Well," she said, "I think we're on the right track. Agent Whelan, that Toyota Camry reported stolen yesterday from behind the Comfort Inn in Covington? They found it this afternoon, south of Houma, pulled alongside a small bayou. They're here. We're on the right track."

A chill raced up Whelan's spine. His arm loaded goosebumps from his wrist to his shoulder, and he stood up.

"Going somewhere?" asked Cannon.

"No," he answered. "I just—how early can we start tomorrow? I need to be out there."

"We all do, Agent Whelan," said Caulfield. "Eat. Franny said you didn't pack a lunch today, and I know you didn't eat at the marina. Eat and sleep well, gentlemen. Replenish your energy. Tomorrow will be another long day."

"I'm already wired," said Whelan.

Caulfield studied him while she picked at her slice of bourbon pecan pie.

A man walked in and distracted her attention. He was six-foot six-inches and must have weighed three-hundred and fifty pounds.

"Cujo?" she asked him.

"Amber?" he replied, heading to their table.

She stood and gave the man a warm hug.

She introduced the agents to him, then him to the agents. "This here's Marcus Freeman. He was a linebacker in high school. One of the toughest SOBs on the field. You should have seen the other teams when he faced off against them." She started chuckling.

"I heard you were back in town—well, in the city," he said.

"Yes, four months now. It's nice to be home. You look good, Cujo. I heard it on the wind you were doing tours out of Baton Rouge."

"Yeah, 'bout three years now. Pays the bills. I got a little home on the outskirts. Not much, but it's paid off. You should come visit me sometime." His eyes darted across hers as his head tilted down and to the right.

Whelan and Cannon exchanged glances. They were curious to see if she would return his flirtation.

SSA Amber Caulfield instead dipped into her purse and brought out her phone. She flashed photos of Eddie Morrison and Connor Whelan to him. "Could use your services, Cujo. We're on the hunt for these two. You seen either of 'em this week? We think they're hiding out in the swamp. We're paying crazy money if your schedule's cleared. Even deputize you."

"I heard. That's why I'm here. I don't mind making twice my normal fare."

He scrutinized the photos. "Naw, sorry. Haven't seen either of them."

"You seen anyone out of the ordinary, particularly this week?"

"Mostly the regulars. However, I did run into Jolie Martín today. She'd picked up supplies in Pigeon and was heading west into Little Bayou Pigeon as I was coming north up the Berwick. I haven't seen her in a few years."

Caulfield twisted her chin side to side, trying to recognize the name.

It triggered a clouded memory in Whelan's head. *Jolie?* He mulled it over while Caulfield spoke with Marcus Freeman.

"You might not have known her," Marcus continued. "She was Raymond's older sister. I think she would have graduated by the time you started high school. She was ahead of me by four years."

"Then she was ahead of me by seven or more. I was a freshman when you were a senior."

"Why did I think you were older?" he asked.

"Excuse me?" she snapped.

"In school. Not now!" His dark cheeks blossomed with patches of red. "You were *fine* in school. I thought we were in the same grade."

"And I'm not *fine* now?"

He paused, staring her down. "You are *absolutely* fine now," he stated, lowering the register of his voice by an octave.

Caulfield bust out laughing, patting Marcus' chest. "I'm sorry, Cujo, I'm messin' with you. So Jolie isn't a regular?"

"Not up north. I've seen her working the bayous before, but she's usually down south. Or at least she used to be. She settled southeast of Houma. I worked that area for a year."

"How was she *working* them?"

"Same as the rest of us, tours and fishing, but I remember hearing rumors a few years back about her running drugs. And she knows these bayous as well as any of us. Grew up on 'em, same as we did."

"She with anyone today?"

"No, she was alone."

Whelan jumped to his feet. "That's her! She's Eddie's connection! I remember her name from a report. I read every word of all the testimonies at the time. It was lumped in with a few other names and possibilities. She's got to be the Unknown Soldier! Jolie Martín!"

Cannon jumped to his feet. "And you know where she lives?" he asked Marcus.

"Yeah, I mean, where she *used* to live. But I doubt she lives down here now."

"Why? Did she tell you where she lives now? When you saw her today?" asked Whelan.

"No, but I don't think she'd be on a supply run all the way up in Pigeon if she still had her old place."

"Why's that?"

"Because it's eighty miles northwest."

"Eighty miles!" said Whelan. "We're searching in the wrong location!"

Chapter 37

Jolie Martín pulled alongside her dock and tied a rope to its cleats. It was well after dark, but she'd taken a few wrong turns trying to get off the heavily traveled bayous as she worked her way home. Seeing Marcus Freeman today stirred her anxiety.

She yanked a tarp off the boxes of groceries and other supplies. Eddie Morrison popped up from the bottom of the boat.

"You said you didn't know anyone in this part of the swamp!" he snapped.

"I didn't know I did. Marcus Freeman was working south of Houma last I saw him. How was I supposed to know he'd moved up here?"

"You're supposed to know this swamp better than anyone! It's what I pay you for."

She squinted at him in the dark. There was less than half a moon out tonight, but she could read his face well enough. "What can I say? It's a small world. And so far, you ain't paid us shit."

"You know I'm good for it," said Eddie. He grabbed her elbow. "You fuck up again on your intel, though, and we're gonna have a real problem, you and I."

Reevus jumped onto the dock from the pier. "You okay?" he asked directly to Jolie.

Eddie released her arm. The man had come out of nowhere and startled him.

"Fine," she said. "We're fine. Everybody's fine. This one's overreacting." She thrust her chin in Eddie's direction.

After unloading the boat and packing half the supplies in the storage shed, the trio entered the cabin.

Eddie smiled for the first time all day.

Connor Whelan was at the stove, frying gator tail nuggets in a cast iron skillet. Whelan's boy was cooking for him. Willingly.

Eddie snickered then threw one in his mouth from the platter already cooked. "Damn, you got skills. Finish that last batch, and let's eat."

He turned to Reevus. "You should run a cooking school, Reevus."

Eddie grabbed a beer and sat on the sofa.

Reevus' eyes flashed toward Connor, then back to Eddie. "Wash up," he snarled. "You're two hours late. If you weren't here in another twenty minutes, we'd have eaten without you."

"All right. Put your big-boy britches on. It's been a trying day. Let me take a piss first."

Jolie and Reevus found each other's gaze as Eddie left the cabin. Reevus motioned her aside.

"What happened?" he whispered.

"Marcus Freeman saw me."

Reevus shook his head, scrunching his eyebrows.

"Cujo."

Reevus' head continued to sway.

"He used to work down south. Remember, he tour-guided all around the coastal area? We traded with him a few times."

"You handled all that. I didn't know nobody's names."

"Well, now you do. He knew us there. And now he knows us here."

"Come eat. Don't matter."

"Yes, Reevus, it does. He *knows* me. My family. From school. He knows who I am. This is bad—dangerous."

"How in the hell would he even know to connect you to a kidnapping?"

"Dammit, man!" she hissed. "You're not listening. He *knows* me. He knows my past, my connections. He knows I served time in my early twenties. He knows I'm a criminal. He knows me and my brother were in the drug smuggling business here in Louisiana. The bayous are a small world, Reevus. And he *knows* me!"

Reevus was still perplexed at her fear. "I don't get it. Your past is your business. How would he connect that boy to you, of all the people in the swamp?"

Jolie sighed, then attempted to explain her rationale. "When Eddie was busted the first time, and the New Orleans operations went to shit, it was all over the news. People pay attention to shit when it's in their backyard. Marcus Freeman was working the same water I was when I was running for Eddie. Then Eddie's convicted, and we move up here. Marcus is smart, Reevus. I'm sure he put two and two together. We disappeared from the southern area the same time as Eddie was sent to prison.

"When I was in town yesterday, I received an internet signal on my phone. The feds are broadcasting alerts for the boy. And there's an Amber Alert now with his name and description. They're searching for him here, in Louisiana. 'Last spotted in Covington,' it said. 'Presumed to be headed south, possibly in the bayous,' it said. I'm sure it's on the nightly news.

"So again, I tell you, Marcus is sharp as a tack, and then he sees me today. And we exchanged pleasantries, and I kept it as brief as possible. But he *knows* me. And even if he doesn't think of me as a kidnapper, he's got a big mouth. Always did. He'll be telling everyone he sees he ran into me. It won't take two days for word to get around. And we've been so careful. Damn. They'll come looking for me for sure. And now they know where."

She watched Eddie Morrison through the window. He hadn't bothered to go around to the side of the home. He was shaking the dew off his manhood over the bayou. She fantasized a large gator would jump up and snap it off. It probably looked like a tasty little chicken wing in the faint moonlight.

Jolie turned her head back to Reevus. "Tomorrow, we're outta here. Eddie's not worth prison. I didn't go the first time, and I'm sure as hell not going now."

Reevus frowned at her. "Let's eat."

Whelan was lying in bed, repeatedly turning left and right. At one point, he stood and paced the floor for five minutes. *I'm not going to get any sleep tonight.*

He'd already researched Jolie Martín in the database. She had a record going back to her days as a juvenile, starting at fourteen, for dealing drugs. Marijuana, then eventually PCP, cocaine, and heroin. She continued into her twenties and was incarcerated three times, the last of which she served five years. She was let out for "good behavior" in an overcrowded prison where cell space was so scarce, convicts were often forced to sleep on the floor.

She was forty-six now, but the last photo on record was from ten years past. She'd disappeared from the system. Not even a recent driver's license and no car registration. Presumably, she'd been running drugs for Eddie during much of that time. Living in and on the bayous didn't require an automobile. You were supposed to register your boat if you operated as a tour guide or professional angler, but it was as though she blinked out of existence.

At 12:18 a.m., his phone rang.

"Georgi? I was just thinking of you."

"Liar," came a voice from the other end. It was not his ex-wife's.

"Hi, Mom. What are you doing on Georgia's phone?"

"I was afraid you wouldn't answer mine. Again," said Kathryn Whelan. "I won't hang on long, I know it's late, but I couldn't take another minute without an update. Even if it's bad news."

"We got a huge break today," said Tom. "A man who knows my lead investigator might know a key figure in finding Connor, personally. He saw her today, and we're shifting our search areas in the morning."

"Honey, that's wonderful. You haven't spoken to Connor again by chance?"

"No."

"Are you eating?"

"Of course."

"Liar."

"No, not lying. I ate dinner tonight. Shrimp Étouffée with rice. Should fatten me right up."

"Uh-huh. Okay, well, I needed to hear your voice. I'll let you get back to it."

"Mom?"

"Yes, sweetheart?"

"How's Georgia holding up?"

Kathryn Whelan seldom sugar-coated her statements. She saw no reason to start now. "Terrible. She's better, I think, with me here. I'm letting her scream at me, get it all out of her system, but she's faltering."

"She should be screaming at *me*. Thanks for being there, for taking the abuse."

"You're welcome. I've taken worse."

He knew she was referencing his father but didn't comment.

"How's Phil?" she asked.

"Amazing. He keeps me balanced. I'm fortunate to have him."

"We all are."

"Mom?"

"Yes?"

Tom froze. He and Kathryn were exceptionally close and understood one another well, certainly better than Georgia and he ever did. He wasn't a "mama's boy," but they bonded during his rocky childhood, forming a tighter relationship than most mothers and sons.

He wanted to share a dozen thoughts, a multitude of prayers to be asked for, and as many sins to be forgiven. He hung on through the end of his breath and was forced to take another. "Just, thanks, Mom."

"You're welcome, son. And Tom, all the other stuff going through your head doesn't matter. You get Connor. No matter the cost, you bring him home."

"How do you know what's going through my head?"

"Because I've known you thirty-four years. You and Connor are the best things that ever happened to me. Don't you forget it. I love you, Tom."

"Love you too, Mom." He ended the call.

He could sense he was getting close to Eddie. A renewed optimism welled up inside him.

At 1:10 a.m., he ran through the shower. The hot water helped soothe away the day.

He lay in bed again, staring at the ceiling. *Fuck it.*

He got up and retrieved his sidearm, the Glock 19 he'd carried his whole career. Many agents switched to SIGs P226s or 228s, but his Glock saved his life many times, and it was like an old friend. He'd heard the fifth-generation Glocks were becoming popular, but there was no way he'd trade up. It'd be like a betrayal.

He snagged a bottle of solvent, his bore brush, an old rag, and a small oil tube from his gear and started cleaning the pistol. He scrubbed on it for nearly twenty minutes, then reloaded it and set it on his nightstand.

At 2:30, he began drifting to sleep. He heard his mother's voice over and over in his head. *You get Connor. No matter the cost, you bring him home. No matter the cost. Get Connor. NO MATTER THE COST.*

Chapter 38

A knock on his motel door woke Whelan up at 6:00 a.m. It was Cannon.

"You just waking up? Couldn't sleep?" he asked, pushing his way into the room. "You missed breakfast."

"I slept three and a half hours, and I'm not hungry."

"You want to shower first?"

"I showered at one this morning. I'm ready. Let's go."

The three agents waited in the parking lot for Caulfield. She drove in at 6:12. "Sorry. I've been on the phone since five a.m., redirecting those I couldn't reach last night. We're moving into the Atchafalaya Wilderness and taking it by storm. I've got the troops going upriver, then spreading out as they hit Turkey Island. Two boats are going as far north as the Grand River, one on the east side, one on the west. They'll work south as the rest of us focus on our new grids. But based on Cujo's intel, they're in here."

Caulfield showed them a tablet with an aerial map already loaded. "Marcus said he ran into Jolie Martín at this spot on the east end of Iberia Parish." She pointed to the map.

"From this entry point, after going west a little ways, she could have traveled north or south, but I'm guessing she's not north of here or south of here," she said, continuing to indicate areas unknown to the three agents.

She drew a boundary line around a significant portion of the Atchafalaya Wilderness. "Logic would suggest she's holed up somewhere in this area.

"That's an awfully large piece of the map," said Garrity.

She pinched across the surface of the tablet, zooming out. "Considering we were going to search all this, I'd say we increased our odds and our timeline. It's about four hundred square miles," said Caulfield.

"Hell of a lot better than five thousand," said Whelan.

"Damned skippy!" echoed Cannon. "We'll take it. Let's roll."

Caulfield whispered to Whelan, "Understand, it *is* going to be a slower search. The swamp is thickest in these parts. Some waterways are so thin the larger boats won't even fit through, and the ones that do will be on trolling motors for much of it. But we're better off than we were yesterday."

Whelan rode with Caulfield in her truck, towing her boat trailer, while Garrity and Cannon followed in their rental SUV.

Caulfield spent the drive on the phone, coordinating the new searches, relaying the best spots to put the boats in from the northern ends of Atchafalaya to those less familiar.

"Six of our deputies are going to need motel rooms this far north," she relayed as they were nearing Pigeon, Louisiana. "The rest can drive or boat to their assignments. Agent Cannon's booking a Best Western in Plaquemine, about thirty minutes from Pigeon. It's the closest we can get. He's securing rooms for all of us."

"Super," said Whelan. "God willing, we won't need them. I'm praying we find Connor today, and tonight he'll sleep in his own bed."

"Amen!" she agreed.

Whelan's phone rang. It was ASAC Miranda Jones, looking for an update.

After he filled her in, she said, "Whelan. I received the title search back on *Sheila's Sunshine*. It *was* Leon Bergman's yacht, not Hector Valencia's. They both lied. And he must have been in deep. I told you he wouldn't have killed himself unless he was seriously involved."

"You were right."

"Yeah. Well, I wanted you to know."

"It's bothering you he grabbed his gun on your watch, isn't it?" asked Whelan.

"It is. I don't slip up often. Took my eyes off him for five seconds."

"Cut yourself some slack."

"I'm trying. Remember Whelan, it only takes five seconds to go between life and death."

"Sometimes less. Have a better day, Miranda."

"Thank you."

SSA Amber Caulfield spent over an hour with eight teams once they arrived at the Berwick River entry near Pigeon, getting all the boats in the water and ensuring all the deputies understood their new assignments.

Three other boats were left: Henrí Saint Amant's, Marcus Freeman's, and her own.

"Franny and Jaques are on the southern end of our new search pattern, Agent Whelan. You can ride with me or Cujo today."

"Wherever you think I can be useful."

"Cujo," she said to him, "you're taking Agent Whelan."

She wheeled on Garrity and Cannon. "You two wanna draw straws?"

Cannon pointed to Henrí's pontoon with the two jet skis on the back. "I used to ride WaveRunners in the summer. I'll be able to handle one of those." He stepped aboard Henrí's boat and introduced himself.

Caulfield poked Garrity's arm. "You're with me. Good hunting, everyone."

Marcus Freeman turned to Whelan five minutes after they were underway to their search zone. "I didn't get a chance to be deputized, but if we get into trouble, I'm packing a .44, and I've got three high-powered rifles under that seat." He pointed to a cushion behind Whelan.

"I'd like to tell you, you won't need those, but if we find them, it won't go down easy."

"So, I guess I'm asking, can I use 'em? My weapons? If necessary?"

Whelan video-called Marshal Pierre-Auguste. To his surprise, he answered. "Agent Whelan? How can I help you?"

"I need a last-minute deputation of my boat captain, Marcus Freeman."

"Hold up the phone."

One minute of the shortest version of a swearing-in Marshal Pierre-Auguste could think of was performed. "Your paperwork is on my desk. You can pick it up when you drop by tonight."

Marcus could see the marshal was on a boat himself, somewhere out here in the swamp. "Uhmm, of course," he replied.

"Welcome to the task force," said Pierre-Auguste, then hung up the phone.

"Yes, Deputy Marshal Freeman, you can now shoot your weapons legally," said Whelan.

"Thank you."

"Actually, I want to thank you, Marcus, for coming in last night. We'd still be wasting time southeast today if it weren't for you. You cut at least one or two days off our search and gave us a name and a face to focus on. I'm in your debt."

"My pleasure, Agent Whelan. I hope we find your boy today."

"Me too."

They were practically silent over the next four hours, whipping through the waterways in a five-by-five-mile block. Twice, they called out for the nearest boat to come and back them up as they searched a small boathouse and an abandoned mobile home. How it became lodged in the middle of a grove of trees was anyone's guess.

"Likely a hurricane," suggested Freeman. "Storm surge can push the water up high. Anything not anchored down can float and find its way into the swamp. I've seen a school bus, several cars, and even a couple of small houses plopped right down in the middle of nowhere, like Dorothy's home landing in Oz."

Whelan stared at the mobile home. He wondered if there might be a wicked witch underneath it. He conjured a picture of Jolie Martín in a witch's hat. He eyed the surrounding area. There was no yellow brick road, only cypress tree knees popping out of the water and a few patches of floating salvinia, a kind of water fern which easily spread in a marsh environment with partial sunlight.

He wished he could float above all this like the good witch in her bubble, find Connor, and click their heels to get them home safely. But his fairytale ending faded as two alligators snapped at each other, fighting for space over a four-foot patch of land where they could rest and take in a ray of sunlight.

Please, God, help me find my son.

His daily prayer of late carried a heavier burden today. Something kept tugging at the back of his mind. Connor was running out of time. He didn't usually believe in a sixth sense, but he could "feel" the clock was running out.

His watch showed 1:15 p.m. There were only a few hours of daylight left.

Chapter 39

"We need a supply run," Jolie told Eddie.

He was sitting on the cabin's front porch in an old wooden rocker. Two cushions weren't enough to block the pain from sitting on his stitches, and he kept shifting his weight to ease the discomfort.

"We went yesterday. What'd you forget?"

"That boy is eatin' all my snacks, and I need more chips. Keep an eye on him while we're out."

"What do you mean, 'we're out?' Reevus can't go. I can't watch the kid myself with my leg in this condition."

"Where's he gonna run, Eddie?" she asked.

She threw her hands in the air and waved them in a circle. "You think he's gonna hop in the water with those gators?"

Eddie frowned. He hoisted himself to his feet. He made sure Connor was inside and out of earshot, then whispered, "Jolie, I'm tired. Those painkillers are making me groggy. I don't trust I can handle him alone in this condition. If I doze off, he'll likely stab me with one of those oversized kitchen knives of yours. If you need more snacks, go. But Reevus stays."

He locked his eyes on hers, which kept shifting her gaze into the cabin through the window screen.

Reevus watched her from the sink as he and the boy washed dishes from lunch. He had cautioned her not to push it with Eddie.

On a whim, he grabbed two bags of chips from the pantry and headed through the door. "Jolie, I told you I saw more chips in the pantry. You've got so much in there, woman, you don't even know what you got. And I threw some in the storage shed 'cause they wouldn't all fit. We're stocked for at least three more days."

Eddie glared at the pair, moving his line of sight from one to the other. His eyebrows raised slowly on his forehead.

Jolie feared he was suspicious, so she quickly added, "Well, the damned boy must have moved them. Fine, we're good for three more days, but after that, Eddie, you both need to be gone. You should be able to travel fine in three days."

"Sure, Jolie. Whatever you say," said Eddie.

He opened the screen door and went inside.

Jolie squinted at Reevus and headed to the storage shed. He was quick on her heels. "Woman, are you trying to get us killed?"

"I'm trying to save us, you fool!" she hissed under her breath.

"From Eddie? Or the Cujo? You're losing it. Your mind's makin' leaps that don't make sense."

"Reevus?" she whispered, "I'm heading out. Right now. Last night, I loaded some rifles, food, and a couple day's clothes for both of us."

"You did?"

"Yes. You were all sleeping. Now, I'm gonna load the boat with a couple of fuel jugs."

She put her hand on his chest. "I care about you. I want you to come with me. But we gotta leave right now. And if you don't get in the boat with me, I'll leave you here. And leaving you here means I'll be leaving you to die. I'm a survivor, sugar. And as much as I care for you, I care for myself more."

"Naw, this don't make sense. Eddie's gonna pay us ten thousand dollars."

"No, he's not, Reevus. You've known me quite a few years. Have I ever lied to you?"

"No."

"Have you ever seen me afraid?"

"Not really."

"Well, I'm afraid now. Look at me." Her eyes darted across his, and she held up a trembling hand.

"I'd kill him myself," she continued, "but he's got folks still loyal to him on the outside. *And* the inside. One of them might come seeking revenge, though I doubt he's worth it. Still, it's not worth the risk. Last thing I need is some pissy little Colombian or hot-headed Mexican putting a gun to my head while I'm sleeping.

"I need us to get out of this alive. I want to be done with him. And frankly, for all my sins, I ain't never killed nobody, not even when they deserved it. And no one deserves it more than Eddie. But I think I'm right with God now, and I don't need that son-of-a-bitch messing that up."

She began speaking to herself more than to him. "I should have left Louisiana. Started fresh. But the bayou is all I know." She tried to justify her reasoning.

"Then you wouldn't have met me," said Reevus. He lifted her chin. "Eddie's not going to kill us. He needs us."

"Not for much longer. He's getting stronger. Reevus, I've never pretended to be more than I am, to be what I'm not. I've been square with you since we met, and I'm telling you, it's now or never. I wish I could have given you more time, but we never had two seconds alone this morning, and now Eddie's clued in. I saw it in his eyes."

"What, are you psychic now?"

She narrowed her own eyes to little slits. "Maybe. Or maybe just perceptive. Reevus, get in the boat. We're leaving."

"Woman, you're crazy. You're imagining things."

"Get in the boat."

"Fine, but I need a couple things, personal things. Give me two minutes."

"Reevus!" she spit. "Get in this boat. *Now.*"

243

His head twisted side to side with his doubt.

Jolie sighed, then gave him a brief, tight hug. She opened the shed and took out two five-gallon red tanks, filled to the top. She walked them both to the pier and set about arranging the boat.

Reevus watched her a minute, then returned to the cabin.

Connor Whelan's eyes grew wide when he walked in. He tilted his chin up toward Eddie Morrison, sitting on the sofa. A pump-action shotgun was pointed toward Reevus, who backed up and positioned himself between Eddie and Connor.

"What's with the gun, Eddie? This boy acting up?"

"There's some acting up going on here, but it's not the kid this time," said Eddie. "Why's Jolie loading up fuel? Didn't we agree we've got three days' worth of supplies? Where's she going with that fuel?"

Eddie stole a peek out the front window, then swung back to face Reevus. He pumped the slide, chambering a shell. "Now, I want you to shout to her and get her inside without moving either of those clogs of yours."

He moved the weapon to point at Reevus' feet. "I'm betting you're partial to walking, so do as I say. Tell her to come inside. Now."

"Jolie," squeaked Reevus' voice. He coughed, clearing his throat, and shouted, "Jolie! Eddie's wondering where you're going with all that fuel! You best get in here and explain it to him."

He gazed through the screen.

Jolie was trying to see him. He was hard to make out in the shadow of the cabin's interior, but she caught the lift of his chin, encouraging her to go.

She didn't waste time with the trolling motor. She let the cord rip on her rebuilt outboard motor and let go of the dock.

The wind dried her tears as she raced away to the sound of two shots from Eddie's shotgun. By the time she thought she heard a third, she was already two hundred yards down the bayou, heading toward a more expansive waterway where she could let the engine fly. Not once did she look back. *Not once will I ever regret my decision.*

She roared at her foolish thought as she realized its deception.

Chapter 40

Caulfield snapped to attention at her boat wheel when she heard the sound of shotgun fire.

"Damn, that was close," she said to Garrity. "I think it was this way."

She steered the boat down a pipeline canal and turned off onto a small bayou.

She lowered her speed to a crawl and got on the radio.

"All deputy marshals receiving this, zero in on the following coordinates." She read them off her GPS. "Gunshots fired. Be advised and proceed with extreme caution."

She guided her Tracker down a smaller waterway off the bayou. When she'd gone four hundred yards, she retraced her route and continued another five hundred feet before doing the same on another offshoot. This led to a small waterway where she could turn left or right.

To the right, there was no sign of civilization, but to the left, and upstream about one hundred and twenty yards, was a small pier jetting out into the water. A tiny dock was tied to it. As she drew closer, the trees gave way to the sight of a minor, makeshift home.

She paused her approach.

Garrity spoke up for the first time all day. "Doesn't look like anyone's there. I think it's abandoned, like all the others we've seen."

Caulfield whirled around in her seat to him. "I didn't know we had Superman onboard today. You scout around inside that shelter with your x-ray vision?"

She turned back toward the front. "Looks like an excellent place to lay low to me."

Once again, she made her call. "All deputies within earshot, cabin spotted at these coordinates." She read the updated numbers.

"All units within twenty miles, proceed to my location. Holding for backup. Please radio me if you're en route."

She received confirmations from Marcus Freeman and Henrí Saint Armant, as well as two others. She couldn't help but breathe a small sigh of relief to know she'd have the backup of at least two, if not three, federal agents shortly. She had confidence in her task force, but they weren't professionally trained for this.

Caulfield was watching the cabin's front door, not forty yards away from her now when another gunshot rang through the air from inside the little shack.

She and Garrity instinctively drew their firearms.

"I don't think we have the luxury of waiting any longer," said Garrity. "Agent Whelan's son could be in there, bleeding out and needing emergency medical care. We should approach now."

"We're sitting ducks. There're no trees by the dock and nowhere else to tie up without stepping into six feet of water."

She pointed to four large alligators resting their heads on the steep shoreline bank. "And I, for one, would prefer not to go into the water with those guys so close. Anyone who ever gives you the line, 'they're more afraid of you than you are of them,' tell them to come talk to me. I've seen some shit."

Caulfield studied the property in front of her. "That's a defendable piece of land she chose. She could blow our heads off now if she wanted. We don't dare proceed without backup. We need extra cover fire."

The sound of another boat motor whirred from behind them, getting closer.

Caulfield whipped around, expecting to see one of her team coming to assist. Instead, it was an old, aluminum Jon boat with someone unknown at the tiller, guiding the craft right for them.

Lowering her weapon at first, Caulfield's eyes picked up on a rifle aimed in their direction, coming low from the woman steering.

When she raised her gun again, the woman raised her rifle, not more than twenty yards from them now.

Two shots rang out. One fell. Caulfield was whipped around as the .22 caliber bullet ripped through her left shoulder. She managed to get one more shot off as her back hit the deck of her boat.

Jolie Martín was still at full speed and shot by the Tracker. Fifty yards past the dock, she slowed and made a tight U-turn, raising her rifle to take another shot as she faced the federal agents.

Her pier was in her way this time, blocking Caulfield's boat and providing protection.

"Shoot her!" yelled Caulfield to Garrity.

"I can't get a shot! Can you move us to the dock? I can get a clear angle if I can get up on it."

SSA Caulfield leaned forward and grabbed the wheel with her right hand, guiding them the few remaining yards. She tied a rope to one of the boat cleats screwed into a dock plank. Her shoulder continued to bleed out, but she ignored it until her Tracker was secure.

"Get out and shoot that bitch!" she screamed, putting as much pressure with her right palm as she could into her shoulder wound.

Garrity jumped onto the dock, hiding his body as best he could behind a piling shooting above the pier.

Two shots came from the woman in the boat, missing their targets.

"You think that's Jolie Martín?" asked Caulfield.

"Has to be. Who the hell else would be firing at us?" shouted Garrity.

He chanced sticking his head out to take a shot, but Jolie zipped in front of them, past the pier at full speed again. She fired three more times but missed them all. Again, she did another turn downstream, and when facing them this time, she stopped her boat entirely. She stood and took careful aim with her long-range precision rifle. There was nothing between her and the agents now.

Caulfield fired continuously, but her bullets fell short at this distance or to the side of her opponent. Garrity fired four shots as well, all of them failing to take down Jolie Martín.

Another bullet ripped into Caulfield, this time getting her right side, above her stomach. It skirted one of her ribs and lodged itself deep into her kidney. Before she could fall, a second cut through her throat.

Garrity fired two more shots, then hopped down beside Caulfield. He watched for five silent seconds as the life ran out of the woman before him, her eyes focused somewhere far above them.

He emptied his clip in Jolie's direction, then hopped onto the dock again and jumped onto the pier. He ran to shore and positioned himself to the side of the front screen door to the cabin. He slapped another clip into his gun and hollered, "Eddie Morrison? Special Agent Luke Garrity with the FBI!"

The roar of Jolie's motor grabbed his attention as she sped by again, firing another shot as she did. It hit the cabin, barely missing his head.

"Damn," he wheezed. "Eddie? You in there? Is anyone in there?"

Another shot grazed his ear. He screamed out in startled fear as much as pain. Whatever waited for him inside wasn't taking shots at him. If he stayed out here any longer, he'd be a dead man soon.

Garrity decided to take his chances.

"This is Special Agent Luke Garrity!" he repeated. "I'm coming in!"

"Where the hell are all those shots coming from?" Whelan yelled to Marcus Freeman. "We have to be close!"

"Yes," he agreed. "I'm working on it. She's got herself zig-zagged into a secure location. I'll give her that."

It took Freeman another three minutes to find the correct series of turns onto Jolie's branch off the bayou. "There!" he pointed. Ahead one hundred and twenty yards was a pier with a small dock attached. Two boats were in sight, a Tracker Mod V, tied to the jetty, and another to the pier's far side.

"That first boat's Caulfield's!" said Whelan.

"They both appear empty," said Freeman.

As they drew closer, the cabin came into view. No one was in sight on the little swath of land between it and the water.

Suddenly, a shot whizzed by his head. He pulled his firearm, unsure where to aim.

"There!" said Freeman, singling out the Jon boat on the other side of the pier.

Jolie Martín was standing in her boat, using the pier as cover. She had enough clearance to hold her rifle over the pier's deck.

"Jolie! It's Marcus Freeman! Who are you shooting at? We're not here for you!" he lied.

"Go away, Cujo!" she screamed. "This isn't your fight!"

Another gunshot came from the cabin, this one aimed at Jolie. She turned and fired a shot toward the screen door, then wheeled back toward Whelan and Marcus Freeman.

"I can't do that, Jolie. These folks have asked me to help find this man's son, and they think you might know where he is. You're not in any trouble, girl. They just want the boy back."

She put her head low, taking aim. Another .22 bullet ripped through the air, striking Marcus Freeman in the leg. "Ain't your fight, Cujo! Now git! Next one's in your head, I swear!"

He dropped to the deck, unable to stand as blood rained over the fiberglass. "Oh shit." A steady stream of crimson was shooting up and over the side of the boat out of his leg.

Marcus clamped his hands against his leg. "She hit an artery!"

Whelan snatched a first-aid kit mounted to the side wall and threw it to him. "See if this has any gauze you can stuff in it." He returned fire toward Jolie, but she was shielded.

"Take my rifle," said Marcus. "That little pistol ain't gonna serve you here."

He fumbled with the latch on the medical kit until it gave. There wasn't any gauze, simply a pack of unopened bandages and some alcohol swabs.

Whelan took his shirt off, then his t-shirt, and stuffed the latter onto and into Marcus Freeman's left leg. "Hold it. Tight!"

Marcus screamed with the pain but did as he was told.

Whelan stood up and aimed the man's rifle toward Jolie, firing a round.

The bullet hit her in the arm, and she dropped her rifle. Two more rounds came flying out of the cabin door, one of which struck her in the gut and spun her around. She grabbed her rifle again and fired toward the cabin.

Another three shots came from the cabin window. All three struck her, one in her other arm, another in her chest, and one in her head.

Whelan grew aware there were two shooters in the cabin. He was trying to see them through the screens but he was sunblind, and the inside was too dark to make anyone out.

Freeman's boat was close enough now to the dock for Whelan to grab it.

Caulfield's boat blocked the cleats, and he couldn't tie off. He stood up to see where the best spot to hook up to the pier might be. Then he saw her. Caulfield's lifeless body in the bottom of her boat, her eyes still open to the heavens above. She was nearly floating in a pool of blood.

"Oh, fuck," he mumbled.

A bullet hit one of the pier's pilings, inches from his head. He knelt and pulled the boat along the dock to the end of the pier. From this angle, whoever the shooters were, they would likely have to come outside to get a clean shot.

"Marcus!" he whispered. "Marcus! How're you holding up?"

"Not too good, sir," he managed. His leg was still bleeding out, despite his best effort.

A boat motor was heard in the distance. Someone else was on the other side of the tree line behind him, on the main bayou, searching for this little offshoot same as they were five minutes ago.

Two minutes ticked off his watch like twenty. No more shots came at them. He chanced standing up and taking a peek. There was no one to see.

"Eddie!" he screamed. "It's all over, Eddie! This place will be crawling with twenty agents in a minute. Give yourself up now before you're killed!"

Another thirty seconds passed, then the screen door began to open.

Whelan was readying the rifle to take a shot.

Garrity's voice rang out. "I've got him!" he said. "Don't shoot, Agent Whelan. I've subdued him. He's coming out with his hands up."

Sure enough, Eddie Morrison came through the doorway, his hands on his head. Behind him was Garrity, pointing a rifle toward Eddie's back.

The sun was harsh, and Whelan struggled to make out the two figures' faces backlit by the bright sky. He held his hand up to block as much sun as he could, but he was staring up into it, trying to make out the men. He thought he had double vision as he tried to separate the two silhouettes before him.

"Garrity?" he asked.

"I'm here." Garrity stepped out from behind Eddie Morrison and held the rifle up. He fired a shot at Whelan. It tore into his right arm, and Whelan lost his grip on his weapon. Another shot nicked his right shoulder above it and flung him backward off the boat into the bayou. He swam under the pier for cover.

"Get on that boat!" Garrity yelled to Eddie, shoving him toward Caulfield's Tracker. "Get the motor running!"

Eddie lowered himself onto Caulfield's boat, careful not to tear open the stitches in his leg. The key was still in the ignition, and a simple push of a button roared the motor to life again. He picked up Caulfield's body and worked it to the edge of the boat, dumping it into the water on the side of the shoreline.

He untied the ropes and hollered out, "Let's go!"

Whelan watched as best he could, but the dock blocked his view of Eddie from his limited position under the pier. He thought to hoist himself up into Jolie's boat and try to grab her rifle. He flung the upper half of his body over the side. A five-gallon jug for boat fuel was lying empty on its side, and the bottom of her boat was full of gas. She had either been trying to fill her engine, or it toppled in the gunfight.

Just as he stretched out his hand to nab her rifle's hilt, he heard a familiar voice.

"Dad!" It was Connor Whelan. "Dad! Dad! Are you okay?"

It was coming from on top of the pier.

"Connor?" Whelan yelled, wheeling his head around to see his son.

Garrity held Connor's arm in one hand and pulled his pistol with the other.

"Dad, be careful!" said Connor. He was trying to jerk his way free of Garrity.

Garrity fired the trigger twice, both shots missing Whelan, who had the sense to drop back down into the water and use the old aluminum boat as cover.

Whelan could see the legs of Garrity and Connor hit the dock as they jumped down from the pier. Connor was thrown onto the Tracker with Eddie, who grabbed him and held him tight.

"Let's go!" Eddie yelled again to Garrity.

Garrity retorted back, "Not yet. Time to finish this."

He turned around and climbed onto the pier again, crossing over to the side with Jolie's boat. Whelan was nowhere to be seen. Garrity fired five shots around her boat, hoping to strike Whelan underwater.

The last shot hit the inside edge of the aluminum craft, causing a spark, igniting the fuel inside. It exploded into a ball of flame, in turn igniting the second tank of fuel. This explosion was more powerful and knocked the pilings from underneath the pier on this side.

Garrity was thrown flat against the pier as it was crashing down toward the back half of Jolie's boat. He hit his head on the side of it and lost consciousness, sinking into the water.

Marcus Freeman's boat was tossed from the end of the pier. It rolled, flipping over, throwing him into the water.

Eddie Morrison stood up and failed to see any sign of Garrity. Smoke was everywhere, and the old wooden pier was on fire. The dock was shaking from the concussion, and he let go, drifting away from the carnage.

He shifted the boat into gear and began to speed up slowly.

Connor stood, trying to see if he could spot his dad.

"Dad! Dad!" he yelled out.

"Here, Connor! Here!" Whelan yelled from the shoreline. He had safely returned to land when Garrity was taking potshots into the water. He had no weapon left on him to fire at Eddie.

Moments ago, he thought he'd felt something brush past him in the water, and as he spotted his son, he saw another commotion on the dock's side of the pier. At least three alligators were splashing and slapping the water as they fought over Caulfield's body. He saw a fourth swim out toward Marcus Freeman's boat. If they were resting hidden from the midday sun, the explosion stirred them into action.

"Connor!" Whelan screamed again. "Connor, I love you! Stay safe. I'll find you!"

"Dad!" Connor yelled back as Morrison raced down the water. "That man, Agent Garrity, is Eddie's son!"

Chapter 41

Cannon heard the explosions and saw a monstrous plume of smoke erupting from the other side of the tree line.

"There! We've got to get over *there*!"

"I'm trying!" yelled Henrí. "This swamp is a fucking maze!"

It took four more minutes before he navigated the correct path and raced to the pier. The smoke dissipated. The dock on the other side of the pier detached in the blast and was drifting freely nearby.

Henrí and Cannon tied up to it and piloted it over by the two remaining pilings, with several planks still attached. What hadn't burned was floating loose around the area. An overturned boat was hugging the surface on the opposite bank of the waterway. Beside it was the body of Marcus Freeman. His left leg was torn off above the knee.

A woman's arm was floating at the shoreline. It was from a black female. Cannon saw the wristwatch and recognized it as SSA Amber Caulfield's. It was her appendage. The movement of their boat caused the water to rock it gently over and over, flapping it against the side of a tupelo tree.

The water was tainted with blood no matter where you looked.

Caulfield's boat was missing.

"Whelan!" yelled out Cannon.

He told Henrí to stay with the dock, then hoisted himself to a horizontal beam still connected to the three pilings standing on this side of what was the original pier. Tip-toeing across to land, he drew his weapon and shouted again. "Whelan?"

Whelan burst through the screen door, running toward Cannon. He threw his arms around him briefly, holding him tight. When he backed away, his eyes were dropping tears as fast as he could talk. "Eddie still has Connor," he began. "Did you see him? You had to have passed him!"

"No," said Cannon. "I'm sorry, Tom, he must have taken a different bayou out of here than the one we came in on. You've seen how nuts it is trying to navigate this swamp. What happened here?"

Whelan gazed at what was left of the pier and relayed what transpired. When he finished telling the story, he wiped at his face with a kitchen towel. It was wrapped around his knuckles, which were bloodied, and he managed to stain his cheeks with a streak of red.

"Tom," asked Cannon, "what's with the blood on your hand?"

"Most of that's Garrity's."

"I thought you said he went down in the water."

"He did. After Connor was out of sight, I jumped back in and pulled him out."

"With the gators?" asked Cannon.

"There were bloodier, tastier choices," Whelan said. "And I needed answers. I just revived him a couple of minutes ago. So far, he's not cooperating. I should have left him in the bayou."

Cannon opened the screen door to the cabin. It was riddled with bullet holes. He assessed the room. In the makeshift kitchen, a black man in his mid-fifties was sitting on the floor, his back propped up against the side of the refrigerator. Both his feet were blown off, from a shotgun by the look of it. His eyes were cast forward in a perpetual state of shock.

Cannon closed them with his fingers. "Who's this?" he asked Whelan.

"I've no idea. Rigor's not set in yet, and the body still has some warmth. I'm guessing he was killed thirty or forty minutes ago."

Cannon turned his attention to Luke Garrity. Whelan had him tied to a chair. He wasn't even attempting to free himself. Where would he go?

"Where's Eddie taking Connor Whelan?" asked Cannon.

Garrity raised his chin. "I have no idea."

Cannon grabbed a folding chair from the dining table and slammed it down on the floor three feet across from Garrity. "You're Eddie's son?"

Garrity started to shake his head but hung it low as he focused on the ground at Cannon's feet with his right eye. His face was hit by Whelan twelve times. He was dizzy, and his breath was shallow. His left cheek was split and popped open in two spots. His left eye was nearly swollen shut and blood was everywhere.

"There's no one here but two people who love that boy," said Cannon. "Neither of us would have a problem tossing you back in with the gators. If you aren't any use to us, you're dead weight."

"You can good cop, bad cop me all you want. I don't know what Eddie plans from here."

"What did he plan *up* to here?" asked Cannon.

"You've been in communication with him the whole time, haven't you?" asked Whelan.

He ransacked Garrity's pants. His phone managed to stay deep inside his front pocket. Like nearly all smartphones today, it was water resistant.

Whelan swiped the screen, and a fingerprint security lock popped up. He held it in front of Garrity. "Which finger?"

"Thumb," said Garrity. "Right one."

Whelan walked behind the chair Garrity was tied to and pressed the man's right thumb against the face of the phone. It unlocked.

Before he did anything else, he went to the settings and disabled all security features. It was easier than cutting off the man's thumb and toting it around the rest of the day.

Sure enough, on Garrity's phone, the texts exchanged over the last week weren't to the Baltimore Bureau office or their special agent in charge. They weren't to Washington or FBI Director Commerson. They were to Eddie Morrison and Sheila Sanchez.

Whelan held the phone up so Cannon could see the text screen.

"You son of a bitch!" said Cannon. He stood and threw a punch into the left side of Luke Garrity's face. It was markedly swollen, and the two wounds from Whelan's punches split wider with Cannon's, meeting in the middle, forming a large gash now two inches long. It would need stitches.

"What's his plan, Garrity?" yelled Cannon. "Where's he taking Connor? Who else does he know in this area?"

Garrity mumbled, "Lawyer."

Cannon threw another punch.

Whelan was leaning on the table.

Witnessing his partner and friend going ballistic on Luke Garrity calmed his own rage somewhat.

"Garrity," Whelan said, his voice low. "I'll throw you hog-tied back in with those gators and let them finish you if you don't give us some answers. I swear it."

"I believe you, Agent Whelan. If you want my best opinion on Eddie's next move, I need to see an attorney and be granted full immunity."

"They'll never grant you immunity. You aided and abetted in the killing of a Supervisory Special Agent with the FBI."

"That wasn't me! That was Jolie Martín. She was shooting at both of us. Check Caulfield's wounds. You'll see they came from Jolie's rifle, not my gun!"

"That'll be difficult to do," said Cannon. "Her body's been torn to pieces. Most of it likely eaten by now."

Luke Garrity absorbed the news. "I was trying to help defend her. I didn't kill her. I would never kill another federal agent."

"You just tried to kill *me*!" yelled Whelan.

"Well, there's an exception to every rule," mumbled Garrity.

Cannon and Whelan stared at him for over a minute, forcing themselves to grow calm.

Whelan took a long breath, counted to ten, then said, "Luke, tell us what happened. From the beginning."

"I will," he replied. He straightened up as much as his bonds allowed. "As soon as you have me in front of a defense attorney and I'm granted full immunity, I'll tell you everything."

"That's not going to happen," said Whelan.

"Then, you'd better start calling in whatever favors you have left. And you'll have to take us back to civilization to get a cell signal. Eddie's got a twenty-five-minute jump on you. How much more time are you willing to give him?"

Chapter 42

Whelan was prepared to make sacrifices to get Connor back. *Whatever it takes.* That meant letting go of his malice toward Luke Garrity and granting him immunity.

"You want us to grant him *what*?" screamed Special Agent in Charge Carson Orville of the New Orleans field office.

"Whatever his involvement is, making sure he's thrown in prison is not as important as saving my son," Whelan snapped back.

"The hell it isn't! I lost my best agent today because of this man's involvement. He's going down, Agent Whelan."

"I'm sorry about Agent Caulfield, sir. She was in a class of her own, truly. And I know she'll leave a huge hole in this department. But right now, we need to focus on finding my son, and if a plea deal is the best way to secure that, wouldn't you want it? For *any* innocent child?"

SAC Orville shot Whelan the nastiest look and stomped out of the room.

The past four hours were hell.

While they were still navigating their way out of the Atchafalaya Wilderness, Whelan notified all of the deputies in the swamp he could reach. He told them to be on the lookout for Caulfield's boat, but held off telling them of her death, saying simply that Morrison took her Tracker and fled the scene. He instructed them to follow and report, but not try to capture Eddie Morrison if seen.

He was terrified they'd start shooting at him and mistakenly kill Connor. Their love for Amber Caulfield might have some of them trying to take the law into their own hands if they knew he was responsible for her death. They'd be given updates tonight by phone when they were home, off the water, and could process clearly.

Whelan knew Eddie would be trying to leave the swamp. If he wasn't spotted by the end of the day today, he likely escaped.

Whelan phoned Assistant Special Agent in Charge Miranda Jones at his office in Kansas City, where all this started. He called her the minute they secured a cell signal after leaving the swamp, and updated her on the day's activities. She vowed to check into Garrity's past and his request for a plea deal.

Now that they were settled back into the New Orleans office, Whelan dialed ASAC Miranda Jones again.

She answered her phone immediately. "Any word? Did you find Connor?"

"No," said Whelan. "What did you dig up on Garrity?"

"He's been with the department for two years like he told you. Before then, he graduated from the University of Maryland, Baltimore. Double major—Computer Science, and Psychology. Went on to get a Master's Degree in Computers."

"And a doctorate in Psychology," Whelan interrupted.

"No. Just a Bachelor's."

"He told me he had a doctorate. Lying son of a bitch."

Jones continued, "He was near the top of his class at UMB, and he passed the bureau's Special Agent Exam the first time out. His career to date was fairly mundane, largely cybercrime. He was closing cases. His file had no marks, and he was being considered for a transfer to the organized crime unit, per his request. That's practically laughable."

"How sure are we he's Eddie Morrison's son?"

"No confirmation we can find yet. His mother was Norma Garrity. She passed away six years ago. We're trying to track down a copy of Luke's birth certificate, but it's not in the database, and we're guessing at the cities and hospitals where he might have been born—we think in Virginia or West Virginia. We're checking Maryland and Pennsylvania as well. She led a fairly unremarkable life as a sales manager for a department store."

"I wonder how he got hooked up with Eddie," said Whelan. "I mean, when they met, and if Eddie tried to recruit him to the family business or what?"

"I can't be sure, but I'm guessing shortly after his mother died. He went off-grid. No job record for three years. Then he's suddenly the CEO of a private company investigating online hacking. Apparently, he's skilled with computers. He worked for nearly a year before applying to the bureau. Between his grades and his latest job, he was a perfect fit for a role with the Cyber division.

"Whelan, Luke Garrity forged the paperwork for the temporary transfer assignment to your team. I spoke with the SAC of the Baltimore office. He clarified that Garrity requested to be at Roffler's home in Gaithersburg Monday. He was going to send another agent, but Garrity told him he was familiar with the area. Then, when you went to Cumberland, Garrity told him you specifically requested him to join you there because you were impressed with him in Gaithersburg."

"Garrity knew where we were going to be headed," said Whelan. "Eddie kept him in the loop. He was one step ahead of us each time we were still formulating *our* next step."

"I heard back from Director Commerson," continued Jones. "Not only had he not assigned Garrity to keep an eye on you and report in, he didn't even know who Garrity was. He had to look him up in the system. He saw the fake assignment filed with his executive assistant, dated the day we went to Miami. Garrity signed Commerson's name. I saw it online, and it was a pretty close match."

"That bastard," whispered Whelan. "Here I thought the director was criticizing all my decisions. Garrity's smart. I'll give him that. I wonder what Eddie promised. Money, you think? Part of the two million they thought they were going to get from Sheila Sanchez? What the hell would turn an upstanding agent? Daddy issues?"

"Clearly. And with Eddie as a father, who knows where the real turning point happened. Sometime after his mother died, I'd guess. Eddie must have kept an eye on her and him their whole lives. I'm sure Eddie talked him into joining the bureau to keep an eye on *you*. I bet if we dug deep enough, we'd find Luke Garrity was using the Sentinel System to hack into your case reports daily, so Eddie knew how to avoid you best. Hell, the last few months you tracked him, Eddie had an inside man updating him on your moves. No wonder you couldn't catch him. Each time you got close, he knew to move on."

"Well, he's lost that advantage now."

Miranda Jones was silent, absorbed in her thoughts for a minute.

"Whelan?" she started. "Eddie zipped out of there, thinking his son died in the boat explosion, right? I mean, you said he witnessed him going into the water as all that fire rained down everywhere."

"Right."

"We might be able to swing an immunity deal after all. If Luke Garrity cooperates, we could use *him* to lure Eddie out of the woodwork. He could call him and say he survived, escaped, and was ready to join him full-time, now that his cover has been blown."

"Yes!" said Whelan. "Miranda, you're brilliant! That will work. Eddie's wounded, and I can't imagine he'd refuse Garrity's help."

"Let me make some calls," she said. "SAC Orville isn't going to let him off the hook easily. Look at me, finding an excuse to speak to Director Commerson twice in one day."

Whelan hung up the phone. He retrieved Cannon and filled him in on the call with Jones.

"So, we're in holding mode," said Cannon. "The paperwork will take time. Let's find a hotel and get cleaned up."

"This is going to work, Phil!"

"I pray it does, my friend."

Cannon led his partner out of the bureau after checking in with SAC Orville. Their renewed optimism went unappreciated as they warned him the call would soon come in from Commerson and they would return to present the offer to Garrity themselves. Orville wasn't happy about it.

"Not much you can do," said Whelan.

When the agents left the building, SAC Orville knew precisely what he could do. After all, prisoners in this situation hung themselves in their cells all the time.

Chapter 43

Four hours earlier, Connor Whelan watched his dad fade out of sight as Eddie sped away in Caulfield's boat.

He swiveled the seat around and faced forward. He knew Eddie had no idea how to navigate the swamp. They zig-zagged often, generally heading west.

When Eddie heard the sound of another boat motor, he veered off from whatever larger bayou he was on and did his best to disappear down a smaller one. He shut his engine off.

Connor started screaming for help.

Eddie put his pistol up against Connor's head. "Kid, you make one more peep, I'll blast you here and now and take my chances. The sole reason you're alive is because you might still prove useful, but if we don't escape this situation, I won't be the only one on the water with a dead son today."

Connor's loathing of Eddie began to swell up in him. He had grown genuinely fond of Reevus, despite understanding on some level the man was not truly his friend. Seeing Reevus' feet shot off was disturbing, even after all he'd witnessed over the last week. He stood and faced Eddie. His eyes narrowed into slits of contempt.

Eddie's eyes went the opposite direction, opening wide. He believed the kid was about to hit him, so he struck first. He took the butt of the gun and smashed it into Connor's right cheek. It was an inviting target since the left one had already been busted twice.

Connor's skin held together, but a spider web of blood vessels broke, and he believed he heard his cheekbone crack. He fell backward, stumbling over the seat, and landed on the deck. He would have tumbled into the water had Eddie not lunged and clenched his pant leg.

"Now, tell me you understand, and you'll keep your mouth shut, kid."

Connor stayed quiet as Eddie raised the gun again. He knew Eddie meant what he'd said, and if he crossed him, he'd be dead in a second. "Okay," he mumbled.

Eddie shushed him with a finger as the other boat's motor roared louder. Whoever was coming was on the main waterway they'd departed. They weren't hidden completely. If someone looked this direction long enough, they would see them tucked behind a small outcropping of brush sticking out over the water.

Connor started standing to get a better view.

"Uh-uh," said Eddie, cocking his gun and pointing it at Connor's rib.

They both watched the larger bayou forty yards in front of them. Ten long seconds ticked away, then there it was, another boat with three men onboard. Then there it wasn't. They hadn't even bothered to glance their way.

The crew was heading to where they'd seen a smoke plume fifteen minutes earlier. They were racing to help a situation already over, unbeknownst to them. It would be two more hours before they received a radio call to be on the lookout for Caulfield's stolen boat.

Eddie expelled his breath. "Damn, that was close, kid."

He waited three minutes, then started the motor and resumed course.

For the next hour, the tears flowed freely down Connor's face. He refused to let Eddie see them, sitting forward in the front seat.

Another boat's motor could be heard, so Eddie hid a second time. He was sure to make at least two turns before drifting alongside some cypress knees and shutting down.

Connor wiped his face with the bottom of his shirt and swallowed his animosity. It was time to get back into Eddie's grace. He studied his captor at the boat wheel. "You're pretty impressive with that," he whispered.

"With what?"

"Boat driving. You must have piloted one before."

"Years ago, when I was young. I enjoyed fishing," he said. "Always kept a boat or two on some lake somewhere."

"I never cared for fishing until this week. Reevus and I had fun. I caught a lot. Ate a lot too."

"And gator," said Eddie. "You're practically a gourmet cook, kid. Maybe you'll be a chef when you grow up."

"Yeah, maybe." Connor gave it some thought. He visualized himself in a large, commercial kitchen, cooking fancy food like he'd seen the chefs do on TV. His mind shifted the servings to gator tail, with a side of potato chips and a Yoo-hoo. The "specialties of the day" board out front had Fried Fish and Gator Tail on the menu, plus a soup du jour. He was then back at a stove stirring a monstrous pot of dark stock full of vegetables, all floating around the head of Eddie Morrison.

Connor smiled at Eddie. "You could join me on the opening day of my restaurant."

"Aww, thanks, kid."

When the coast was clear, they got underway.

The Atchafalaya River came before them soon. It was nearly a thousand feet across at this point. Eddie studied the flow and tried to see the next bayou he could go down. The tree lines on the other side were as thick as what he'd been dealing with, and he couldn't tell when he would be able to get off the river.

He held his gun on Connor again. "Down low, kid. Curl up beside me, and don't come up until I tell you."

Connor sighed but kept his mouth shut as he contorted himself at Eddie's feet.

Eddie pushed the boat onto the river and let the motor rip as fast it could carry them. It felt like flying. After a minute, he saw two boats headed in his direction. He crossed their path early and hugged the opposite shoreline as close as possible without slowing down.

The boats passed him. One had a family with two kids and two dogs onboard. They waved at him. He waved in return. The second boat had two fishermen, who also waved. They were all part of one big river family, celebrating the day, being courteous, showing proper "friendly river etiquette."

A broad bayou offshoot to the west came up, and he guided the boat onto it. After two miles of winding northwest, it narrowed to a trickle, barely fifteen feet wide. They hoisted the Mercury engine and made their way with a trolling motor. After another half-mile, it merged with a pipeline canal. It was forty feet wide, allowing them to start the main motor again.

A mile later, another vast waterway presented itself, five hundred feet across.

He chose to go north again. Connor twisted himself down low, and they were off. Three boats passed this time. They were southbound and too far away to worry about waving.

"I think you can sit up, kid. But behave yourself."

"Of course."

"I may be crazy, but I think I'm hearing cars."

Connor agreed. "Over those trees." He pointed to their left.

They continued three more miles.

"Oh, thank God," said Eddie.

A boat ramp presented itself. It wasn't official and was carved out of mud instead of asphalt, but he'd take it. There were nine trucks and SUVs, each with a trailer, parked in chaotic order around the edges of the makeshift road. Eddie pushed up on the throttle, giving them enough speed to beach themselves on the ramp.

"You ready to get off this water?" he asked Connor.

"Hell yeah."

"Me too, and here comes a fresh truck."

"Oh, wait." Connor realized what that meant. "Can't you hotwire one of these? Do you have to kill someone else?"

Five minutes later, it was over. Eddie shot rounds into the heads of a thirty-four-year-old man and his five-year-old boy.

"Pop'em in the head to make sure they're dead," he said.

Connor found himself nodding in agreement. He wanted to feel sick to his stomach, but the emotion didn't come. All he truly wanted was to get on the road and get somewhere they could eat. It was after 5:00 p.m., and that same emotionless stomach was growling, reminding him it was empty.

They drove sixteen miles north on the Bayou Benoit Levee Road until they hit Interstate Ten. They continued west into Lafayette, where they got off to find food and possibly a cheap motel. They'd need to switch up cars as well.

"What are you hungry for, kid? Fish and chips?" Eddie joked.

"There!" said Connor. He was pointing to a local pizza joint.

"Sounds fantastic to me. I was getting tired of all the fried shit, too. Do I need to throw you in the trunk, or can you stay tucked in the backseat?"

Connor crossed his heart and threw his right palm in the air.

Eddie called the number on the door and asked if they could run it out to his car. Fifteen minutes later, a girl came out with a large pizza box.

Afterward, they stole an SUV from a neighborhood three blocks from the pizza joint. The woman was startled when Eddie marched right up to her in her driveway, offering to help her with her groceries. The blood spatter on the driveway reminded Connor of his pepperoni slices as he took another bite. He was too hungry to respectfully wait until Eddie hid her behind a front hedge.

They were soon westbound on I-10 in their traded-up SUV, eating slices of pizza and sharing swigs from a two-liter bottle of Pepsi.

The sun was setting, and Eddie let Connor sit in the front passenger seat.

"We've got a long day ahead of us tomorrow," said Eddie.

"We do? Where are we going?"

"Houston."

"Texas?"

"Yeah, kid. It's about three and a half hours from here. I'll treat us to a room tonight, and you can sleep in a proper bed instead of that cot. I've made us over four hundred dollars today."

He meant he'd stolen that much from his victims, but Connor declined to say as much out loud.

"What's in Texas?" he asked.

"Oh, lots of things. It's large and spread out—a good place to go off-grid. We can disappear. I've got one friend left in the whole world who might help us. He operates a cattle ranch in the south. Maybe we can be ranch hands."

We're an "us" now? Connor wasn't sure he liked Eddie's tone. It was too jovial. "What if he doesn't agree to help?"

"We'll take our chances. But he owes me one. I think he'll be ready to pay up," Eddie smiled wide with his unshared memory.

Something was off. "Eddie, how many painkillers did you take with dinner tonight?"

"I had three left, so I took them all."

"I figured."

"Relax, kid. You'll love Texas. We might just get a little ranch of our own and settle down there."

Huh?

Chapter 44

Whelan observed himself in the mirror of his hotel room. He hadn't eaten much this week, despite what he told his mother. His pants were loose, and he had to yank his belt to the next hole.

The agents showered and grabbed dinner at a nearby diner with a meatloaf special. It reminded Whelan of his ex-wife's, but Georgia's was better. He fought melancholy memories while battling despair.

Whelan held up his coffee cup. "Here's to Agent Amber Caulfield. May she rest in peace."

Cannon raised his water glass, and they toasted their colleague, slain in the line of duty.

"I only hope she was already dead by the time those gators got hold of her," said Whelan.

"Let's focus on what we can do moving forward," said Cannon. He knew how his partner could dwell too long on things beyond his control.

There was no word yet from Director Commerson, so they returned to the New Orleans field office to see if Garrity felt like sharing any new information now he had some downtime to think.

It was 9:25 p.m., and much of the staff was gone. There was a skeleton crew working the night shift.

They rounded the corner to the holding cells. The hallway was dark, but the end cell with Garrity spilled light from his ceiling lamp. The bars cast long shadows on the opposite wall. In the middle of them, a man's silhouette rocked gently from the breeze of an A/C vent, two feet above the floor.

"No!" Whelan ran down the hall.

Sure enough, Garrity was hanging from the top horizontal bar of the cell by his bed sheet, wrapped tight around his neck.

"Get someone down here!" he barked at Cannon. "We need them to open this door!"

Whelan slipped his arms through and wrapped them around Luke Garrity, hoisting him up to relieve the weight off his neck.

"Garrity! Garrity! Luke! Can you hear me? Wake up, Luke!"

Whelan was frantic. "Cannon! Hurry!"

He got a better grip on the man. "Garrity, wake up. You son of a bitch. I need you. Time for you to make up for your crimes, you fucking piece of shit. Wake up! Damn you, Garrity, don't you dare die on me right now."

He couldn't tell whether the man was breathing.

After what seemed like an eternity, Cannon came racing down the hall with another woman.

"Oh, shit," she said as she fumbled with a set of keys. After trying six of them, the door swung open. She retreated to the front office to call for an ambulance.

Cannon grabbed Garrity from the other side, giving Whelan a respite.

Whelan climbed a notch on the bars and untied the sheet from the top rail. They lay the man on the ground, and he listened to his chest for a heartbeat while Cannon checked his pulse. Nothing.

He began CPR, pushing for four minutes, as Cannon breathed into his lungs at twenty second intervals.

For the second time today, Luke Garrity jolted back to life with a cough and a sudden air intake, thanks to Special Agent Tom Whelan.

The following three minutes, Garrity couldn't speak a word. His windpipe was crushed, and fought to stay open. Ice water helped, and he was able to murmur his first words. "It was Orville."

"No," said Whelan reflexively.

"And two agents," Garrity whispered as they helped him sit upright. "They wanted it to look like a suicide."

He pointed to the bed in the cell, positioned beside the door.

"We were supposed to think you stepped off that?" asked Cannon.

Garrity nodded. He eyed the clock on the wall outside his cell. "It's been eight minutes. Thank God you came back tonight. I can't believe I held on as long as I did before passing out."

"Passing out?" said Cannon. "You were dead. You must have run out of air in the past couple of minutes."

"Dead?" said Garrity. He shook his head in disbelief. "Couldn't have been."

"Why not?"

"I didn't see anything. No bright light, no angels...."

Whelan looked at Cannon. "Go check with the front desk. See when Orville left the building."

Cannon ran up the hallway. "Did SAC Orville leave here in the last few minutes?" he asked the woman who opened the cell door.

"He did. You just missed him," she answered, oblivious to his reason for the question. "Ambulance is on the way."

"Do you have camera footage of the cell Luke Garrity is being held in?"

"We should."

She tapped away at her keyboard. "That's odd. The picture went dark about twenty minutes ago."

She gawked at the screen in disbelief. "Yes, it sent a signal until nine-eighteen, then—nothing. I'll have the tech guys take a gander in the morning."

"You do that," he said, then returned to Whelan and filled him in.

"Shit." It was about all he could say. "We need to get him out of here. Now."

They were all in agreement. "Garrity, can you walk?"

"I think so."

Cannon and Whelan helped him to his feet. When they turned out of the holding area, they searched for another hall which might lead to a side door instead of going through the front. They found one.

It opened to the sound of sirens coming down Leon C Simon Drive, a half mile away.

"Get the car," spat Whelan to Cannon.

He ran around the side of the building to the visitor parking lot and fetched the car. Garrity reclined as far as he could in the back seat. Whelan and Cannon covered him with dirty clothes.

As they approached the exit gate, Whelan flashed his credentials to the guard. He was waved through in time to avoid the ambulance turning onto the property.

From his rearview mirror, Whelan saw it enter the lot and race to the main door.

"Shit," he mumbled. "Shit. Shit. Shit."

"We're going to catch hell, aren't we?" asked Cannon.

"It'll come down to his word over Orville's. With no camera evidence, yeah, we're screwed."

They retrieved their belongings from the hotel as fast as they could, hopped on I-10, and headed west out of New Orleans at eighty-five miles per hour.

Whelan called ASAC Miranda Jones in Kansas City and filled her in on all that transpired.

She listened quietly, then said, "Whelan, I'm going to file a transfer request. I'm typing the email now and sending it to SAC Orville. You'll be cc'd along with Director Commerson. It won't protect you fully for yanking him out of there without the proper authorizations, but it might provide plausible deniability. You can swear you were under the impression it was a done deal. Still, you'll likely receive a documented reprimand at the least."

"What about the worst?" asked Whelan.

"A demotion, or outright firing. But I would guess if you're right about Orville, he won't make much fuss over this. He won't want the formal investigation. But Whelan, if you're wrong, he'll come after you like a shitstorm."

"I understand. Thank you, Miranda." He hung up the phone.

The threesome drove in silence for an hour. Whelan wasn't sure where they were headed. He wanted to put distance between himself and New Orleans.

A highway sign snagged Whelan's attention: Louisiana Airborne Memorial Bridge—Atchafalaya Basin. They were about to cross the third longest bridge in the United States, heading west over and into the Atchafalaya Wilderness once again.

Into the heart of darkness, Whelan sighed. *Whatever it takes.*

Chapter 45

Connor was asleep when Eddie drove up to a Motel 6 in one of the eastern suburbs of Houston, Texas. It was nearing 1:30 a.m.

Eddie carried the boy inside their room and placed him in the bed farthest from the window. He covered him and inspected Connor's cheek, where he'd struck it about twelve hours ago.

A colossal bruise was developing, and the broken blood vessels were like a tattoo. His other cheek wasn't healing well, where he'd popped it open below the eye with his ring six days ago. It was trying to scab over but needed the help of a butterfly bandage to stay closed. Their supply of them was used up. Below the eye, it was deep purple, with yellow and green starting to develop. His split lip was healing some, but it cracked open again whenever Connor opened his mouth more than an inch.

Eddie created a freak only P.T. Barnum could appreciate.

"Sorry, kid," he mumbled before handcuffing the boy to the headboard.

He checked Connor's arm where it tore open a few days ago from the broken chair at the cabin. It stayed shut from the tight compression of an ACE bandage and didn't appear infected.

Exhausted, Connor slept through the inspection.

Eddie managed to grab a hot shower before falling into his bed. He put his growing arsenal on the floor alongside the front wall. SSA Amber Caulfield had two pistols and two rifles on her boat. In addition to what he'd been lugging all over the country, he was now up to eight pistols, ten rifles, and four shotguns.

Maybe I can sell some of these for some quick dough.

He counted his cash on hand. He was back up to $1,238. Drifting to sleep, he questioned what his next steps were. *What am I doing?*

Drowsiness from the long day and his painkillers took over. His last thoughts before crashing were of his own son, Luke, whom he'd come to know recently.

So many years wasted. And now he's gone forever.

Eddie jerked to consciousness around 10:00 a.m. He thought he heard gunfire.

The boy was still in the other bed, awake and watching some cowboys riding horses on TV. They were shooting at some Indians fleeing an old rustic town.

"Morning, kid."

"Morning, Eddie," Connor replied. He didn't take his eyes off the screen.

"You like old westerns?"

"Nope. There's nothing else on. I think we have ten channels. It's this or the local news, or the national news, or the weather channel. Weather news. Woo-hoo."

Eddie stood and grabbed the remote out of Connor's hand. "Well, aren't you curious what they're saying about *us*?"

He flipped to a local channel. Five minutes in, there was no mention of them. No Amber Alerts. No "wanted" signs with his face on it. He continued flipping through all the channels. Nothing.

"They don't know where we're at." Eddie became excited, even snorted a little. "They have no clue we're in Houston. Kid, we may have gotten away clean!"

Connor looked at the man for the first time this morning. He wanted to say many things to him. *I hate you. You're a psychopath. I miss my mom. I hope my dad kills you.*

The one thought he voiced, however, was, "I have to pee."

"Oh, sure, kid."

Eddie released him so he could take a leak. "And run through the shower."

"Why bother?" asked Connor. "My clothes are filthy. You want me to put those back on?"

"I'll pick you up some new duds."

Connor wanted to argue, but his face hurt, and a shower sounded refreshing. "Okay."

Eddie handcuffed Connor to the shower curtain rod.

There was a large truck stop adjacent to the motel's property. They both needed fresh clothes, and these stations always carried a small section of items.

He lowered a ball cap on his brow and spent five minutes picking items off the discount rack. He also grabbed packs of socks and underwear for them both, and more bandages, including butterflies. With the addition of coffees and bagel sandwiches, he kept the purchase to one hundred and seventy-eight dollars.

Eddie was focused on keeping his cash wad at over a thousand bucks. It was like a magic number he couldn't fall below, or he'd realize he was in real trouble.

He walked back to their room as fast as his injured leg would allow. When he got there, the door was wide open. He found the curtain rod pulled from the wall and lying in the bathtub. Connor Whelan was gone.

Eddie threw all his bags into the room and ran down the hallway, frantically scouting the handful of cars remaining in the parking lot this late in the morning. He ran around to the other side of the motel.

Connor was wearing nothing but a towel wrapped around his waist and was approaching a man getting into his car.

Eddie kicked his wounded leg into gear and reached the pair in another six seconds.

"Connor!" he yelled. "What are you doing out here all naked, boy?"

The stranger climbed out of his driver's seat and studied the oddly matched duo.

"I'm sorry," said Eddie. "My grandson is autistic and doesn't like to put on his clothes some days. Come on, Connor, let's get you back to our room and get you dressed."

"I understand," the man said. "My nephew is autistic. He's five. You know, they're making strides in identifying and helping those with this disability. They now estimate one to two percent of the population has autism to some degree. Isn't that fascinating?"

Eddie shifted his eyes to Connor, who was spinning his head around like he was searching for the best route to make a run for it. He gripped the top of the boy's left arm above his wound, now exposed without any wrapping.

The stranger's disposition altered when he saw Eddie's forcefulness with Connor. "He's got one nasty looking wound there," he commented.

"You know autistic kids. Always hurting themselves."

"No, not really."

"Well, wait till your nephew's twelve instead of five."

"What happened to his face?" the man asked.

"We were in a wreck. I can't get him to keep his seatbelt on."

"Did you *handcuff* him? He's not an animal, he's a child!" the man screamed at Eddie, then turned to Connor directly.

"Are you okay?"

Connor bounced his pupils back and forth between the two men. Eddie's free hand automatically went for his rear waistband, where Connor knew he kept his pistol. His thoughts darted chaotically. If he blurted out the truth, Eddie would kill another person, but this man looked strong and perhaps could overtake Eddie. Maybe he could get away while they fought?

He thought about how he'd gotten the charter plane pilot killed earlier in the week, and let a tear roll down his cheek. The salt stung his wound.

"I'm fine, thank you for caring," he said, then turned to Eddie. "Let's go, Granddad."

The pair retreated as the man jumped in his car and drove away.

When they were back in the room, Eddie flung Connor onto the floor. He pointed his gun at the boy's head.

"Do it," said Connor.

"Why are you testing me, kid? I've been good to you. Bought you clothes. Bought you breakfast. I give you a minute of my trust, and you betray me. I thought we were moving past all this nonsense."

"I already have a dad, Eddie. I can't replace your son."

The weight of Connor's statement froze Eddie. He lowered his weapon. "You're not replacing him, kid. But since your dad took my boy, I'm taking his."

Connor felt brave this morning for some reason. "First, you took me before my dad met your son. And my dad didn't 'take' him. He jumped back onto the pier and started firing at my dad. All on his own. He tried to kill him. Those gunshots are what got him killed. He blew himself up. I was there, Eddie. So were you."

Eddie continued staring at Whelan's son.

Connor thought he'd push his luck. "And what's with this 'you and I are going to live happily ever after on some ranch' shit, anyway? You plan on keeping me forever?"

"What the hell got under your skin this morning?" asked Eddie.

Connor lowered his chin. "I got a good look at my face. You've made a monster out of me. The man in the parking lot confirmed it."

"Well, Frankenstein's monster was pretty popular," Eddie tried to tease him. It didn't go over well.

"Kid, those scars will heal fine. In a few years, you'll hardly see them."

"A few *years*?" Connor screamed.

"Maybe sooner. I brought you some more butterflies. Let me help you fix them up."

Eddie opened the package and took Connor to the bathroom. He wiped the boy's face with some alcohol swabs. The burning made Connor flinch, but he stood still and took it. Fresh bandages were applied, followed by a drop of antibiotic ointment left in the first aid kit.

"There, kid, good as new. Now get dressed. That guy you bothered might report us to the police. We need to hit it."

"Sure, Eddie. Whatever you say. You said you bought clothes?"

Eddie retrieved the bags he bought. He gave Connor's to him in the bathroom, then stepped out so he could dress privately.

Connor put on a T-shirt and some sweatpants that fit fine and he was grateful for fresh underwear.

Eddie changed his own clothes and packed the car right outside their room.

"We're going to have to grab a new car this morning," he hollered.

Connor sighed. He looked at his arm. It was scabbing in a few places across his self-inflicted gash. Before he cleaned it, applied fresh gauze, and wrapped it up again, he ripped off one of the smaller scabs. Blood welled instantly.

He dipped his index finger into it and wrote on the mirror. *Fuck fingerprints.*

When he finished, he stepped out. "Okay, I'm ready. And hungry. You said you bought breakfast?".

"Yeah, it's in the car. We can eat on the way."

"Then let's go. I'm starving."

He closed the door behind him and hopped into the backseat.

Eddie grinned. The kid was learning when he could and couldn't sit up front without being told.

They peeled away in search of another vehicle, eating a cold convenience store breakfast.

It would be another two hours before maid service would find the message on the mirror.

CONNOR WHELAN WAS HERE. TELL FBI. GOING TO CATTLE RANCH S. OF HOUSTON. TELL MOM I ♥ HER.

Chapter 46

Whelan received a call at 12:20 p.m. from ASAC Miranda Jones. "Whelan? Connor left us a message. You've got the bravest, smartest kid I've ever known."

She relayed the note he'd left on the Motel 6 mirror.

The three agents had holed themselves up in a Red Roof Inn five miles east of downtown Houston off I-10.

"I told you, I *know* Eddie," Whelan said on the phone. "He has one uncaught ally left. That man's rumored to be in Houston now. We're going to head south and start poking around some ranches, but honestly, I expect there will be tons of them. I need you to come through with the immunity deal for Garrity."

"Whelan, I'm sorry, but I don't think they'll ever agree. Commerson said no. Garrity's too involved with Eddie. There's a wave of bodies from Maryland to Miami, and I'm sure more will turn up in New Orleans. They're not going to let him walk. For anybody."

Whelan looked at Garrity. "That's fantastic news, thank you!" he said, then hung up the phone.

"Garrity, they've agreed. You'll have your deal, but only if we get Connor back alive *and* capture Eddie."

"I need to see the paperwork," he said. "Have them text it to my phone."

"It's not in hand yet. The judge will sign it this afternoon as soon as he's cleared his docket. His clerk is drafting it. But we aren't wasting several hours waiting for it. You're going to have to trust me."

"I'm not sure I can do that," said Garrity.

"Luke, I saved your life yesterday. Twice. You can trust me."

Garrity thought about it. "Okay. So, what do we do?"

"You make a call. You tell Eddie you crawled out of the water and shot me."

"Shot you? That'll make him ecstatic. And how did I get out of the swamp?"

"Another boat rescued you. You told *them* Eddie killed me, and they needed to continue trying to find Connor. They took you back to your vehicle so you could phone in and get new orders from your superiors. Then you told the deputies you were being called back to New Orleans to deliver an update in person, but they were to stay in the swamp and keep searching. Afterward, you high-tailed it out of there and drove to Houston, knowing Eddie would be heading there."

Whelan paused. "*Would* you have known his next step?"

"Not as well as you, it seems. But Eddie did mention a past connection in Houston as his last resort should Jolie fail him. Some guy named Rico. He never mentioned a last name. Said he owed him a favor for keeping him out of prison. That's all I know."

"Okay, that's helpful."

Luke Garrity noticed his reflection in a mirror on the wall of their hotel room. His left eye was swollen shut, and the side of his face was black and blue. Whelan and Cannon beat the tar out of him the previous day. He felt conflicted between despising them and feeling gratitude for saving his life. Twice.

"How am I going to explain all this?" he asked, pointing to his face.

"The truth. You were in an explosion, and your face hit the side of that boat."

Garrity rehearsed the scenario in his head before shifting his thoughts to his new future. With a plea deal in the works, he could start fresh. Go back to California and restart a career as a computer hacking consultant. Big corporations paid top money for that kind of thing.

Cannon was watching Garrity's cogs turn. "Luke, I'm curious to know how Eddie recruited you to join his 'family' operation and leave a life in the FBI, doing a job you loved, to endorse a life of crime."

"I don't exactly *love* this life," started Garrity. "Truth is, I did join the bureau because Eddie wanted an inside man."

"But you joined before he even escaped. Oh shit, you *helped* him escape prison twenty months ago, didn't you?" asked Whelan.

"I pulled some reports and provided intel on who might rat out who. I only passed along information. He did all the hard work himself. He finagled all the arrangements."

"Because you helped him."

"And that's why I need total immunity for all my involvement."

Cannon and Whelan thought about that.

Garrity seemed concerned. "Agent Whelan, they are writing my deal up for *total* immunity, right?"

"Yeah," he lied. "You won't serve a day for anything relating to Eddie Morrison. In fact, they were talking of putting you in the witness protection program, should you need it, in case you thought Eddie and his goons might track you from prison and try to harm you later."

"I'll give it some thought," he said.

"So Eddie promised you what?" asked Cannon. "When your mother died? When you had a career catapulting you into the sweet life."

"I didn't have that yet, when she passed."

Garrity cleared his throat and took a sip of coffee. "My mother was struggling financially. She helped me with college as much as possible, but it was expensive. I earned some minor scholarships, but they barely made a dent. I still had to take out a ton of student loans. Four years left me with over a hundred thousand dollars to pay back. I hoped maybe she had a life insurance policy, but no. And when I thought I could sell her house, I discovered she owed the bank more than it was worth. She'd taken out a home equity loan. Thank God I wasn't on the deed, or they'd have come after me for the debts she owed.

"About two months after that, Eddie approached me. I'd never met him. I'd heard my mother mention him a few times over the years, but it was never favorable. Eddie made no excuse for not being in my life. He blamed my mother for it and said he respected her decision to keep me away from his life of crime. I didn't know what to think. Then he wants to pay off *my* debts—all of them. Catch me up to zero. He wrote me a check for $123,000, no questions asked, and demanded nothing in return. Said it was less than he'd have paid had he ever bothered to provide child support."

"He didn't say you needed to pay him back?" asked Cannon.

"No. But a month later, he offered me a job. Said if I worked for him, I could make a million dollars a year."

"Nice," said Whelan.

"Right? The most I was being offered for a job in computers as a college grad with no real-world work experience was forty-five thousand. It didn't take me two seconds to say yes. And he said I could manage one of his operations anywhere I wanted. California was always on my bucket list to check out."

"And the fact you were working for one of the largest crime syndicates in the country didn't faze you?" asked Cannon.

"I had no idea how large an operation he ran until several months later. I wasn't even sure how we were committing crimes. We were taking overseas orders from some Chinese outfits, similar to Alibaba, and wholesaling here in the U.S. at a markup—an amazing markup. I worked seven hours, four days a week, and received checks based on a million-dollar salary. With so much free time, I was taking Spanish lessons. I enrolled in a pottery class. Hell, I was even learning to surf."

"*You* took a pottery class?" asked Cannon.

"Yes. There was this place at the mall offering classes three nights a week. You've seen how popular those painting classes are? Everyone's drinking wine and painting the same image? Same concept, only with clay."

"That seems like a rather creative outlet for someone into computers. I would have pinned you for a gamer."

"Well, you don't really know me, *do* you, Agent Cannon?" snapped Garrity.

Whelan watched the pair exchange despising expressions. "Okay, so you go from that to enrolling in the FBI so you can help Eddie escape and keep your eye on me. How do you bridge to that from surfing and Spanish lessons?"

"A couple years into the job, Eddie said he needed me in Cumberland. His California plans weren't materializing. I always loved Maryland and was delighted to go home—well, more or less. This time we moved product by train instead of boat, and the stuff wasn't coming from China as much as Canada and across the Atlantic. I started to see the criminality of the operation—altered invoices, payoffs to those we needed to turn the other way, failure to record delivery destinations properly, but I was hooked on the income. And then came the teddy bears."

"Teddy bears?" asked Whelan.

"An entire rail car showed up one day, full of teddy bears. Well, of course, I'm good at my job, so I'm taking inventory, and this box is marked incorrectly, and I wind up slicing into three teddy bears when I cut through the packing tape. Three hairy bear bellies are split open, along with the kilo of coke they each contained. I felt like a fool, for not having realized until then. How many shipments of drugs had I sent through and repackaged for other territories thinking they were Kewpie dolls and totem poles? Every product we'd received from China while still in California played through my head. And not once had I ever questioned why Hello Kitty's head seemed to rattle when you shook it. They were full of pills! Fucking Eddie had me smuggling drugs, and I was clueless as a child."

"A million-dollar salary can blind a man, I'd imagine," said Whelan.

"Yeah. I tried to leave once, but Eddie reminded me how well he kept records and had documentation on all my involvement, should the 'need' ever arise to use it. And more than once, I'd heard of people 'disappearing' from the operation, never to be seen or heard from again. I was enjoying my life. I was still putting in less than forty hours a week. Cumberland was beautiful. Then, you happened."

He paused a few seconds before continuing. "You took down his whole operation. Eddie went to prison, and I was out of a job. I thought I'd be making that kind of money a lot longer. I didn't bother saving any of it. I've got a house in Baltimore that's paid off, and it's great, but I blew the rest. It's surprising how you can go through a million bucks on fun and fine dining."

"I was in Cumberland," said Whelan. "I never saw you there."

"Yeah, I came in right after you went to Miami. They'd talk about you like you were some kind of superstar in that outfit," said Garrity. "If they'd only known. Ah, well."

Cannon wanted to throw another punch into Garrity's face but restrained himself. He put Connor Whelan in the forefront of his thoughts. *He* was the priority right now.

"Shame on you," Cannon said. "I grew up without a mother or a father. I had nothing. I certainly never had a million dollars. I had opportunities to go down misguided roads, take an easier path on the wrong side of the law. What gave you the right just because your mom died and you missed your daddy?"

Luke Garrity thought about his question. "I don't know, Agent Cannon. All I can venture is that you had someone who made a difference for you at some point in your life. Some role model or inspiration that I never had. I made easy choices. Easy isn't usually right, and it's fraught with uncertainty and regret."

Cannon expected a smart-ass comment, not some half-realized, philosophical truth full of vague existentialism. It left him speechless, pondering the man before him. No, he really *didn't* know him at all.

"Thank you, Garrity," said Whelan. "I appreciate you sharing your story. It doesn't excuse any of your actions, but it gives insight into your relationship with Eddie. Are you ready to make the call?"

Garrity took a deep breath and held it. He nodded with a slow exhale.

Whelan handed him his phone.

Cannon and he took a few steps back, so Garrity could have some breathing room to conquer his nerves.

He dialed the number. "Hello, Eddie. It's Luke. I'm still alive."

Chapter 47

Eddie hung up the phone. He was as gleeful as a newly adopted puppy. Connor had never seen him like this.

"Luke's alive! He survived the explosion!"

"He did?" asked Connor.

"He's on his way. He's close! He'll be here in a couple of hours."

Connor was fixated on the large swing gate in front of them. "Where exactly is *here*?"

They'd been traveling out of Houston, heading south, for over forty miles. Much farther, and they'd hit the Gulf of Mexico.

A little sign beside the gate had two letters centered among some fancy scrollwork. RS.

"This is Rico's ranch."

"RS?" asked Connor.

Eddie snorted. "An old nickname. Rico Suave."

"How's that a nickname?"

"Kid, you missed the 80s and 90s. Good times."

Connor's face was blank.

They waited another ten minutes until the gate opened. As they drove through, Connor saw a camera on top of a post for the first time. There was a matching one on the driver's side.

The road was dirt and wound around some trees. Small ponds were scattered about, and the fields were full of green grass sprouting from an early Texas spring season. Everywhere you looked, there were cows and occasionally a bull.

A sprawling estate, the five-thousand-foot main home was surrounded by other smaller homes for ranch workers, housemaids, family, and guests. They made a compound, all surrounding an enormous in-ground swimming pool. On each side to the east and west, there were stables full of horses and, behind them, roofed cowsheds. And if that wasn't enough for Connor to take in as they drove around to the backside of the residence, there was a dairy barn and a slaughterhouse. The entire ranch was in pristine condition, like it was ready to be featured in a magazine.

"This is unreal," he couldn't help but mutter.

"Where do you think all the milk you drink comes from, kid?" asked Eddie. "The hamburgers you eat?"

Connor was impressed. "I think I'd have hidden out here before choosing the swamp."

Eddie sobered. "The 'swamp' was closer. And I wasn't in shape to make it any further. *And* I thought we'd be safe there. Oh, why am I defending myself to you?"

A man came out from the stables to greet them. He was Mexican and barely cleared five feet in height. He wore a wide-brimmed, leather Stetson hat, hiding his face in shadow from the midday sun. It was already ninety degrees in the early April of South Texas.

He gave Eddie a cold handshake. "Why are you here, Eddie? And with one hour's notice? You're lucky I don't have any visitors today."

"I need to hole up for a day or two, Rico. Then I'll be out of your hair."

"You'd better. In two days, I'll be heading up to Nebraska for a week. I'm an honest man now, Eddie, and honest men work hard. Two days and my debt is paid."

"Yeah, sure, Rico. Whatever you say." He took in the view of the gorgeous Spanish style home and matching casitas. Roofs were covered in multi-color barrel tiles, even the stables.

"Nice outfit you have here," continued Eddie. "If I didn't know better, Rico, I'd say you must have been skimming off the top when you headed up my Houston operation."

Rico's eyes narrowed, and he nodded to the two men behind him, who approached quickly on horseback. They carried rifles, resting on their saddles. "No, sir. I never hid a dime from you. Remember, you paid well, and my bonuses were generous. I kept what we agreed on. And you have copies of all my ledgers to prove it."

Eddie ignored the henchmen. "I didn't pay you *this* well. To buy all this? Uh-uh."

"It's not mine yet, Eddie. It's the bank's. You only paid me enough to put twenty percent down."

Eddie laughed. "Well, I guess that does make sense. An honest man now, you say? What a shame. A ranch like this?" He failed to finish his thought, letting it hang in the air. It was surely unscrupulous.

"Look, Rico, my son, Luke Garrity, is coming to meet us here," continued Eddie. "Make sure he gets through that gate of yours, okay? We'll need two rooms, and I need double beds in one of them at least."

Rico handed him a key. "Casita tres. It's got all you need. Dinner will be at six in the main home. You'll be my guest this evening. The doors are open, just come on in. The dining room is easy to find."

"Thank you, Rico."

The man started walking back to the east stable. "Two days, Eddie," he hollered without turning.

Eddie and Connor made their way to Casita number three. It was tastefully furnished, with two bedrooms, each containing two queen beds. There was a kitchenette, a substantial living area, and two full bathrooms. It was clean and well-maintained. A small patio was on the backside with an outdoor dining set and attached by a short walkway to the main pool deck.

Connor turned on the television. A satellite dish brought in over four-hundred channels, and he rapidly grew lost in channel surfing.

Eddie called Rico again and made a few requests. Within an hour, a woman dropped off a large bag with clothes fitting Connor and himself. They were "borrowed" from some of the workers. Shortly after, came another knock on the door.

"I'm Doctor Guerra," he introduced himself.

"Marvelous, Doc, let's go in here," said Eddie. He led the man to one of the bedrooms. Eddie dropped his pants and plopped face-first on the bed.

The doctor inspected Eddie's wound. It was healing pretty well, though a couple of the stitches had torn loose and were seeping pus and blood. He cleaned it and changed the bandaging.

"I don't think it needs to be restitched. You'll have quite a scar, but I wouldn't worry about it. Who would ever see it?"

He handed Eddie two bottles. "This one is an antibiotic. Better safe than sorry. And this one is the painkillers you asked for."

Eddie popped an oxycodone. "Thanks, Doc. Much obliged."

After the doctor left, Connor approached Eddie. "You shouldn't overdose on those. One of my friend's mothers did. It wasn't pretty. Now he's living with his grandmother."

"Thanks for worrying about me, kid, but it's okay. My grandmother's dead."

Connor squinted, uncertain whether to comment.

"Hey, kid," said Eddie, "turn the television off for now. I've got a surprise for you."

Eddie rifled through the bag of clothes and found a bathing suit. He tossed it to Connor. "Here. Go try out that pool. Might as well take advantage of the full hospitality of the resort."

"Resort!" said Connor. "I've been to a resort. This place looks like they'll put us to work, milking cows or worse."

Eddie sniggered. "I can arrange that if you want, milking a cow."

Connor thought about it. "Naw, I'm good."

He put the swimsuit on and headed out the back door.

"Have fun," said Eddie. "I'm going to get some rest. Oh, and kid, you try running away here, there's a whole ranch full of rifle-wielding hombres who'll take you down in two seconds. And there's cameras everywhere. Best behavior now. We don't want to wear out our welcome."

Eddie lay on one of the beds, letting the pain-relieving tablet do its job.

Twenty minutes into his pool time, Connor was joined by a thirteen-year-old Mexican girl. She came out of a set of doors on the west end of the main home.

"Hi," she said, "I'm Carlita. It's wonderful to see someone new here."

Connor stopped swimming and stood up in the shallow end. He had his dad's height genes, and with his face beaten and swollen, he appeared older than he was. Girls weren't on his radar like video games, but he was aware they existed. "Hello. I'm Connor Whelan. FBI agent Tom Whelan's son."

Carlita giggled. "What an odd way to introduce yourself. I'm Rico's daughter." Her English was perfect.

"Rico Suave's?"

She laughed again. Connor decided she was pretty.

"Rico Sandoval's. This is his ranch."

"Oh. Sorry. I was told the S stands for suave."

She shook her head, then dipped it back until her hair was all wet. When she came up, it fell neatly behind her head. "What happened to your face?"

"Eddie Morrison."

"Oh," she said, "I don't know him. I'm sorry."

"Carlita, do you have a phone I can borrow for a minute?"

"No. I'm not allowed. My dad doesn't like drawing attention to us."

"Is there one in your house? It's important I make a call," pleaded Connor.

"To FBI agent Tom Whelan?"

"Yes! I've been kidnapped! Eddie Morrison is holding me against my will. I need to get a message to my dad, tell him where I'm at."

"Sorry. I'd be grounded for a year. My dad already spoke to me about your situation. There's nothing I can do."

"Isn't being grounded for a year worth it to save someone's life?"

"Save your life? You're not in any danger here."

"Eddie's trying to kill me!" Connor hissed.

Carlita wiped her smile off her face. The boy was cute but not worth getting in trouble over. "I made a mistake joining you. I'll let you swim in peace."

She climbed out of the pool and headed back inside.

"Carlita, please!" Connor was desperate.

He jumped out of the pool and ran up to her as she arrived at the door to her bedroom. His hand spun her around.

"Please!" he repeated. "Eddie *is* going to kill me. He can't let me live."

Carlita jerked her arm back. She opened her bedroom door. Her dad, Rico, was standing there with an old .22 Ruger revolver in his hand. He aimed it at Connor. "Boy, if you touch my girl one more time, you won't have to worry about Eddie shooting you. I'll take you out myself."

Connor was at his wit's end. He started sobbing and ran back to his casita.

The girl and her dad both stared after him.

She turned to him and asked him in Spanish, "Is there no way we can help that boy?"

Rico shuddered. "Not without risking our lives."

Chapter 48

Whelan viewed the monstrous swing gate through a pair of binoculars while hidden behind some brush two hundred yards away.

"What do you suppose RS stands for?" he whispered to Cannon and Garrity on either side of him.

"Rough Son of a bitch?" offered Cannon.

"Rancho Sur," said Garrity. "According to Google Maps."

"Look at you, being helpful," Whelan said sarcastically.

"Don't get too excited. I'm not making a move until we get a text from the judge my plea deal's been signed."

"Garrity, I told you, we don't have time to wait for that. It's coming. It'll be here after two."

Whelan glanced at his watch. He had three hours until his bluff would be called. *This will all be over long before then.*

"Are you sure you don't want to bring a SWAT team in for this?" asked Cannon.

"I'm sure. Surprise is on our side right now. If an armored truck were to bash through that gate, it would be over for Connor before it started. There are cameras everywhere."

He handed the binoculars to him.

Cannon surveilled the property. "Damn. They have them mounted on top of the fence about a hundred yards apart. How are you and I going to get in?"

Whelan studied the layout of the land. They were uphill slightly, giving him an advantage. "There's some kind of electrical box. It's on their side, though. Maybe we could—oh, wait. One of the cameras isn't flashing a red dot."

"Where?"

"Over to the right, third camera from the gate. See how they're all flashing a little red light below the lens? I'm assuming that means their functioning. That one's not. That's our entry point."

Cannon spied it through the binoculars. "How sure are you the red means they're operating?"

"Somewhere between positive and no fucking clue."

"Good enough for me," he agreed.

"Okay, Garrity," said Whelan. "Give us twenty minutes, then approach the gate. I'm assuming you're on the guest list. Hopefully, that gives us enough time to be in position."

The two agents made their way to the blind spot in the perimeter.

"How do you know Garrity won't take the car and run?" asked Cannon. "That's what I'd do. You know, if I were in his shoes."

"I've been watching him all week, profiling him. Skilled liar aside, I don't believe it's in his character to live a life on the run. The whole country would be searching for him. He has no ID or passport to travel internationally. We stripped him of his cash and credit cards.

"Deep down, he's not very tough, or loyal. I think at this point, he wants to prove himself to Eddie, only if it will benefit him personally. Otherwise, he'll sell out his daddy to save himself. If not for the events of this week, I might feel sorry for him. He strikes me as someone lost, who's waited his whole life to prove his worth. This is his chance."

"How will you explain to him he didn't get his plea deal?"

Whelan turned to his counterpart. "I thought I'd leave that to you."

The men hopped the fence and began jogging lightly forward. The aerial map on Google, while likely outdated by a couple of years, showed the main house about a mile ahead. They held a steady pace, staying off the road and sticking to tree cover as best they could.

The compound came into view. They circled to the rear, hiding between the trees, and entered the east stable. Four horses were in stalls, and ranch hands were leading out two others. Once outside, they mounted them and trotted to the west.

Whelan and Cannon hid behind a stack of hay bales. As soon as the horses and men left the building, they slipped inside and ran down to the last stall, closest to the residential areas. An empty stall at the end had a barred window, providing a view of the compound.

"I count four possible areas where they could be holding Connor," said Whelan. "Assuming he's not in the main house."

"They're guests," said Cannon. "Makes sense they'd be in one of these guest houses."

They made their way to the closest one. "Casita 3," it read above the door. Positioning themselves on either side, Whelan tried the nob. It turned freely.

Stepping inside, the home was small but tidy. The first bedroom had no occupants, and the bathrooms were empty. The door to the second bedroom was shut. Whelan counted down from three on his fingers and flung the door open. Cannon stepped inside, his pistol ready to shoot.

Again, no one was inside. A bag, stained with blood and dust, was on one bed. The other was recently slept in, based on the crumpling of the bedspread and pillows.

Whelan looked out the back window. A large pool could be viewed from here. A few chaise lounges were scattered about. No one was in sight.

"Slow time of year for company and entertaining?" asked Cannon.

"Maybe. I think in South Texas, it's pretty much year-round, though. I guess there are no visitors right now, aside from Connor and Eddie. If I knew Eddie Morrison was coming to my home, I'd clear out any other guests too. I expected to see some cattlemen here, though."

"They're probably all out working, doing whatever ranchers do."

"Let's move on."

Again, Casita 4, like 3, was unoccupied. No bloody bags were in this one.

A much larger building was adjacent, facing the pool's end and the main house. There was no sign above the door. Whelan decided these were the sleeping quarters for the permanent ranch hands. Six bedrooms, each with a tiny on-suite bathroom, and either two double beds or two sets of bunk beds in each one. They were tidy, though a couple of beds remained unmade.

A closet in the hall was converted into an armory. A large gun safe was still open. All the slots were empty save two. These held semiautomatic rifles with 30-round magazines. Ammunition boxes and extra magazines were scattered on its floor. Whelan was more interested in why the other eight slots in the rack were missing their weapons and who was wielding them.

There was a kitchen and a spacious living room inside. The TV was turned on, broadcasting a Spanish telenovela. The kitchen smelled like fresh popcorn. Whelan opened the microwave door, and a fully popped bag was inside, unopened. Three empty bowls were waiting on the countertop.

"Connor and Eddie wouldn't be here," said Whelan.

Cannon agreed. "No. That leaves those other two buildings on the far side of the pool. I'm guessing Casitas Uno y Dos. If he's not there, then he must be in the main house."

"I'm getting a bad feeling," said Whelan.

"What?" asked Cannon.

"Miranda is always telling me to trust my gut."

"Okay. What's its advice right now?"

"To watch our backs. I think it's against the odds not a single ranch hand is in here right now. You'd think they work rotating schedules. This building sleeps sixteen at a minimum. *Some* should be here. Some were, in the last few minutes, I think. Two of those beds were slept in recently—an afternoon siesta. And someone was making snacks in the kitchen."

"Maybe they got called out on an emergency? Dropped everything at the last second?"

Whelan peeked out the window on the far side of the building. He scanned the other buildings as best he could from his vantage point.

"Shit! I think *we're* the emergency."

Cannon thought about his comment. "Why? What are you seeing?"

Whelan handed him the binoculars. "See those exhaust vents on the roofs of each building? On the corners? I thought that was such an odd placement. Look at the one closest to us, on the casita."

"Shit. A flashing red dot inside." Cannon tilted his head, and his brow tightened. "They've been watching *us*, haven't they?"

"Yes, and by now, Garrity should have been granted access. They have to know we came with him."

A speaker crackled in the ceiling above.

Eddie Morrison's voice came through. "Indeed, Agent Whelan. It's all over now."

Whelan and Cannon's heads jerked about like robots as they scanned the room for a camera. Obviously, they were on video *and* audio, though it was well hidden in the room.

"Where's my son, Eddie?" Whelan shouted into the air.

"He's fine. He's in my protective care. Both of my boys. And you thought Luke was going to help you?" He shrieked.

The high pitch indicated to Whelan Eddie's nerves were on edge, and he was unsure of his statement.

"Luke led you right to me," Eddie continued. "You thought he'd assist you after what you did to his face? The left side couldn't be worse if it went through a meat grinder. Hell, he can't even see out of that eye. Now, why don't you two come on out, and we can have this conversation in person?"

"Show me Connor!" snapped Whelan. "I want to see him right now. Bring him out by the pool, and I'll surrender to you, Eddie."

Cannon shook his head at his partner.

Whelan shrugged and lowered his voice. "What choice do I have? Phil, I'm sorry I led you here into this nightmare of my own making."

Cannon put his hand on Whelan's shoulder. "*You* didn't make this. Eddie did. And you didn't lead me here," he whispered. "We both chose to pursue this. We walked the steps we thought best to save Connor."

Whelan nodded.

"My son, Eddie!" he repeated. "Bring him out now, or we'll find out who the better shot is soon enough."

"Hold your horses," said Eddie.

Two painfully long minutes ticked off the clock.

A French door on the main house opened to the enormous covered patio. Luke Garrity walked out, pointing a rifle into Connor Whelan's back, pushing him around a wicker seating area and fire pit toward the pool.

Connor's face was still swollen. Both his cheeks were black, blue, red, yellow, and green. It was an agonizing rainbow of afflicted torture. Veins on his right cheek spread from his nose to his ear. There was a new line of blood running down from his lip to his chin.

Whelan saw Connor the day before but wasn't able to make out his son's face this clearly. *And Eddie has the gall to complain about Luke's face?*

"I'm going to kill you, Eddie," he mumbled.

Cannon sighed. "Whelan? Are you ready?"

"I think so."

"What's the plan?"

"I'm not sure. We're going to make it up as we go along."

Chapter 49

Connor Whelan turned his head around far enough to see Luke Garrity. "You don't have to do this. This isn't our fight. Why don't we step aside and let our dads hash it out?"

"It's our fight now. We made choices."

"*I* didn't make any choices. My only choice all week was to go along and stay alive. You know, Eddie's not so bad once you get to know him. Why, we've gotten along fine this week. All things considered."

Luke gawked at the boy's face. "Splendidly, I'd say. What did you do to deserve the bloody lip?"

"Oh, that's my fault. I pointed out to Eddie my dad is going to kill him today. He popped me in the lip. Again. It was starting to heal from the last time, too."

"You said the two of you got along fine."

"Yes, well, our relationship is complicated. Aren't all son's with their dads?"

"Eddie's not your dad," said Luke.

"Exactly."

Luke Garrity focused on the odd boy in front of him, less than half his age yet seemingly with more wisdom than most men he knew. Confusion wrestled his mind. "I think my mother might have saved me from a monster."

Connor touched his right cheek, still sore as hell from the butt of Eddie's gun. "Yeah. You don't know the half of it. A monster psychopath."

He let out a short, high-pitched note of laughter.

"I'm not sure why you're still alive," said Luke.

"He needed *me* to get to my dad."

"I mean *now*."

"Because it's not over yet."

Connor gazed up directly into the man's eyes. "Luke?"

"Yes?"

"Whose side are you on here, anyway?"

Garrity reflected on his question for an exhaustingly long ten seconds. "I'm still deciding."

He coughed to clear his throat, and tried to push away the doubts he struggled to keep at bay. "Keep marching. Go to the left. We'll stop halfway."

Garrity walked him down the first half of the pool deck, alongside the swimming pool. "Okay, stop. We'll wait here. He should be able to see you fine from here."

Connor scrutinized the building in front of him. He couldn't see through the sun's glare on the windows. If his dad *was* watching him, he couldn't tell.

They stood in silence for over three minutes. It was torture.

Connor couldn't take it. "What are they waiting for?"

"I'm unsure."

Eventually, Whelan came out of the building across from them. His pistol was tucked into the back of his waistband. His shirt was untucked and covering it. He quickly assessed the surrounding areas.

Three men, presumably ranch security, stood on the pool deck on either side of him, all sporting matching semi-automatic rifles like he'd seen inside. Two more men were on horses to the west of the building he'd vacated. They held bolt-action rifles aimed straight at him.

I count eight. Not impossible.

"Connor?" he said. "You okay?"

The boy was clearly not "okay," but what else could he ask?

Connor Whelan wasn't sure how to respond. He spoke gently. "Thanks for coming to get me."

"Of course, son. I love you. You're going to walk away from this."

"Okay." Connor was suddenly petrified. A lump grew in his throat, choking him. Seeing his dad so close after the week he'd experienced was numbing. He sensed this was all coming to an end, and he didn't trust the outcome. His mind began shutting down.

"Your mom loves you too," continued Whelan. "You're going to see her tonight."

The thought was too much for Connor to accept. He couldn't even nod. Doubt quelled all hope. The brave façade he'd put up all week collapsed.

"Eddie!" shouted Whelan toward the house behind his son. "What's wrong, Eddie? Eight men holding guns on me, and you're still too afraid to face me?"

After a pause, Eddie Morrison came out of the main home.

"Where's your partner, Agent Whelan? Holed up in the house, trying desperately to think of a way out of this situation?"

"No. There's only one way out of this situation."

"I'm afraid so. It was a fun hunt, Tom. You kept me on my toes the past few months. Well, I might have had an edge on you."

Both men looked at Luke Garrity.

"I've got a terrific son there," Eddie said loudly. "Well, two of them now."

Whelan raised his eyebrows high, his eyes opened wide, and he lowered his chin in question to Luke.

Garrity took a deep breath and gave a nod in return. He then wrapped Connor's shoulders in his arms and dove them both into the swimming pool.

Whelan turned immediately to the men on his left, yanked out his pistol, and began firing. One fell while the other two returned fire, but lacking significant weapons training, their shots were scattered, striking potted plants and pool loungers or zinging into the water. None connected with their target.

As the men on horseback galloped behind the home to help join the men on the east side, the other three men on the west side were attacked from behind. Cannon came rushing through a side door and unleashed one of the rifles from the gun safe inside. The second rifle was strung over his shoulder.

Cannon's first two shots each brought down a man. The third turned around and began firing, one shot hitting Cannon on the right side. It spun him around, but he recovered promptly and kept firing. Thankfully, lugging a Kevlar vest around the country paid off.

Eddie Morrison stood in shock at the other end of the pool for the first ten seconds of the gunfight before coming to his senses. He turned and ran to the French doors. He heard a click as he grabbed the handle and raised his head to find Carlita's face staring back at him. She'd locked the deadbolt.

He raised his SIG and fired two shots at her. They bounced off, one nearly striking him.

She retreated further behind the bulletproof glass, giving Eddie the finger as she left.

"Fucking kids!" he cursed, running around to the side of the main home, desperate for a way to escape.

Whelan hit another one of the security personnel on his end of the pool from behind the cover of a large concrete planter. He exchanged shots, emptying his clip. He loaded another one with a smack into the bottom of his pistol as one of the two on horseback came around on his left side. He fired, knocking the man off. The horse was frightened and darted toward the main home.

The second horse was no longer in sight.

"Cannon!" he shouted, unsure of his partner's whereabouts. "The other horseman is coming around to you!"

It took another ten shots to fell the last man in front of him.

The sound of silence clamored in his ear until he heard water breaking the pool's surface, followed by gasping.

Connor and Luke came up for air, unable to hold their breath any longer.

Whelan looked on in horror as the water surrounding them was crimson and growing darker.

He dove in and swam to his son. He put his arm around his chest and brought him to the edge. He lifted him to the pool coping, then jumped out of the water and hoisted his son to his feet. Whelan began stripping his clothes, searching for bullet holes.

Cannon subdued the last horsemen, then jumped into the water to help a struggling Luke Garrity reach the shallow end and climb out of the pool. He was bleeding from two wounds, one to the stomach, the other to his chest. Cannon laid him down and began applying pressure.

Garrity found the gaze of the man he'd spent the week with. He grabbed Cannon's upper arm fiercely. "I never did have that plea deal, did I?"

"No, Luke. You didn't. You were always going down."

"I knew it. We make our choices," he coughed. After a few more seconds, he smiled and released Cannon's arm, his eyes fixed on a better place beyond the sky above.

Cannon closed the man's eyelids, then returned his gaze to his partner and friend, Tom Whelan, and his son Connor.

Whelan had Connor stripped to his skivvies. He spun him around and checked every inch of his body. The blood in the pool had stained his clothes, but it wasn't escaping his body anywhere.

Whelan grabbed his son and brought him tight into his arms.

Connor stood still, unable to return the affection. Instead, he raised his arm and pointed to the southeast.

"What?" asked Whelan.

He wheeled around when he saw sheer terror envelope his child's face.

Eddie Morrison was riding the first horse across the pool deck on the other side of the water. He held his firearm, aiming at Whelan. Two shots rang out.

The horse bucked, and Eddie hit the ground. One shot was from Eddie. It missed Whelan and Connor by inches. The other came from the patio.

Rico Sandoval lowered his rifle.

Cannon and Whelan spun their heads toward him, unaware of the stranger's presence.

"Enough is enough," he said, then tipped his hat to Whelan before returning inside the main home.

Connor forced his way out of his dad's arms and ambled around the pool until he stood above Eddie lying on the ground.

The man appeared frailer than he had all week and certainly more frightened.

He'd been struck in the chest by Rico's bullet. It pierced his heart, then his right lung, before exiting from his back.

Connor put his foot on Eddie's chest, just below his heart. He stepped down, watching the blood spurt faster, like a fire hydrant opened on the corner for the kids to play.

Eddie attempted to speak but coughed up blood as he took in air. He managed to gargle his last words. "Fucking kids."

Somewhere in the distant background of Connor's auditory perception, he heard a voice screaming, "Get away from there."

He glanced around and saw Eddie's gun, the SIG P226. It was the same issue as most FBI agents carried. He wondered if Luke gave it to his dad at some point—perhaps some twisted gift for all the Father's Days he'd missed.

Connor picked up the gun and studied it for a second. He enjoyed the weight of it in his hand. He aimed it at Eddie's head and pulled the trigger. It struck true. He fired again. And again. On the fourth squeeze, there was simply a click. The clip and chamber were empty. Three would have to do.

"Connor!" screamed the same, distant voice.

He looked up. It was his dad, staring in disturbed bewilderment.

Connor let the gun fall to the ground. "You gotta pop'em in the head to make sure they're dead," he said.

"He's dead, son."

Whelan dropped to his knees and grabbed Connor in his arms once more. Again, his son felt lifeless.

Connor made no effort to return the hug. He stared into his father's eyes with cold numbness.

"Connor!" Whelan shouted from twelve inches away. "He's dead, son. Look at him. He can't hurt you any longer."

Connor turned and took a peek at what was left of Eddie Morrison's head, then swung his neck back around to glare at his father. He was eerily quiet. Not even a loud breath escaped him.

Whelan rattled his shoulders and shouted again. "Connor, he's gone! Eddie's gone. Forever. You're safe. I've got you."

He threw his arms around his son and embraced him so tightly he feared he might crush the boy.

Connor tried to pull away, but Whelan refused to let him go.

"You're safe. I love you. You're safe. I've got you," he whispered over and over into his son's ear.

Finally, Connor's body reacted. It jolted to life as if mighty Zeus struck him with lightning. He began sobbing into his dad's neck. The tears fell fast, and soon he was crying hysterically. He threw his arms around his dad, squeezing tightly.

Tom joined him in the waterworks. The pair howled and blubbered until, eventually, they were spent.

They released their grasp.

Cannon was standing to the side until it felt safe to come in for the huddle. He threw a giant pool towel around Connor's body and gave him a long hug of his own.

"You guys ready to get out of here?" he asked them both, standing up from the ground.

The Whelans nodded.

Tom wrapped an arm around Connor's shoulder and led him to the patio.

Another pool towel was thrown over the face of Luke Garrity.

Whelan knelt, putting a hand on the man's chest. He looked up and said, "Find a place for him, Father. He earned it in the end."

Rico Sandoval opened the door for them, and Cannon led Connor inside to get cleaned up and dressed.

"I've got to call his mother," Whelan murmured to Cannon as he passed, choking on his voice.

"Sure. We'll be fine." He closed the door behind him.

Whelan fell into a wicker loveseat on the patio. He was breathless as another wave of emotion overtook his body. He struggled against the weight of the phone, the weight of the call he had to make, and the impending reaction.

He pushed the second speed dial.

It rang three times—an eternity.

"Hello?" came her soft voice.

"Georgia? I've got him."

Chapter 50

Whelan was on the phone with ASAC Miranda Jones from a private charter plane. It was nearing 7:00 p.m., but he was determined his son would see his mother tonight and sleep in his own bed.

Connor was passed out in the rear of the plane. He'd been treated for his injuries and was sleeping off some painkillers.

It had been a long afternoon, debriefing via video conference with Director Commerson and his own SAC, Alan Kendrick, of the Kansas City office. Agents Whelan and Cannon each separately reported their story of the week's events. They lined up as expected.

Even Connor Whelan was given a few minutes of time. Director Commerson had three kids of his own, all grown now, but he remembered what it was like to be a father of a twelve-year-old boy. Kids grew up much faster today than they did even twenty years ago.

Connor experienced five years' worth of life lessons in one week. He'd witnessed nightmares even most adults couldn't handle.

"So Commerson was gentle with him," Whelan told Jones on the phone. "I was impressed with his patience and compassion. We've got an exceptional man leading us. It was largely him stroking Connor's ego about how unbelievably strong he must be."

"That's kind," said Jones. "I'm glad he took the time."

"I couldn't say anything in front of Connor, but truthfully, no one is that strong. He's going to need counseling. We both are. Eddie Morrison was a total mind-fuck. Connor told me how he'd play 'daddy' with him one minute, then fly off the handle and strike him the next. Miranda…"

Whelan choked up before swallowing it down, "Eddie left his face as broken as his psyche. The doctor told me it would all heal fine, but he will have physical scars matching his emotional ones. My beautiful boy."

"Just keep reminding him they're battle scars, proving what a badass he is. And that he's earned them and should wear them proudly."

"Yeah, when he's ready. Right now, he needs the sympathy he deserves."

"Tom?" started Miranda. "Did he ever say how Lil' Baby was involved? Connor's the lone witness to what went down there."

"Apparently, Eddie contacted Lil' Baby, asking for help—cash, weapons, anything he could offer, given his desperate situation. Lil' Baby lured him to Cacapon, telling him there was still one stash there never discovered by the Feds. That much was true.

"But Lil' Baby's real intention was to kill Eddie and hold Connor for himself in exchange for a full pardon of all his crimes. He thought he'd walk a free man and no longer be on the run, living in the shadows.

"Connor didn't hear the conversation where it all went south, but it only took Eddie several minutes to start realizing Lil' Baby was playing him."

"Well, I'm glad Eddie is put to bed," said Jones. "I can't say I'm sorry he's dead, either. So what was the deal with Rico Sandoval? He was Eddie's last connection in the world. What changed his mind and made him decide to help you?"

"I'm not sure. He could have easily killed Cannon and me instead of Eddie. We killed his security detail. I'm surprised he didn't put bullets in both of us. He could have—we never saw him coming. But what was he going to do? Kill a child? In front of his own? Connor said he had an encounter earlier in the day with Rico's daughter, Carlita. I think the whole situation tugged on his parental heart-strings. It was too close to home, literally. He saved our lives. Perhaps it was a way for him to make amends with his past.

"We have nothing on him directly connecting him to Eddie. It's why he slipped through our fingers before, during the big bust a couple years ago. The attorneys back then couldn't make anything stick. He was free and moved to Mexico. He returned to the U.S. six months ago after a legal name change. I was notified, but he'd already had his day in court."

"I doubt anything will stick this time either," said Jones. "He can deny any knowledge of his involvement and come up with any story he wants. It's his word against a dead man's now. I'm betting they don't even pursue it."

"I'm okay with that," said Whelan. "As I said, we owe him our lives."

"Well, you're off the hook with SAC Orville. I received a transfer approval for Agent Garrity in my inbox not twenty minutes ago."

"Interesting. I thought he'd put me through the ringer," said Whelan.

"Apparently you were right about him. He was probably shaking in his boots over his actions more than you. By saving Garrity, you saved him from a murder conviction, if it had ever gone that far. I'm sure once he had time to calm down and think about it, he was ultimately grateful to you."

"I won't hold my breath for a thank you card."

"Cannon said you bonded with an agent who was killed, Amber Caulfield. Would you like to talk about her?"

"I would, thanks. She was sharp and full of wit—reminded me of you, actually."

The pair continued to visit for over an hour.

"Well, I guess I'll let you go," Whelan said. "We're getting ready to land at Reagan National."

"I look forward to reading your full report. Take a couple of days and get Connor situated back home."

"That's the plan."

Whelan grabbed a rental and made his way to the house he once shared with his ex-wife.

Georgia Whelan was waiting with Tom's mother, Kathryn, on the front porch. She came running across the yard when they pulled up. More hugging and crying ensued, and then it was Grandma's turn.

Though 10:45 p.m., Connor's mother insisted he eat before bed. She didn't know what else to do for him. She made turkey sandwiches for everyone, and they did their best not to talk about the horrific week. Scoops of chocolate peanut butter ice cream were devoured afterward.

It was nearly 1:00 a.m. when Georgia tucked Connor into bed as though he were still five instead of twelve, almost thirteen. She kissed his forehead and left a nightlight on.

She also left his door cracked so she could hear him in the middle of the night should he need her.

Kathryn had already gone to bed. She was sharing with Georgia. Tom would be taking the sofa tonight. He was content to do so.

When Georgia walked back into the living room, Whelan stood. "I guess it's time to say goodnight."

"I guess it is," she said, unsure. "Maybe I'll sleep tonight, without the nightmares."

Whelan pointed toward the hall where Connor's room was. "His will just be starting. You know I'm a light sleeper. I'll be in there pronto if I hear anything. You focus on you."

He reached out and stroked her hair.

She was bittersweet. "Tom, are you certain Eddie can't hurt him any longer?"

"From the grave?"

"I mean, there's no one else, in Eddie's gang or otherwise, who'll be coming for him?"

"We got them all this time."

He gathered her to him, holding her close. Neither wanted to move, but eventually, Tom was stronger.

Planting a kiss on her cheek first, he took a step back and said, "Well, goodnight, Georgi."

She smiled. "I think it will be. Goodnight, Tom."

Four months later, Whelan was sitting in the bullpen of the Kansas City office. It was the first time he'd been free of any caseloads since Eddie Morrison. He was going through his mail, mostly junk.

On the bottom of the stack, a brochure for Kittimer Cruise Lines caught his attention. A picture of their new pride and joy, the *Kittimer Journey,* was on the cover. It was quite a vessel. He flipped the pamphlet over. It was addressed to Miranda Jones at her home address. She'd left it for him with a Post-it note: *I'm ready for some R&R. How about you guys?*

He smiled and picked up the phone.

"Cannon? You have some time off coming?"

"It seems I do. In fact, last week, SAC Kendrick told me to 'use it or lose it.' Why? What did you have in mind?"

THE END

Thank You

Thank you for reading **EDDIE MORRISON**! I hope you enjoyed it and are loving Agent Tom Whelan and his team.

I had a wonderful time writing this for you. Heavily action oriented, this one proved to be more of a thriller than a murder mystery, though the murders sure racked up, didn't they?

If you haven't read the first Agent Whelan mystery, **12 PILLS,** or book two, **MURDER AT PARKMOOR,** you can find purchase links on my website, www.kirkburris.com. You can also subscribe to my newsletter if you'd like to stay updated on new releases, public appearances/signings, and special promotions!

If you enjoyed this story, please tell your friends and family, and most importantly, **leave a review** on the site where you purchased this book! Reviews go a long way to help indie-authors like myself build an audience so we can keep writing for you.

Lastly, the fourth book in the Agent Whelan Mystery series will be out in 2024! I've just started plotting and writing it for you. It promises to be a fun ride with another twisty murder to solve.

Be on the lookout for the new release:

THE KITTIMER JOURNEY

Have a blessed day!

Kirk Burris